Shelby's Creek

AGENT IN PLACE

Mark Matthiessen

ISBN: 1544900619
ISBN 13: 9781544900612

Praise for <u>Shelby's Creek</u>:

SHELBY'S CREEK
Mark Matthiessen
4 Stars

"Matthiessen's debut novel about life during World War II is a compelling, emotional read. The story takes place in both Iowa and France, and is told in alternating chapters, which juxtaposes the peacefulness of American farm life with the horror of war, building momentum and maintaining tension. The main characters are written beautifully, real and honest. The first in a series, this book will grip readers and not let go, leaving them anxiously awaiting the next installment."

-RT BOOK REVIEWS - 09/26/16

"An appealing, meditative tale about life during wartime...the discussions of obligation, ethics, and resistance are quite nuanced and engaging."

-KIRKUS REVIEWS - April 19th, 2016

". . . an engrossing tale."

-MIDWEST BOOK REVIEW

"Shelby's Creek is a work of love of family and the farmland of Shelby County. The characters are realistic with authentic problems of the time placing the reader into each situation. Each setting vividly exposes the time and place making the reader feel as if they are the character, creating an enthralling historical journey."

-COUNCIL BLUFFS NONPAREIL

"Shelby's Creek" is rich in detail, full of character development and gives its readers a unique glimpse at life during World War II . . .can't wait to read the next entry in Matthiessen's series."

-SIOUX CITY JOURNAL

"This riveting story juxtaposes life on an Iowa farm with the struggle of the French Resistance during World War II. A great read with amazing detail about life in Iowa . . . and life in Paris under the Nazis."

-SHENANDOAH VALLEY NEWS

"As a Shelby County native, I know how much our farmers love their land, and Mark eloquently captured their emotions with rich prose. He added such beautiful detail of our flora and fauna. I am excited to know he will delight us further with a second book.
It truly was great!!"

-Shelby County Iowa Attorney, Kathleen Kohorst

"Well-written; interesting characters; look forward to the next book"

-WWII 8th Air Force Staff Sergeant, Elmer McGinty

"My overall impression of the novel, "Shelby's Creek" is very good. The action moving from Iowa to France and back again keeps things moving along. The descriptions of people involved in action make the story more vivid, especially the French partisans . . . Then, back in Iowa all the details of the farmers, their families and how they make a livelihood from the fertile land makes the story come alive."

-WWII Air Force Captain, Al Crisi

"The first in a series of WWII historical novels, Mark Matthiessen's Shelby's Creek is a moving tale of the powerful and unshakeable bonds of family and love that extend across the globe and across generations to bind us to each other, and that empower regular people to transcend their limits and heroically take part in the making of history. Shelby's Creek tells the story of the French resistance by following the unforgettable France Deschamps, freshly widowed and still raw with pain, as well as the story of the pacifist farmer Valentin Schmitz, on the other side of the world on his farm in Iowa, as he contemplates the unthinkable: leaving the safety of his farm and entering the war of his own accord to find and hopefully save his relatives, who, as Jehovah's Witnesses, have been forced to hide from the Reich——and who, for all he knows, may already be dead. A thoughtful and well-crafted story. I look forward to the next entry in the series."

-BookFuel Editor, Justin Luzader

"A beautifully designed story bringing the characters, their lives and ties to life very realistically. The pace moves along superbly switching back and forth from Iowa to France truly captivating as the characters become more familiar and you get absorbed in their stories. The realism of the descriptions really allows the reader to become immersed in the story as if they were a part of it.

Really looking forward to the next in the series."

-Pauline Rawson, Independent translator, Toulouse, France

Love the way this book is written - true-to-form; well-explained. Beautiful the way the two worlds of France and Iowa are told and the way family is penned - truthfully - honest.

Look forward to the next book in the series.

- Staff Sergeant Larry Ralston - 29th Division - served under General George Patton in Germany.

* Shelby's Creek is listed with the Boston Public Library
* Shelby's Creek is listed with the Omaha Public Library

For Mom

Acknowledgements

*T*hanks to Brice Delcourt, for being a gracious Gallic guide in researching France.

Thanks to Clarke co-alum Dominique Winders for your translations, your cell phone, your time and indelible assistance.

Thanks to the Greatest Generation personalities from France, Germany and America for providing their stories, including World War II D-Day hero, my friend, Mal Walker.

And thanks to Miss Bouchez for your support, integrity and mellifluous voice.

"This story is inspired by a generation called America's greatest and inspirited by true events and true accounts."

— *Valentin Schmitz*

"So I must write to show people later on what these times are like."

— *Helene Berr*

"We owe our World War II veterans . . . a debt we can never fully repay."

— *Doc Hastings*

"Solitary trees, if they grow at all, grow strong."

— Winston Churchill

Air Flight——Atlantic Ocean/Celtic Sea
May 1943
0600 Hours

Chapter 1

*V*alentin Schmitz opened a briefcase from D.C. and looked over the OSS files for Paris.

He'd read recently about there being no resistance in Paris. Well, either the reporters or their reportage were wrong: 08/21/41 – Hauptmann Scheben assassinated at Boulevard de Strasbourg; twelve prisoners executed in retaliation in response to Fuhrer's demand for "merciless reprisals" to nip resistance in the bud. 10/20/41 – Feldcommandant of Nantes, Lieutenant-Colonel Holtz assassinated. In retaliation, twenty-eight communists shot at Chateaubriant, including a farmer guilty only of not turning in his hunting rifle . . . In all, some seventy-five resistant attacks in 1941.

"Unbelievable," Valentin whispered and then turned the page:

07/42 – General Ernst von Schaumburg, commander of Gross Paris, attacked with grenade; the commander survived, many hostages did not. 12/26/1942 – Monarchist Fernand Bonnier de la Chapelle assassinates Petain's deputy, Darlan . . . .

Valentin looked out the plane's window and wondered how long it might take to get *back* to Shelby's Creek.

He opened files dated 1943: 01/43 - Six enemy units assaulted by partisans; mid-Paris, midday. 02/15/43 - Officers Nussbaum and Winkler assassinated in ambush in Tuileries. 03/10/43 - Resistance activity increases in Paris in response to Hitler's intensified labor draft. 04/30/43 - Sixty resistance actions against enemy in bloodiest month of Paris resistance . . . . Final note: as of May 1943, an estimated fifty thousand partisans have been deported; twenty thousand shot.

Darn, Valentin thought. Not *only* is there resistance in Paris - there's *hell* - and *I'm* about to enter the mess. What the *heck* am I getting myself into? Sure, I owe Grandpa and Grandma Lambert. Sure, I owe Paris. Heck, I owe France, home of Mom, where Dad risked his life in World War I, where I've spent much of life before World War II. *And* I owe just as much as Dad and Grandpa for freedom. Yes, its about flying that flag on the cabin - its duty in exchange for free choice - choice to go to church or synagogue - to be lawyer or farmer - to call Jesus son of God or your senator son of a gun. "Doing right for rights," Grandpa always said. And like Grandpa - like Dad - it's my turn - **time to pay dues - hell or high water.**

But the knot in his stomach stayed tight and he inhaled deep, released a breath slowly, released his grip on the folders and closed his eyes to rest.

An hour later, he stirred from a sound nap and glanced out the window as his plane descended from London's cloudy sky.

His plane taxied to a stop.

He stepped out of the aircraft.

The air felt cool, drizzly-damp, and strange - not a strangeness as when he flew from mid-winter, scent-dead Iowa to scent-lively Florida, wafting sweet with camellias, and petunias. Nor a strangeness as Yellowstone's early autumn's dying-flora resins, or Paris's late-winter birthing blooms. No, this strangeness seemed heavy and tense - as a minor storm before a major storm. Yes - the air - smoky stale - sweat stale - blood stale - bomb stale - apropos to war - nothing fresh about it.

Gosh, he thought, I've got to get back home.

I've *got* to get *back* to Shelby's Creek.

"There'll always be wars because men love wars. Women don't, but men do."

— Margaret Mitchell

London, England
May 1943

Chapter 2

"Hello sport," said a young, slim, Brit-uniformed man who checked the ID tag on Valentin's neck. "Jump in the jeep."

"I must give Britain credit," said Valentin, "neither Luftwaffe nor Kriegsmarine has broken your back."

"Thanks mate - things been rather quiet with the Luftwaffe till our RAF hit historic Lübeck - like hitting Hit's hornet's nest. In turn, the Luftwaffe hits us periodically - bloody Baedeker Raids."

"Pretty bad?"

"It's not like mass blitz bomb raids from two years ago, but they still happen per Hit's whims."

They drove past a sign that read "Danger——Unexploded Bomb." People walked around the bomb as though walking around a construction site.

The driver pointed to a bombed-out three-story house and explained the two London Home Guard gunners standing in position, holding weapons, ready to take stations inside the skeletal three-story house. The guards blended into the destruction, their faces blackened, their bodies covered in torn tile and wallpaper. The driver pointed to either side of the road where men with spades dug into the earth to fill holes left by bombs.

The driver pointed. "As you may or may not know, the dome of St. Paul's is the heart of the Brits. And St. Paul's survived the blitz - as long as she stands - we stand. As you can see, her skeletal-frame epicenter took a bit of a hit, but her dome is sturdy as the grit of a Brit."

"I like that - grit of a Brit."

"Yes, we took a bit of a thrashing a couple years ago with those Luftwaffe air raids. But today, we're sound as a pound - keeping our chins up, old boy. How can we not? If our few daring RAF boys can hold off and obliterate those bugger Heinkels and Stukas in the Battle of Britain, least we can do is stay chipper."

"I remember reading Churchill's speech to the House of Commons about the RAF: 'Never was so much owed by so many to so few,'" Valentin said.

"Prime Minister Winnie, yes, deah ole Winnie and the whole of London owes those boys in their Spitfires and Hurricanes. Inspired the whole of London to fight; even my silly sod little ones are firewatchers and when I'm not driving, I'm spotting, keeping an eye to the sky, night and day, for those Luftwaffe buggers. I 'elp tie those big tethered kite balloons to piano wire that we hoist for the Luftwaffe to tangle up in. We call them balloons 'sausages.' Krauts *love* sausages, but they *don't* love *these* sausages. They get their planes too low and get knotted up in those balloons in a bomb raid and they're the ones getting bloody bombed to the ground."

The driver yawned wide, rubbed his eyes. "I'm a bit bleary-eyed right now, ole chap; took my all-night-guard, all-night watch last night. S'pose it'll continue for a tick or two, second front permitting . . . ."

"Second front?"

"You know, Allied invasion 'cross the Channel."

"Where's the first front?"

"Well, Allies cleaned up Axis in North Africa last month. They started with Benghazi, Tripoli, Kasserine Pass, Tunis, and then Bizerte. To me, that's the first front. Once we get the second front under way, this bugger of a war will be over."

"Where are we headed exactly?" asked Valentin

"That's for me to know, bloke, and you to find out. We'll be passin' your embassy soon, then Grosvenor Square."

"What devastation," Valentin said, looking at the bombed-out burnt ground.

"Yeah, just last night the Balham underground station turned truly underground with a massive crater in its belly. If you're in the wrong place at the wrong time, Bob's your uncle."

"What are people carrying - those canisters strapped across their shoulders?" Valentin asked.

"Gas masks. In London, they're as common as an umbrella."

The driver swerved hard and fast around what appeared to be a large canvas cattle tank.

"What's that?" asked Valentin.

"The Fire Service uses portable reservoirs to douse constant incendiary bombing . . . ."

Then they drove through an area where military personnel seemed everywhere, including women and Valentin liked to see this, liked the idea of women in authoritarian positions, wondered if there'd be war if women were in charge of things. Certainly there'd be more soldiers alive - mothers certainly don't want to see lives they brought into the world taken out before the world is ready to take them out and thought of the French adage - *a jeau de massacre* - war as a man's quest. Yes, with women in charge - more tea parties - fewer wars . . . .

His thoughts turned from tea to blood as he observed whole buildings condensed to busted bricks and pilings, broken beams, layer upon layer of fallen plaster walls, streets stained with soot from fires and bombs. And he imagined screams of Londoners as their homes exploded into fire, night after night. How these people survived, he didn't know. How they could still be free and *not* occupied by the Third Reich, he didn't know.

To the side of the street, he spotted an old man in a civilian suit wearing a British helmet, aiming binoculars at the sky. "Who is that man?"

"Part of the British Home Guard - air raid wardens, spotters, chaps too old to fight but capable of watching the sea for enemy ships and the air for enemy bombers and parachutists."

The driver stopped the jeep. "Here we are - 64 Baker Street. Right - off you go. Walk past the front of that building with the plaque that says, 'Inter-Services Research Bureau,' and go down that alley to another plaque that reads, 'Marks and Spencer Department Store, 82.' Find the side door, open it, go inside."

"Thanks."

"Not even the blimey Krauts have learned of this location, so keep it hush-hush. New guests such as yourself are rarely received here, but they're anxious for you. So don't look so bloody lost you silly sod - off you go."

Yeah, Valentin thought, I may look lost but looks are not half of how I feel. I've *got* to get back home, he told himself.

I've *got* to get back to Shelby's Creek.

"... If the British Empire...lasts for a thousand years, men will still say, 'This was their finest hour.'"

— *Winston Churchill*

London, England
May 1943

Chapter 3

Valentin glanced up and down the street and noticed all the American uniforms and suddenly didn't feel so alone.

He walked between two tall buildings down the deserted alley and nodded to a large man by the door that looked closely at him and at his ID number. The man opened the door and Valentin stepped inside where another man greeted him. "Third door on the left - don't knock, just go in. Find the secretary."

Once upstairs and inside the room, Valentin saw several men around several desks in quiet discussion. Some men were in uniform, some suits; all sat at a large conference table, drinking coffee, smoking.

"You look lost," a man said.

"I'm looking for the secretary," Valentin said.

"Over there," the man said, pointing to a lean, buxom woman filing her nails. "Be careful, she's a bite that stings - a real honey trap - and rightly so. She's got one helluva fuselage - hubba-hubba."

"Fuselage?"

"You know - body - like fuselage is the body of a plane and the fine body of a woman. Were you raised in a barn? You seem a bit green, hayseed. But she's not green. She's no broad with canned goods - that broad's a heat wave, got an advanced degree beyond cuddle-bunny victory girl. She's a full-fledged Spam-basher . . . you might wake up the next morn as a 'scratcher' though . . ."

Valentin grimaced and walked to her.

As she noticed him, she looked down and popped a mint in her mouth.

In the background the radio played, "God Save the King."

Yeah, God save the naïve son of a gun that tangles with her, Valentin thought. And he could tell she purposely ignored him now, as the gaze of her eyes looked shallow as she typed gibberish on her typewriter.

"Hello," he said, showing his ID.

She looked up as if surprised, batted her eyes, wheeled her chair back to show a slim, corset-tight waist below her perking, packed chest. "Welcome to ISRB," she said as she checked his ID and a clipboard, stood, held out her hand and batted her eyes as if a lash fell into them.

Yeah, she knows how to work those baby blues, he thought.

"Forgive me for staring," she said, whispering in a growling tone. "I'm not used to seeing big, strapping lads coming in here looking so lost."

"That's okay." he said, shaking her hand, looking around.

"Yes, Mr. Harrison will be with you shortly. Have a seat over there if you like or stand and talk to me as I like," she said now, winking her smile growing.

He looked down, felt slightly embarrassed for her.

"I've got your ID, but what's your name?" she asked in another throaty, growling whisper.

"I'm not to tell my name."

"You're American?"

"Yes."

"You look German," she said and winked and smiled again. "Are you a spy?"

He shook his head and grinned.

"Are you the strong, silent type?"

He shrugged.

"You know what Winnie says ... 'A silent man is silent only because he does not know what to say, and is reputed *strong* only because he has remained silent.'", she said and shot a rubber band at his chest. "I was just testing how *strong* you are."

He checked to see if anyone had seen the infraction, picked up the rubber band, and placed it on her desk.

"Well, you also look American for many reasons," she said.

"What are those?"

"Well, your long frame, your square face, but...your pant legs *aren't* pulled up."

"Pardon?"

"Most Americans, especially big Americans, wear their trouser legs short as if cooling their ankles."

"Well, ma'am, I move fast and my ankles stay cool."

"If you move so fast, I'd think your ankles would be hot," she said and her confident smile turned into a hearty feminine laugh.

"It's funny, we have an expression in America where we call tall people with long legs and long pants 'highpockets,'" he said.

"Well, Mister Highpockets, you also look American because of your nice teeth. We've heard rumors about these good-looking, sanitary American soldiers with nice teeth who *can't* speak *any* foreign language."

He grinned and wondered if she was testing him for the OSS.

"They'll have to stain *your* teeth if you *don't* want to look American," she said. "Start drinking more coffee or tea."

He nodded.

A British officer walked by and she feigned typing, flipped the carriage on the typewriter, rang its bell.

"See," she said, smiling, "*that's* what you do to *me*, Mr. Yankee…you ring *my* bell."

He looked away and fiddled with his hat.

"Pardon," she said, "I *mustn't* clatter on like this. Mr. Harrison, my boss, your boss, will be like a horse chomping at the bit. I should call him about you."

He forced a ghost of a grin and looked around, feeling somewhat nervous.

A phone on her desk rang.

"Yes, sir," she said. "Right away.

"Um, Mr. Media Number 2057," she said, "Mr. Harrison said he'd be ready in five shakes of a lamb's tail. Do you know *how* long *that* is?"

He shook his head.

"Well, in England, a lamb shakes its tail once every minute unless he's *really* happy. I suspect our lamb is *not* so happy, so we've time to chat. America?" she asked, brushing his forearm with her hand. "Yes, I've *heard* about *you* Yankees."

"Yes, *we're* a *fine* baseball team."

"Come on, tell me just your *first* name, sport," she said in a low growl.

"Valentin."

"Ummm, any relation to the great silver screen lover?"

"That's Valentino."

"I don't mean the name - I mean the lover part." And she lit a cigarette, held it aslant to her face like Bette Davis and licked her lipstick-heavy lips.

"Coffee?" he asked, now spotting a pot and cups on a nearby table beside marmalade and muffins.

"Only if you hurry back, but promise first you'll stop to see me *after* you see Harrison, won't you?"

He forced a grin and went to the coffee.

"If you *or* your baseball team needs *anything*, I'll be *here*."

He walked to the table, grabbed two cups and poured coffee.

"That's blackstrap coffee," said a man with an American Boston accent.

"What do you mean?" asked Valentin, not looking up.

"It's as thick as the bimbo dust that secretary's wearing, but she can make a good blanket wife. That's right; she's *more* than just khaki-whacky. That broad's got khaki fever for *all* men of *all* uniforms. Heck, that chippie could open up her own cathouse - as popular as she is with the Yanks and the Brits - probably make more money than a secretary too. Still, with all of her belly cousins, one can't wonder if she's got the drip . . . ."

"The drip?" asked Valentin.

"You know, 'ladies' fever,' 'Old Joe,' 'packet'. You seem awfully green, highpockets. Where you been the whole war, raised in a barn?" he said, now laughing like a loud Peter Lorre.

Valentin nodded and returned to the secretary with two cups brimming with coffee.

"Chesterfield?" she asked, punching a pack of open cigarettes until one poked out from the pack.

"I don't smoke."

"Don't smoke? I don't think I've ever met a chap who doesn't smoke. I'd be glad to get you started."

He shook his head and she puckered her lips around her cigarette, tattooed it with lipstick, took it from her mouth, and handed it to him while batting her eyes. "Are you sure?"

"Sure as eggs is eggs."

"*You* don't know what *you're* missing Mister 'eggs is eggs,'" she said, enclosing her moist lips gradually over the cigarette, inhaling slowly, not taking her eyes off him.

He looked outside the office window that showed a procession of soldiers marching down the street. "Excuse me, but who is that?"

She walked up close, pressed her chest against his shoulder, leaned hard into him. "They're the first commando unit of the Fighting French Army under de Gaul."

"They look well-trained."

"They're not. But I am . . . so, its Valentin . . . and who's Valentine are you?" she asked, winking again.

"Well, I um…"

"Valentin? As in, 'will you be my Valentine, Valentin?'" she asked as her eyes suddenly bulged and her face froze as a man walked in through the office door.

The man stood nearly as tall as Valentin, but half as wide in the shoulders, wore a British uniform and a pronounced frown.

Valentin thought he seemed all John Bull British upper class, but class changed to jackass as he approached the secretary.

"Keep flirting with *my* biddy and you'll find *my* brolly up your butt," the man said, staring hard at Valentin.

"Your what?" Valentin asked, calmly as if receiving communion.

"My brolly. My bumbershoot. My bloody umbrella, for God's sake."

"Oh - sorry old sport, didn't catch your lingo, and wasn't trying to catch your girl either," Valentin said, or anything she might offer to catch, he thought.

"Hanging around puff rapscallions again, I see, Madeline. Who is this?" he asked, pointing to Valentin.

"Just a soldier, Edward."

"From America?"

"Yes, from America. Stop being so bloody stiff upper lip, Edward."

He walked closer to Valentin, his head high, his teeth clenched. "I don't like tin-tank Yanks - they're all on skirt patrol."

"Stop it, Edward," she said. "We were just talking."

"Bull and baloney," he said, his eyes widening, his face blushing.

"Dear, I'm *just* conversing with this gentleman," she said.

"I *won't* tolerate your puckish behavior, Madeline," Edward said, not taking his eyes from Valentin. "It looks more like this tin-tank is lookin' for...a belly cousin - and by the looks of him, you'll be catching a packet from this one."

"Edward, how dare you," she said, nearly shouting, her face flushed.

"Why, you're just a bloody social gadabout aren't you, Madeline, my dear?" said Edward.

"Stop it. I said stop it," she said, now turning to Valentin. "You'll have to forgive Edward. He doesn't use his loaf often and is even more often a bit of a twillip!"

"She's a slugabed you know," Edward said, "stays in bed till noon if possible. But then maybe that's what *you're* looking for, Yank . . . You Yanks are everywhere . . . the pubs, clubs, you're oversexed, overpaid, and over here and *I* don't like it . . . ."

"Edward," she said, "stop it, he didn't do anything."

"She's my popsey, she's my homework, and she's NAFF and don't forget it!" he said.

"NAFF?" asked Valentin.

"Not available for forn. . ." said the secretary, now rolling her eyes at Valentin. "Were you raised in a barn?"

"Seems to be the going assumption..."

"So back off, you rajpot," said Edward.

Valentin looked calmly at Edward. "I'm not sure what a rajpot is, but I'm sure if I knew, you *might* just make me sore." And he stepped within inches of Edward. "I'm sorry we got off on the wrong foot, Edward. Yes, I've heard about American fliers over *here* last summer, arrogant with their cash and their mouths. But I'm *no* fly-boy, I haven't sweet fanny Adams to spend, and I'm only over *here* long enough to get down *there* and back over *there*," he said, pointing south to France and west to America. And as he pointed, he pointed with his thumb sticking out above his fist, now tight, round, big as a boule ball, just shy of Edward's jaw.

"Do you both think I'm a bloody git and don't know what's going on here?" Edward said.

Valentin glanced at the man, at his soft hands, hands of a banker or jeweler - waxen-pale, dark-hair dotted, frail, veins invisible, manicured. And he glanced at how the man's coat fit loosely about the shoulders where deltoids and biceps should show - and where a slight pot-belly did show. Well, he thought, if Edward *didn't* settle down, his arm would soon be pinned behind his back until he *did* settle down. No, this wouldn't be a punching match, *not even* a row; *he* knew it, the *Brit* knew it. So Valentin stood still and, to show good will, extended his hand.

Edward looked at Valentin's hand, massive compared to his own, tanned, scarred, blood-gorged.

After a second of heavy weather, the Brit held out his hand.

Valentin took it and heard the Englishman's fingers and wrist make funny, popping sounds with the handshake.

Edward watched Valentin's cheek muscles flex and his eyes hold steady.

Edward blinked fast, his face flushed and he backed up half a step.

"Secretary Ingersoll?" a voice came from the open door of an office.

"Yes, Mr. Harrison?" she said.

"Send in 2057."

"Yes, sir."

Valentin held his stare with Edward, held the Brit's hand firm.

"I apologize," Edward said, his face still blushed, his hand still making popping noises. "I've experienced bad times with American soldiers here."

"I understand," Valentin said. "I accept your apology, but you should check if the lady will do the same."

Valentin let go of his hand, turned to the secretary, nodded and said, "Miss."

"You'd better get a rift on," she said, smiling big as ever, "the director will be in a swivet if kept waiting. Good luck to you and sock it to the bleedin' sods."

Now she stood within inches of Edward. "You just truly buggered my day Edward!" and she slapped him.

Valentin walked over to the office door that read, 'SOE Harrison.'

And he thought how walking through that door would put him yet further *and* farther from home. Gosh, he said to himself. I've *got* to get back home. I've *got* to get back to Shelby's Creek.

"The English have a miraculous power of turning wine into water."

— Oscar Wilde

London, England
SOE Headquarters
May 1943

Chapter 4

Valentin knocked on the door.

"Come in, deah lad," a low, gruff voice said.

Valentin opened the door and stepped inside an office that smelled of cherry-scented cigar smoke and liquor, perhaps bourbon, perhaps brandy - he didn't know.

A short, stocky man stood, walked forward, held out his hand. "Hello, so glad to see you. I'm Paul Harrison of RF division, Special Operations Executive."

Valentin nodded and shook Harrison's hand, plump and soft, revealing no semblance of any callus from ever lifting a five-gallon bucket of corn, a pitchfork full of manure-laden straw bedding, or a bale of hay. And, like his hand, his face showed puffy and fleshy, with blotchy-patchy brick-red skin. A red bulbous nose and watery, bright-blue barracks-bags eyes seemed connected to the brandy breath that now polluted the air more than the tobacco smoke. And those bright blues darted constantly away as though the man had something to hide or would have something to hide, Valentin thought and nothing looked predatory about those evasive eyes - automatic, mechanical, as though he'd been evading truth all his life, coasting through on lies to convenience vices.

"Wind in your neck!" said Harrison.

"Beg your pardon."

"Nevermind, lad," said Harrison as he shuffled behind Valentin and locked the door. "Well, don't frig about lad, get a rift on, come in, have a chair."

Valentin sat in a chair farthest from Harrison to avoid the cigar smoke and liquor breath as much as possible.

"I say, we'd been absolutely *twiddling* and *twitching* waiting your arrival," Harrison said, burping now, discharging more brandy breath. "Deah God, man, you're no bantam; must be more than a sapling's height and must weigh awfully close to twenty stones - in shape. I must weigh twenty stones but a squat twenty stones - sitting behind this desk eating tarts - whereas you work toward the common weal."

"The common what, sir?'

"God save the Queen, what do they feed you in Iowa, it is Iowa isn't it? You look like you eat cast iron, steel cables, and all that sort of thing for breakfast. You're absolutely a box of birds ready for a donnybrook."

Valentin grinned and thought how Harrison should do a few "organized grab ass" push-ups and pull-ups for his potbelly, but he guessed exercise to some was hard as stopping with one tart, one scone, or one of anything. Yes, this Harrison fellow was definitely a chair-borne commando, experiencing warfare from a desk, not a field.

"Are you puckish, Mister Schmitz?"

"I beg your pardon."

"We've no crumpets this morning, but we've other fare on the far table. I say -scoff a scone and jam, ole sport; they're awfully good. Or I'll just eat them all to the point of being pogged and end up with a gutbash. Yes . . . the scones are considerably toothsome," he said, his blivit face lighting up with each bite like a toddler gorging on an Easter basket.

"No, thank you."

"Better stock up when possible, ole boy – most food in occupied countries is *ghastly* these days."

He then went to a large safe, turned the tumbler clockwise and counter-clockwise, cussed at it, kicked it, turned the tumbler again and again. "Hmm yes," he said aloud, "you've caught me a bit unbuttoned but...ah, there it is," he said as he pushed down on the handle, opened the door, pulled out a folder. "Consider yourself lucky, my good fellow. SOE takes in American recruits now."

"SOE?"

"Yes, SOE, created under ole bulldog Winnie himself. 'Set Europe ablaze,' he says, and when the bulldog barks, we absolutely listen. We've hundreds of agents in France right now . . . a bunch of raffish rogues . . . but that's what this man's army needs . . . Care for a cuppa? Or a brew?"

"A brew?"

"So sorry dear chap - Brit slang - a cuppa is tea - a brew is coffee."

"No, thank you."

Harrison then held up his cup of tea and his cup of coffee and grinned big, his rust-colored teeth showing sustained stains from both drinks. "I'm double-fisting this morning ole sport, but they say *force* liquids, *keep* the kidneys *cooperating*." He then puffed on his cigar, sipped on his coffee and bit into his scone and Valentin watched his face light up with each puff, each sip, each bite - as if some inner-voice regulated his senses to react with pleasure - as if these were the *best* pleasures late life had to offer and he *best* suck in *every* second.

"The French," said Harrison, "also have this independent F-Section force - they're for de France - but for de Gaulle? Who bloody knows? Damned frogs. Neither pro, nor anti-Gaullist - don't know what they are other than *frogs* - should have a bloody leap frog contest to work it all out." And he roared with laughter as scone fell from his mouth.

"A lot of politics, uh?" said Valentin as he looked away from the man's foul eating habits.

Harrison sucked in a big gulp of tea and spoke, his spit shooting across the table. "Bloody French fight with their *mouths - not* their *minds* or *hands* - that's why they've *not* won a bloody war *since* nitwit Napoleon."

Valentin felt his face flush with annoyance, stood military-straight, began to speak his mind… "Well, the French that helped America's revolution against the bloody Brits. . . . ."

So, you're a birdwatcher?"

"I beg your pardon," Valentin said, wondering how this Brit knew of his fondness for birds - wondering just how much MI6 then truly knew about him.

"Yes, a birdwatcher - British phrase for 'spy'."

Valentin rolled his eyes, scolding himself for being remiss with the Brit penchant for claptrap, mumbo jumbo, looney lingo, *British blather*. . . now acutely in accord with his French mother's contra-Brit sentiment.

"Yeah, *I'm* a *birdwatcher*," Valentin said in annoyed, humdrum agreement.

"America sent you 'cross the pond to us, uh dear chap?" asked Harrison. "Just like Virginia Hall - bloody fine agent. Deah God, did you know she calls her wooden leg Cuthbert? Did you know Cuthbert means conscientious objector? Isn't that a bloody rib tickler? That Hall's got some sense of humor, I must say."

He then opened a drawer, pulled out a bottle and held it up. "Care for a bevvy?"

"Beg your pardon?"

"Beefeaters breakfast - nothing compares…awfully good way to start the day when the day's a bloody war."

"No thanks."

"It's a load of guff if anyone says a good tipple is just for high tea . . . Bull and baloney . . . any time's a good time for a brew up in bloody war - and I'm not talking a skinful or being trolleyed or rat-arsed, my good man - just lubricated."

And he lifted the bottle to Valentin.

"No thanks."

"Like Wilde says, 'I occasionally take an alcoholiday'. . . And mind you, I don't care for Oscar, that bloody anti-Brit . . ." said Harrison as he burped and poured gin into his coffee.

Valentin grimaced.

"Good show - two fingers for the pour - one finger for the stir," Harrison said as he now twirled his finger in his coffee like a swizzle stick and then sucked on the dripping digit as if to absorb every trace of alcohol. "I say, jolly good idea not to get too chummy with John Barleycorn - but chummy ole John kicks crap when I need it and I need it with this bootleg coffee . . . Though one must avoid being all stonkered around Buckmaster - wouldn't look too favorable - your poggled head on the desk for a zizz, and ole Buckmaster walks in. I must say."

And he took a sip of coffee and smiled. "Have a fag?"

"Beg your pardon?"

"A cigarette?" he said, pulling a pack of Player's Navy Cuts from his pocket and jutting fat, nicotine-soiled fingers toward Valentin.

"I don't smoke."

"You don't smoke? I say, you must be the *only* bloke in Europe that *doesn't* smoke. A bloke that doesn't smoke - I say, sounds like catchy lyrics to a song."

"Maybe we should contact Hammerstein."

"Hammerstein? Sounds like a bloody Kraut."

"Have you seen my last name, sir?"

"I say, I *haven't*, my good man."

"Well, it sounds as *much* a bloody Kraut's as Hammerstein."

"Yes, well, a spot of tea perhaps?" Harrison asked, pouring milk into his teacup.

"No, thank you."

"I teach agents *not* to pour in milk *before* tea as those Kraut buggers sniff that English sort of thing out *right away* and here *I* do it. Speaking of which, *how's* your dental work?"

"I beg your pardon?'

"That's another dead give-away, if you show dental work - other than false dead man's effects - you may be considered an English spy - and if you *don't* eat with knife and fork, you *are* considered an American spy."

"Cavity-free sir and I eat with *both* utensils - *like* a human being."

Harrison sounded off with a sort of Santa-esque "ho, ho, ho", as the room echoed with his laughter and Valentin squirmed back in his chair to dodge the boozer's liquor breath.

"Well then, let's not fart arse around and get on with it, shall we?" Harrison said, his voice and face exuding an air of haughty expectation. "A quick bit of SOE history: we're not the blue-eyed boys with the establishment. Our task is in building an *effective* underground force in France . . . ."

"Underground?" asked Valentin now wondering about Rosy, the OSS man Captain Kraus told him he'd be working with. Why instead is he working with this SOE officer?

"Now," said Harrison, "we've *already* developed this SOE file card for you in relation to what your Captain Kraus provided. That Kraus seems to be a top-level contact, a big bean - gets things absolutely done, I must say."

"Yes, sir," said Valentin, still feeling confused.

"Been beavering away on your file - says you speak perfect French."

"Yes sir."

"What we have here is a Yank speaking French with *no* Yank accent?"

"No Yank accent - no American accent - no Yank American-Iowa-farmer accent."

"Brilliant! Have you ever heard an American attempt to speak *amateur* French? An abomination! Simply an abomination! It's like a horse trying to sound like a cow for Christ's sake. Quite…quite…rare as hen's teeth I must say."

"Yes, sir."

"And German - you speak German?"

"With a Bavarian accent."

"A *tri-lingual* agent - a polyglot? You ever hear about Emperor Charles V? Spoke Italian to women - German to his horse - Spanish to his God."

"Yes, sir".

"I say, Schmitz, you are the *zenith* of *all* new agents - tri-lingual, tri-cultural, a 'Gallicized' Yankee, if you will. Plus, you're **not** a bloody Texan. Can you imagine having a Texan stuck in France trying to speak French? Ha, I must say, that's *bloody* rich. John Wayne in Paris would stick out like Winston Churchill in San Antonio."

"Yes, sir," said Valentin, grinning now, picturing Wayne riding a stallion down the Champs-Élysées with his ten-gallon hat and Churchill on a ranch, holding a stogy in one hand, a branding iron in the other over a calf.

"You lived many years in Paris?"

"More like many seasons."

"You trained at Fort Claiborne two years?"

"Nearly two years."

"You received a 3 - A hardship deferment from military service because your civilian job is essential to the war effort? "

"Yes, sir."

"May I ask what job?"

"Farming."

"Corn Conroy, I must say. *Can't* fight if we *can't* eat and *that* sort of thing."

Valentin sighed, slouched slightly in his chair.

"You received *high honors* from your composite battalion on the firing range at Camp Claiborne. You are *absolutely* all wool and a yard wide."

"Beg your pardon?"

"I must say - guerilla warfare, radio communications, and highest marksmanship score in your unit, extremely accurate at up to two hundred yards - beastly. You're *no* bolo - can hit a frog hair from two hundred yards. By jove, a total of 598 points out of 600 in the World Marksmanship Championship. I say, old chap, you could knock out a bird's eye from here to Bletchley. Good God, I'm a *complete* washout compared to you, lad. With this sort of talent, we'll positively provide you with all the lashings to get the job done."

Valentin looked out the window and thought about Florine waking soon to milk the goats.

Harrison tapped on the folder, pushed scone crumbs from his desk and stared up at Valentin. "You are absolutely a capital fellow - *no* ordinary stumble-bum - blood's worth bottling, I must say...a few rungs higher on the military ladder, I must say."

Yeah, I'm a regular Chevalier, thought Valentin.

"Now, you won't be alone in occupied France, ole sport. Quite soon we'll drop two SOE-trained agents named 'Tommy' and 'Alfred' to join Resistance circuits - similar to your MO. Alfred - now *there's* a lad with a God-given talent to assassinate!"

"God-given? God *gives* such a talent?"

"Hmmm, yes...considerably. And, by jove, we also just dropped eleven SOE-trained female agents. So far, they're *still* alive. In fact, Diana Rowden is a courier to Paris and you may marry up with her on occasion. Her name will change, but here's her photo - memorize it. Not a bad honey trap either, uh ole sport?"

Valentin remained stoic as he memorized her face.

"Here are two photos of two more female agents you may marry up in Paris. This is Nancy Wake, otherwise known as the White Mouse to the Gestapo, who has a huge ransom on her head. And this is Julia Child, who works mostly with the OSS, but we keep tabs."

Valentin studied each face with each name.

"Believe it or not," said Harrison, "our man's army also has a woman named Violette Szabo, the *best* shot in SOE. The two of you should *quite literally* marry up - could be as two peas in a pod. And she's not *only* SOE's *best* shot - she's SOE's *best* looking broad."

Valentin looked out the window again.

"You know, *that's* what this man's army needs - *more* marksmen. Look at Switzerland - built deep tunnels in high mountains - loaded them up with highly-trained marksmen and powerful artillery. After a few failed days, those Kraut buggers realized they were up against a formidable foe *not* to be reckoned with."

"Yes, sir."

"Well then, let's get on with this cloak-and-dagger business, shall we? So you *specialize* in assassination?"

"Sir...I..."

"And you have your own bandook, a specialized Mannlicher rifle, I see. Well, ole sport, we don't want you taking pot shots at big wigs with an eighteenth century blunderbuss, now do we?"

"Sir, I'm no assassin."

"Well this report says you're a *highly skilled marksman*, old boy. I'd scarcely assume you're going into France to shoot *pheasants* for *Petain's* dinner."

"Beg your pardon?"

"You want to fight for the French Resistance, do you not? What's the *crab* in it for you sport?"

"Beg your pardon?"

"Sorry, I'll speak American English. Why do you want to fight? Adventure? Intrigue?"

"No, family in Paris that needs help . . . ."

"Here we're fighting on every bloody continent except Antarctica - that's sixty-one countries, three quarters of the human race - and you want to help your family in Paris? Noble, dear chap, absolutely noble. Not for pelf and power, good show, yes, we all fight for family first, country second, truth be told."

"Yes, sir."

"Your parents are deceased? No siblings? No wife? No children?"

"No sir."

"So," said Harrison, "you're a farm lad from Iowa about to embark on a spy mission in the hurly burly of Paris. Do you think a country boy is ready for the city life?"

"I've been accustomed to the hurly burly of Paris for some time. And to me, it's not hurly burly; I've always found more quiet and peace in Paris than most *small* towns."

"Yes, well, good luck lad on that 'peace' part in Paris these days," said Harrison as he gulped down his coffee as one finishes a mug of beer. "Fair warning, ole sport, the bugbear is that agents average *six months* in France *before* they're denounced, captured, or…must return to England where they'll get the bowler hat back to civilian life. *None* believe they'll die. *None* believe they'll be caught. But Herr Hit has a new top secret executive order: SOE and OSS agents are to be shot following interrogation. So - stay *away* from those Gestapo and SS buggers. They get hold of you and God falls off your mattress; it's all over, I must say. *Six months, six months.*"

"Good to know, sir."

"Fair warning also: an agent's life can be absolutely boring and lonely ninety-nine percent of the time."

"What about the other one percent, sir?"

"Bloody scary as hell, dear boy. I was an agent of SOE - within two months we were all betrayed - old sweat before we made it over the hump. The Gestapo knows my face. Other than boobs on a boar, few things are considerably less useless than a blown spy. I must say, I feel awfully lucky pushing a pencil in London instead of pushing up daisies in France - or being a kriegy in Krautland."

"Yes sir."

"Ted Wilkinson, by jove," said Harrison suddenly, his eyes popping, his fist punching the air. "Bloody Ted Wilkinson is who you remind me of, lad."

"Beg your pardon, sir."

"Wilkinson is from America - Missouri, I believe - a state below you, I believe. He spoke French, like you, a Midwesterner, like you - trained by the RAF and SOE - like *you* will be."

"SOE? RAF, sir?"

"Yes, fine gent, *damned* fine gent that Wilkinson bloke," said Harrison. "He lasted a long time in the field too…anyway…haven't heard from that deah lad for some time…perhaps betrayed…perhaps a kriegy in Krautland…quite the bloody curious situation."

"Yes, quite," said Valentin, now longing more than ever for Iowa - as Wilkinson must be longing for Missouri - *if* he's still alive.

"So, you shoot, speak, fight, and kill. By jove lad, you and Napolean are pissin' through the same straw. Capital, yes, capital . . . now, we've learned Paris's

Hôtel Meurice is to receive dignitaries and elite enemy officers in the next two months. We need someone to take them out."

"Take them out?"

"We'll set you up safely in Paris to deliver *important* kills on *important* targets."

"I don't kill, sir."

"Pardon?"

"My objective is to get into France, find my family, and get all three of us out of Europe, back to Iowa, T.N.T."

Harrison's face colored crimson. "We've *all* got a job in this bloody war and I'm *not* asking you to do someone *else's* job. I'm *not* asking you to be a *bloody* Joe Soap."

"I ***won't*** kill."

"All due respect, Schmitz...you Yanks are *all* the same - you take war *so personal*. Do you think we Brits had time to take war *personal* at Dunkirk? Do you think we have time to take war *personal* when the bloody Luftwaffe is bombarding us? When war comes to your front yard, you put all that *personal* crap behind you and you do what you must to survive. It's *not personal*; its *bloody business* to stay *alive*."

Valentin looked down.

"Lad, this isn't the same secret service that sent in Agents Kubis and Gabcik to assassinate Heydrich. They had *no* backup to get them out. You'll have *as much* backup as a well-organized infantry company."

Valentin said nothing.

"I understand if you're a bit timid, lad, but we must *absolutely* take out these targets and there's *no* operative in the Resistance or SOE with *your* skills at *this* time. So, *you* are vital to *us*, but *we* are risking a *lot* for *you*."

"Yes, sir."

"We have a major offensive in the works called 'Operation Ratweek,' where we're planning assassinations on the enemy and collaborators. Your skills will prove quite handy... you have several days of training at Hampshire to consider what we've discussed . . . take the 'turnip course' where you live off the remote Highlands and wild turnips . . . take a crash course in demolitions, plastic explosives, counterintelligence, interrogation training . . ."

"Yes sir."

"Buckmaster's obviously going to love you. Get on good terms with Buckmaster, ole boy, he'll dole out solid gold cufflinks to special agents."

"Buckmaster?"

"Yes, ole boy. Maurice Buckmaster, former employee of the Ford Company in France, one of your *main* contacts. He'll be pleased to learn of an American on his team. In fact, other than 'Moe' Berg, you'll be the *only* male American OSS agent in Paris at this point . . . ."

"Yes, sir."

Harrison stood and went to the table for a scone and put jam on it. "Now, they'll suspect you're English if you speak *only* with your mouth. They'll know you're American if you speak *only* with your mouth. Talk with *every* agile limb and facial feature you have, like the French."

"Yes, sir."

"Know that your enemy will detect an American demeanor immediately. Hell, any European can detect the American smug mug."

"Smug mug?"

"You bloody well know what I mean - that insular, capitalistic, independent conceitedness that you buggers portray as if you must answer to no one, regardless of authority, rank, or advanced position in society. Oh, you respond favorably enough to your boss, but less as a show of respect and more as a show of butt-kissing for self-possessed advancement."

"You don't say?"

"But since you've a military background, I sense that superiority sense has been wiped from you. Good God, thanks to military brainwashing!"

"Tally ho, my good man," said Valentin, tongue in cheek.

"So you know now *how* to walk and talk like the French - animated nonverbal - animated verbal - body back - your gait more Walker, less Morgan, less quarter horse? You know how *not* to act American - active mouth and inactive limbs - a fork for all food - inquisitive, friendly; face legible as a book; moving like a race horse stretching for the finish line?"

"And how *not* to act British," said Valentin - "Pretentious, pompous, self-righteous, somber-faced silly with a wily wit, dry and dour, a pace so proper, a frame so erect, as if expecting a knighting any moment. . . ."

"Hmmm, yes, considerably," Harrison said, "and all that sort of thing."

"Bloody right, sir," said Valentin, now grinning. "And God save the Queen while you're at it…"

"Hmmm, yes…well, we've had you vetted and found you to be a 'genuine Joe' You help us, we help you. Oh, and keep an eye on those partisan wastrels. We're *not* made of money in London."

Valentin looked out the window.

"So, enough of this bobbery and tomfoolery - let's not shilly-shally around - following is the doctrine established for all volunteers of the Free French movement - one, volunteers will sign up to fight until the liberation of France is secured - two…"

"I *can't* sign this. This *doesn't* apply to me at all. I'm a *different* kind of volunteer . . . ."

"Do tell old man . . ."

There is a quick knock on the door.

"Deah God, what is it now?" Harrison said as he pushed his chair back with great effort and shuffled to the door. "I'm not to be bothered," he hollered through the door.

"You *will* be bothered or I'll **kick** your door in," said a voice, unmistakably American, thought Valentin.

Harrison opened the door and his ruddy face changed to a ruddier glow as a tall man wearing a pressed suit walked in and hollered, "What sort of *flimflam* are you trying *now Harrison?*"

"In wartime, truth is so precious that she should always be attended by a bodyguard of lies."

— Winston Churchill

London, England
SOE Headquarters
May 1943

Chapter 5

"**I** must say, this is rather *awkward*," said Harrison.

"You lousy Crumpet-Stuffer," said the tall man.

"Well, blue pencil, you ruddy blokes hornswoggled Hall from us, our most prized female agent."

"Baloney. Virginia came to us. Just because you gave her a British medal for bravery, doesn't make her British - she's from Baltimore, not Berkshire. And this agent's from the United *States* - *not* the United *Kingdom*."

"I say," said Harrison, "...you know of SOE's bad luck with incompetent crack-pot agents in the field of late. Besides, OSS and SOE work together now. And so, we thought..."

"You thought **what**? You've got a bloody 'cheek' trying to steal **our** boy."

"I say, you stole our last stellar agent and we just thought..."

"You just thought **what**?" said the tall man as he stepped in front of Valentin with his hand extended. "My name's Rosy. I'm Captain Kraus's friend. The OSS and Dulles has first dibs on you, **not** the SOE and Buckmaster. I apologize for being late, and **this** SOE mess."

"Beg your pardon, old chap," Harrison said. "...SOE mess? OSS is *more* of a mess."

"Not **today**," said Rosy as he nodded to Valentin and then toward the door.

"By jove, we don't want a hoo-ha with you lads," said Harrison, "but you *can't* blame us for trying . . . I guess I truly cocked up this one. No hard feelings," he said offering his hand to Valentin.

Out of courtesy, Valentin shook Harrison's hand, avoided looking at his face, looking instead out the window - preferring the clear blue skies over *his* blood-shot eyes - preferring the songs of the birds on the trees to this bullcrap Brit. And as he released Harrison's soft hand, he thought how the world needs *more* farmers with calloused hands, *fewer* fools with soft hands.

"Well, I must say, you extracted the urine from me again, Rosy," said Harrison. "Cheerio then," he said, now walking the men to the door, his body a bit tippsy-wobbly.

At the door, Valentin stopped and turned to Harrison. "Oh and by the way, ole boy, this Corn Conroy actually prefers a shot of 'John Barleycorn' with the likes of Lafayette over the likes of Cornwallis any ole day - and fine fare from a Frog over pea soup from a Brit as well - absolutely!"

Rosy grinned as he watched Harrison's face redden. "Let's get out of here pell-mell," said Rosy, now leading the way down the hallway.

"Now that we've got the stalled project back on track, how are you, Schmitz?"

"Right as rain now, sir."

"Darned SOE," said Rosy. "Soon as anyone who speaks French arrives in England, he's reeled in by British Secret Services. I wished OSS weren't so darned dependent on SOE in England, but we put up with *their* antics because we need *their* plane and boat transportation for OSS drops into France."

"Just glad I won't be under the command of all those obviouslys, scarcelys, awfullys, considerablys, absolutelys, and bloodys."

"Yeah, a lot of bloody abuse of English adjectives by English blokes, that's for sure. When I return stateside, the only time I want to hear the word 'bloody' is when someone's ordering a vodka and tomato juice."

"Yes, sir."

Valentin looked ahead and saw the secretary waving at him and then handing him a note that showed her phone number.

Valentin nodded and the two men kept walking.

"It's none of my business," whispered Rosy, "but that's *one* skirt I *wouldn't* chase."

"Why's that?"

"That secretary's definitely a beaut worthy of nooky, but a sign should hang around her neck, 'Enter at your own risk.' Most Brits around here refer to her as their 'Piccadilly Commando,' - her flat's like a skivvies house."

"You don't think her phone number is worth keeping?"

"*Only* if your date is followed up by a doctor visit and most doctors prefer to care for war-wounded."

"You mean she might have the 'drip'?"

"The drip?" said Rosy, laughing. "Nobody says 'drip' anymore. When you say the 'drip', it sounds like you were raised in a barn."

"Good to know," said Valentin, rolling his eyes and tossing her phone number into a trash can, remembering Katherine's photo and letters in a similar trash can in the cabin at Shelby's Creek . . . .

Just then, a short, stout, muscular man ran up to Valentin. "Are you the marksman?"

"Oh, this is Agent Lewis, from MI6," Rosy said to Valentin. "He's a marksman as well."

Valentin glanced at Rosy, frowned, and wondered why he was being labeled "marksman."

"Hello, ole sport," said Lewis. "I say, you're not staying around the pubs around Beaulieu?"

"We're staying near the Northumberland pub tonight," said Rosy.

"Jolly good. A chum of mine will wet one's stripes tonight at that very pub. Join us and I'll buy you a brew at, let's say, 02100?" said Lewis.

Valentin hesitated as he sized up Lewis. Yes, there was something wrong about him, something he didn't like in the shiftiness of his eyes and impish smile on his boxer-rugged mug.

"You might as well relax and learn a thing or two from MI6," said Rosy.

Valentin hesitated and then nodded. "Yeah, okay, see you at the pub - 2100 hours." But he already regretted it.

Lewis nodded, smirked, and walked away.

"Lewis seems okay," said Rosy, "besides, he's dropped into France twice already and may share some insight with you."

"He's with MI6, uh?"

"Yeah," said Rosy, "MI6 doesn't care much for us OSS folk - they think we're FUBB."

"FUBB?"

"Mucked up beyond belief - same as FUBAR, mucked up beyond all recognition - same as MFU, military muck up - same as SNAFU, situation normal, all mucked up - same as SUSFU, situation unchanged, still mucked up - same as TARFU, things are really mucked up - similar to SFA, sweet muck all."

"What exactly is MI6?"

"Britain's age-old intelligence service. They regard us as new kids on the block. They think we're badly informed and bad-mannered. One of their officers, a Sir Claude Dansey, seems to be the ring-leader for this attitude. Personally, I'd like to take him behind the barn for a 'dance.'"

Valentin thought it funny how Rosy referred to "dance" the same way he did in dealing with a jerk. But he did not find it funny how Lewis referred to him as a marksman. Yeah, I'll be having my own "personal dance" with Lewis tonight as sure as a nimbus brings rain. And by the looks of Lewis' boxer-mug and solid build, there might be a storm when it rains.

"I don't know how you ended up here at Baker Street with Harrison," Rosy said. "SOE must have coordinated with MI6 on this one. Understand that most agent volunteers are clumsy rookies -when a star athlete like you becomes a free agent, all teams vie for him."

"Boy there are a lot of secret agencies to remember: MI6, SOE, OSS, F-Section, de Gaulle's exile secret agency..."

"Yeah and the Brits get along least with most . . . ."

"A lot of politics, uh?"

"It's like an old lady's club. You hear rumors that MI6 is monitoring Napoleonic de Gaulle who is conspiring with Russia because America is conspiring with Vichy when in reality America may be France's only hope for a free France again. But France needs a hero and the *voice* of de Gaulle on BBC may be *that* hero while D-Day English, Canadian, and American soldiers will die for *that* voice. Hopefully de Gaulle *remembers* this."

"Hopefully the free world **remembers** this."

"For now, your agent pseudonym is Farmer."

"Yes sir," Valentin said and thought how, right away, he liked Rosy. Yes, he seemed more machine than man - yes, his discipline subtracted character, but the former is what you want from Patton on the battlefield — which is what you want to win and to survive - which is all he wanted - win, survive, and get back to Shelby's Creek T.N.T. Yes, T.N.T.

"It is not the beginning of the end; it is the end of the beginning."

— Churchill

London, England
Northumberland Hotel
May 1943

Chapter 6

Rosy parked his jeep at the back of the hotel and he and Valentin walked into the pub's back entrance.

Valentin scanned the bar - hazy-smoky, beer-smelly, and busy with sailors and soldiers wearing different uniforms from different nations. All were drinking, most were smoking, some singing - a couple fighting. In a larger back room, an even more motley crew of soldiers were busy with what looked like flower girls, dancehall girls, and dance-in-a-room girls, singing, swinging, and partying as if D-Day had passed into V-E Day.

"Looks like I owe *you* a beer, Farmer," said Rosy.

"Well, would a *genuine* German *ever* turn down a beer?" asked Valentin.

"SSShhhh, don't say that too loud around here," Rosy said.

"Oh yeah."

"Two bottled sunshines," Rosy hollered to the bartender.

"Bottled sunshines?"

"You really need to catch up on slang, Farmer," said Rosy winking, "people might think you were raised in a barn."

"I think I *was* raised in a barn," Valentin mumbled.

Rosy grabbed the two beers, handed one to Valentin.

"Good Lord," said Valentin, grimacing. "This beer is warm. Warm beer is worse than cold tea."

"Welcome to Britain," Rosy said as he led the way up to the second-floor stairs where the aromas of food wafted on the stairwell from the second-floor restaurant.

Valentin wasn't sure, but thought he smelled vegetables - possibly peas - possibly tarts - none of which appealed to him as much as the beer, even if it was warm, for it calmed his nerves.

They topped the third level and Rosy turned down a hallway and opened a door that led to a large room converted into an OSS office, complete with large desks, large files, and a dozen chairs.

Rosy turned on a lamp light that showed his desk, clean except for pens, paper, and a large ash-filled ashtray. He took a key from his pocket, jiggled it in a hole in a file, and pulled out a folder marked "Farmer," and handed a paper from inside it to Valentin. "Here's your own personal poop sheet - study on your own time."

"Can do."

"Now, I'm known as your operations officer or 'Joe handler.' I coordinate your cover story, flight plan, communications, documents, clothing and training. Whatever you learned in the Army is valuable, but your code of conduct, unlike the Army, will definitely *not* be by the numbers."

"Yes sir."

"Your mission will be to penetrate occupied France and join up with a French Resistance cell in Paris."

"Yes sir."

Rosy walked to a table fully set for dinner with fake food and utensils. "First things first. You've heard the expression, 'Words fitly spoken are like apples of gold and settings of silver'? Well, settings of silver are set that way for a reason that Americans seem to have forgotten:

Lesson 1: Eat the European way with fork in left hand and knife in right. How Americans ever started eating differently, I don't know. I guess when we crossed the pond we crossed our silverware too. OSS has already lost two American agents from eating the 'American' way.

Lesson 2: If you drink milk with tea or coffee, pour the milk into the cup *after* tea or coffee. Any wrong move under a watchful Gestapo eye might spell doom."

He then fished into his front pocket, pulled out and punched at a pack of Chesterfields. "Cigarette?" he asked, already holding out a lighter.

"I don't smoke."

"I...don't think I know anyone who doesn't smoke...mind if I do?"

"Help yourself."

"Lesson 3: Americans have the point of pie or cake toward them; Europeans don't," he said, pointing to a wax cake model.

Lesson 4: We work with small Resistance groups, not *only* for security, but it makes hit-and-run raids *more* effective. And we *always* run. *Any* attempt to stand your ground results in *disaster* against a superior force.

Lesson 5: Language. I know you speak French, but be aware of speaking non-European colloquialisms. Your enemy speaks French as well as the French. And once in France, speak only French.

Lesson 6: Stay away from women. Women spell danger; a spy already has enough of that.

Lesson 7: In public, never stand still as if waiting for someone, never walk too fast, never whisper - this all draws attention. And for *God's sake*, **don't** whistle or stand with your hands in your pockets; they'll think you're a *bloody* Brit.

Lesson 8: Take different routes at different times every day to work, to your flat, to your cell's meeting place.

Lesson 9: If in doubt in a multifarious situation, trust your gut.

Lesson 10: Where you live is *your* business alone and change flats every month.

Lesson 11: Keep your person clean. *Never* carry anything seditious - a note, a gun, a weapon of any kind. Three years ago agents dropped into France with a Gestapo welcome because an address book was confiscated on a detained agent the week before. And last year, an agent was caught with the address of a safe house in his pocket and the Gestapo transformed the safe house into a *souriciere* or *mousetrap* to catch a dozen more agents.

Lesson 12: **Never** tell anyone your true identity or your true history, **especially** a beautiful woman.

Lesson 13: Trust **no one**; turncoats are **everywhere** - from Paris booksellers to Paris waiters, from cab drivers to desperate children, from

French police to French priests, all may be in the pay of the Gestapo. A trusted source may change at any time. Entire networks are betrayed by one captured member that can't tolerate torture or that accepts money in exchange for freedom and a new life in a new country. There are two secret-agent adages: First, three can keep a secret if two of them are dead. Second, dubito ergo sum - I doubt, therefore I survive - *the golden rule* of all secret agents.

Lesson 14: Keep radio communication to a minimum. Use a quiet alarm clock to time your transmissions; a second too long may be the second the Gestapo direction finding teams bust you. Also, the enemy loves to play a radio game referred to as Englandspiel. In this game, the enemy conceals the capture of a radio operator, keeps the radio link open, receives our intelligence, and provides misleading intelligence back to us. To fight Englandspiel, our radio operators now have security checks, which may include a mistake or a special word in every transmission. The absence of a security check indicates to London that the operator's in trouble and, in turn, they may play their own Englandspiel back to the enemy.

Lesson 15: If arrested, you're on your own; we disavow any knowledge of your existence. So don't get arrested. It'll probably spell your doom. You are, after all, an undercover agent, **not** military personnel. *Neither* the prisoner-of-war status under the Geneva Convention *nor* the Reich protects your rights. If caught, you may be shot on the spot. If caught listening to BBC, you may be shot on the spot. If caught with a radio transceiver, you may be shot on the spot. If caught out after curfew, you may be shot on the spot. If caught with Resistance paraphernalia, you may be shot on the spot. If caught distributing tracts, you may be shot on the spot.

Lesson 16: See your enemy indifferently. If you show hate, you become suspect.

Lesson 17: Some OSS field personnel get personally involved with their Resistance cell. This involvement is a human weakness that can prove *dangerous **and** deadly.*

Lesson 18: Be as objective as possible at all times.

Lesson 19: We provide funds, *but* to justify the money, we ask for intelligence in return. How you gather intelligence - bribes, blood, or blackmail - I don't care; we *need* Intel for *doe-ray-me*. I provide you with French Francs. Some agents receive hard currency to exchange on the black market, but this raises suspicions; there are plenty of suspicions already. Speaking of suspicions, don't grow a beard; it arouses suspicion. If you must, dye your hair, grow a mustache, wear spectacles, a derby, limp, and carry a cane. Your cell will provide new ID papers to match the new getup.

Lesson 20: Learn to see without turning your head. Walk on the same side of the street as approaching traffic to help you spot a tail in the windshields of the traffic. And take a circuitous route always to make sure you're not tailed. If tailed, however, slip into an alley, a café toilet, a back row of a bookshop and put on a beret you'll always have in the seat of your pants, or a fake moustache you'll always have in your pants pocket, or a pair of spectacles you'll always have in your front shirt pocket."

"Why no fake beard?"

Rosy shook his head. "No Frenchman wears a beard in France unless he's Monet, Van Gogh, or Renoir - and they're all dead.

Lesson 21: When you destroy a message, *never* crumple it, but tear it in pieces and scatter the pieces hither and thither or eat it. It's much better with salt, by the way.

Lesson 22: Don't go into a night club, a black market café, or a first-class railway carriage - as they are raided.

Lesson 23: Know the sounds of your safe house and be ready to move if you hear a strange sound.

Finally, Lesson 24: *Most* agents are captured within *six months*. Some of our top agents in Algiers, Barcelona, Vercors, Italy, and even Switzerland have gone missing this month and we may *never* hear from them again. Like I said, as an OSS agent, *six months is your life expectancy*."

"Good to know," said Valentin as he swallowed hard on his beer.

"Starting tomorrow, you'll take crash courses with OG, which trains in demolition, ambush, compass runs, and special night simulation operations. You'll also learn about sentry and key figure elimination."

"You mean assassination?"

The phone rang. "Excuse me," Rosy said, picking up the phone and just as quickly putting it down. "Research and Development will bring your cover credentials."

Valentin nodded.

"We understand you wish to find your grandparents. We can't assist you to any great length. We have greater priorities right now. But we'll assist you *as much* as we can *for your help in turn*. Any questions?"

Valentin shook his head.

"Mandatory OSS training usually lasts three weeks, eighteen hours a day and includes interrogation exercises, code work, memory tests, land survival, killing, and radio operation. Kraus and I agree you can skip much of this. Few OSS agents, hell, few SOE or MI6 agents have *your* expertise. You'll study Morse code and state-of-the art radio operations. English Major William Fairbairn, author of a renowned book on dirty fighting, will be one of your instructors tomorrow."

Rosy put out his short cigarette and lit another. "So what are your thoughts?"

"Scared as hell."

"I'd rather hear that than hear you're gung-ho with *no* fear. *Those* agents fall first. What's your *biggest* fear?"

"A situation of kill or be killed."

"You'll be in that situation," said Rosy, now handing over a folder. "This is your cover. Know it with conviction - even in the case of a shock raid, in the middle of sleep, in the middle of dinner, all of which will happen *several* times *before* you leave."

Valentin nodded.

"Your cover is Phillipe Delcourt, a *real* French soldier who escaped at Dunkirk. He is *not* regular army and there are *absolutely no* records of his participation. He lives here in London now, awaiting D-Day. His features and stats are similar to yours. He is from the north, Lille, where the French are bigger and blonder like you. Know that Americans raided the steelworks at Lille in early October with a hundred bombers. Only half the planes reached the target and few bombs fell within five hundred yards of the steelworks. You, Phillipe Delcourt, were in Lille at this time and witnessed the Luftwaffe driving the bombers back to England. Understand?"

"Yes."

"Memorize your home street address in Lille and the side streets. Your ID paperwork includes the service faux papers that include membership in a sporting club, a Polo club, a worn identity card, a railway pass, baptismal certificate, tax receipts, a medical report, a railway pass, and a ration card, all stamped with authenticity. *'Pocket litter,'* as we call it, includes these train tickets from Lille and a Lille opera stub. Your card identité has your photograph, name, thumb print, marital status, place of birth, date of birth, physical marks, and nationality. Your work permit states your place of employment and trade qualifications. All identity cards have been dirtied to look authentic. All appropriate passes have a forged signature of an enemy officer at the bottom with a replicated authorized stamp. *Please* guard all of this with care. We *don't* have many covers that come *close* to your large stature."

"Won't the enemy have such records that may show differences?"

Rosy shook his head. "We do our homework, Farmer. It's true that the Gestapo in Paris has access to all French public records since Europe keeps files of family nationalities. But the civil register in Lille with Phillip Delcourt's original records were destroyed in a bomb raid."

"Yes sir."

"Memorize some basic information such as Phillipe Delcourt's mother's maiden name; his father's middle name; his siblings' names, their locations; his grandparents' locations, alive or dead; where his maternal Grandpa was born; where his paternal Grandma died. You'll know where you bought your clothing, your shoes, why you have not collected your rations, your tobacco. You'll also know Lille. The two most important things to know: Lille is a large industrial town and it's where the Free French leader Charles de Gaulle was born. Oh, and here's a tobacco card."

"I don't smoke sir."

"You can't resist saying '*sir*' and you *never* smoke? Were you raised at West Point or a convent?"

"No, sir. Shelby County, Iowa."

"Now - I understand you speak fluent French and German and we thought initially you'd work well with the Deutsche Institut as a language teacher. But that'd limit movement. Plus, we learned of your journalism experience. So, you'll work as a reporter for a pro-Reich gutter newspaper called *Les Nouveaux Temps*. You'll be known as an ultra-collabos - a Frenchman who contributes work for the enemy. So, you may not be the most popular Parisian, but its **excellent** cover and it's the **safest** paper for you to work with as we have people on the inside. Take care what you write. *Le Soir* just lost three agents that printed obvious anti-Hitler sentiment - they were caught **and** executed. Here's a copy of that *Le Soir* edition. *Just this small column cost three men their lives.*"

"I guess sometimes the sword *is* mightier than the pen," said Valentin softly as he shook his head.

"For *Les Nouveaux Temps*, you'll serve both as interpreter and journalist for entertainment - and being a bilingual journalist keeps you immune from compulsory labor for the enemy - even if they up the ante on age."

"Why is a journalist so respected?"

"Well, the enemy believes the pen is mightier than the sword, especially when **that pen** prints propaganda. As a journalist for a pro-Reich paper in Paris, you have a **high-priority occupation** and are therefore **exempt** from the draft."

"Yes sir."

"Your occupation gives you **carte blanche** in Paris. Just know the French Gendarmerie hunt draft dodgers and your STO documents and papers may be checked often. Just **never** forget your papers. To be caught without your papers **guarantees** you a one way ticket on a cattle car bound for a concentration camp - without a trial, without a rebuttal. But once your face becomes familiar, your role will **not** be questioned."

"What is compulsory labor?"

"The Fuhrer needs to replace soldiers lost in Stalingrad and on the Russian front by recruiting French men for his factories, which proved good for us because it inspired more French men to fight with the Resistance - *rather* than work in Reich factories."

"So, the Resistance grows stronger?"

"There are an estimated forty thousand active partisans in Paris. *Even* the metro staff in Paris has resistors now. Speaking of which, you'll use the metro a lot in Paris since most above-surface transportation has been immobilized due to gas rationing and bombing raids. The metro is your most efficient mode of getting about, other than a bicycle, *gold* these days."

Rosy put his cigarette out and lit another. "What do you think?"

"I could use a six pack of beer about now - warm *or* cold, I don't care."

The phone rang. Rosy picked it up, listened and put the phone back down.

"As we speak, on the fourth floor of Brook Street, near OSS headquarters at Grosvenor Square, 'moles' are customizing clothing accouterments to appropriate your cover. Our garments store gives utmost attention to every label and every seam so it will be as though your fictitious Lille mother bought it for you '*made to order*' from the *corner tailor*."

"Impressive."

"Oh, before I forget, word is that the Gestapo is recognizing wrist watches supplied by the OSS," said Rosy.

"I have this pocket watch that's over sixty years old," Valentin said. "My Grandpa brought it from Germany when he came to America. There's *nothing* on it that implicates that I'm from America, as it was made in Germany."

Rosy nodded. "We actually have a division called the Bach section that will check everything on your person before you go. For example, if you start to smoke, hold the angle of the cigarette like a European.

Valentin looked at his fingers and the oil still under the nails from the farm and wished there was *fresh oil* on them *now* from the farm.

"You'll *parachute* into France. Landing agents to the Channel coasts by boat is too risky due to heavy coastal patrols. Besides, your target drop date will be a full moon phase - full moon - only by air - no moon - only by sea."

"Yes, sir."

"Once in occupied France, you'll rendezvous with a reception committee for a few hours and then hike, finally rendezvous with a SOAM boat on the Seine."

"SOAM, sir?"

"Service des Operations Aeriennes et Maritimes - developed under the direction of austere RAF guidelines along with Service des Operations Aeriennes et Maritimes - which provides vital aid to the Resistance with Allied agents, supplies *and* most importantly - transport of *all* these things throughout France via a boat or plane."

"I drop from what type of plane, sir?"

"A Halifax. Supply canisters must also be dropped in many zones on the same night."

"What about my *personal* equipment, my bore brush, my rifle. . ."

"All will be packed in kapok material in reinforced, lined wicker panniers and sent ahead to Paris...your rifle will *always* be handled by the *best* people. They will disassemble it, clean it, oil it, check the bore, the mechanisms - no worries."

"I have a request that it be lubricated only with the finest oil, not that petroleum jelly Cosmoline crap."

Rosy nodded and made a note. "I *respect* a man who *respects* his tools."

"Yeah, that rifle is *special* to me, *irreplaceable*," said Valentin, thinking how there was *nothing more* he wished to say to Rosy or *anyone* else about it. Some things *cannot* be explained - some things may drift out that window of your heart if you open that window too much. No, nobody could understand his rifle. Just like nobody could understand why Shelby's Creek was the **most wonderful** place on earth, and the **only** place he wished to be - **right now**.

"Kites rise highest against the wind, not with it."

— Churchill

London, England
Northumberland Hotel
May 1943

Chapter 7

"Any questions, Farmer?" Rosy asked.

Just then an air raid siren sounded, followed by a second.

"That's no drill," said Rosy. "That's '*Condition Red*.' When the second siren comes on, lights go off," he said. "No lights. No targets."

Valentin immediately fished in his pocket for his pencil flashlight and kept his finger on the switch.

Rosy shut off all lights and found his way now with his own pencil flashlight. "Better get to the cellar."

The wailing, warning sirens continued.

Then - the faint drone of planes followed by falling bombs – whistling - the whistling building to crescendo - crescendo ending with a thunderous explosion -followed by windows breaking, rubble crumbling - the large pieces thudding hard and fast - the small pieces rocketing up and drizzling down like large hail on a tin roof.

Rosy and Valentin rushed to the first floor pub level.

All around, windows crashed from constant bomb concussions.

Valentin glanced out into the streets.

"Come on, Farmer, down the cellar," Rosy said.

"You go. I'm going down the metro." And he rushed outside to a lady sprawled on the street, her three children trying to pull her up.

"I'll help you, Madame," Valentin hollered and she nodded, her face desperate.

He lifted her up. She took her toddler girl by the hand and he lifted the two smaller boys into his arms and rushed toward the metro.

People darted in all directions like angry ants, into one another, away from one another, into and away from explosions and bombs.

"Down the shell! Down the shell!" people hollered and pointed to the metro steps.

Valentin hurried down the stairs, just ahead of a cloud of coarse dust from bombed brickwork.

Above the steps - onto the streets - many more whistling missiles - wobbling, careening helplessly until helplessness found a home with a tremendous boooooooommm.

Valentin set the boys down.

They all huddled against the walls where bricks spit dried concrete and dusty brick breath from the bomb concussions.

No, neither the bricks nor the people around the bricks would ever be the same, he thought, as he looked at the children's wide, crying eyes and heard the elderly folk's raspy screams.

Then the bombs stopped, the bomb concussions stopped - but the sirens wailed on and on.

Valentin looked farther down the tunnel where many citizens settled down, as if camping out, with water and tins of food beside them. Some lay next to the track - on blankets, coats, or the bare concrete, beneath a string of light bulbs. Some lay on their backs, some on their sides, most showed a demeanor of calm now as though they were having a picnic, as if this were now part of a daily schedule. Some, mostly children, held their ears. Some, mostly adults, sat on chairs, leaned against walls, crocheted, read, waited... waited. Mothers fed bottles to children as they sat, legs splayed, hair a mess. Children wore infant gas masks and it looked funny to watch mothers strap the masks on - as if they were putting a fish bowl over their child's head. One little girl sat in a corner and played with a wind-up music box and smiled - the only smile in that tunnel. Then her mother put a gas-mask fish bowl over her and her smile left.

He took off his coat and put it on the floor for the children to sit on.

"Thank you," the mother said.

He nodded. "Please *keep* my jacket. I have more. I'll see if anyone else needs help," he said and walked down the tunnel as it suddenly shook now from an explosion just above ground followed by another and another.

49

He returned moments later. "Actually, everyone in this tunnel seems less rattled than I," he said.

She nodded. "You sound American. We Brits have been going through this since '40; we've a lot of practice." She then opened up a huge bag filled with blankets, canned goods, a can opener, bottles of water, and several gas masks.

"Good Lord, ma'am - *how* can you carry *all* those items? That bag *must* weigh a ton."

She nodded. "Everyone down here comes as prepared as possible in case - after the bombing - there is no home to return to."

"I think I'll walk down this opposite way and check on things," he said.

He walked several meters for several minutes.

At one juncture, a teen boy played accordion next to an old man who played harmonica. What a wonderful way to divert people's attention, he thought, but, after a moment, he realized that sight was more pleasing than sound as the boy was off key and the old man couldn't harmonize or carry a tune in a bucket. So he moved away from them - almost preferring the thumping of bombs to the thumping of their instruments.

Soon he was within another station tunnel where people crowded the tunnel halls. He found it extremely strange to see everyone settled in as leisurely as in their living rooms - women darned wool, children played with toys, old men smoked on a pipe or closed their eyes as they leaned against the walls. The ones that *didn't* preoccupy themselves or *didn't* close their eyes took on a raised-brow, forehead-furrowed, mouth-twisted, wide-eyed look - and jumped every time a bomb hit. It seemed, *even though* they'd brace for the bomb as they'd hear the whistling, they'd *still* jump - like being in a storm, seeing the lightning, expecting the thunder, but shuddering anyway when it rumbled because it was always *more* than you braced for.

And the bombs dropped again and again.

He stopped at a large poster on the metro wall that showed a battleship and fighter planes flying above it with the logo, 'Mightier Yet!'

He stared at the poster for some time and wondered what poster might be here if it weren't for the war - perhaps it'd be an ad of Sir Thomas Beecham's next concert - perhaps it'd be of a London Tower exhibit - perhaps Chanel's next perfume – perhaps Rolls' next Royce. Instead, it was a poster about "might."

Well, he guessed *might* makes "*right*" with what's *wrong*, even if *might* is *wrong*. In the case of the Allies, *might* would be *right* - in the case of the Cains - *might* would be *wrong*. Gosh, he hoped the Cains *weren't* using their power back home to spray chemicals; chemicals that would wash into his land, pollute his water, air, farm.

Then the bombs stopped.

The wail of the sirens died.

The citizens stood and walked up the steps, out into the streets.

Valentin wondered if he should return to the mother and her children, but sensed they'd be fine. They'd been through this before - they'd be through this again. Besides, he didn't want to feel any attachment, didn't wish to feel responsible to those adorable children or their lovely mother. How does Saint-Exupery say it, "You become responsible, forever, for what you have tamed." No, I don't want to "*tame*" anything in this war - and I want to become "*responsible*" **only** in procuring a one-way ticket *back* to Shelby's Creek.

He topped the metro stairs and watched fires burn from several buildings where black smoke funneled skyward.

Then the sirens went off again and people on the streets quickly retreated back down the metro stairs and Valentin followed them. He knelt down beside an elderly man sitting still on the floor, smoking a pipe, reading a book.

"Excuse me," said Valentin. "What now, more bombing?"

"Not necessarily, my good man... But we'll be fine down here. I do wish to finish my book and pipe before I go, however... I say, it'll be several hours *before* the all-clear siren sounds."

"Several hours?" said Valentin.

The old man nodded as he inhaled deeply and exhaled a wafting wave of whitish pipe smoke.

"Several hours...several hours...that's *several* hours I could be *at* Shelby's Creek," Valentin mumbled.

"Beg your pardon," said the old man.

"Nothing, sir," said Valentin. You *wouldn't* understand...he said to himself.

"Mad dogs and Englishmen go out in the midday sun."

— Noel Coward

London, England
Northumberland Hotel
May 1943

Chapter 8

The air raid sirens went silent for some time.

Valentin walked up the Metro steps and back into the Northumberland pub.

Rosy walked up to him to shake his hand. "Already the hero," he said. "You're a helluva lot braver than I. Let me buy…"

"It's time for that pint!" someone shouted.

Valentin and Rosy looked behind them to see Lewis, the MI6 operative they'd met earlier at 64 Baker Street.

"I say it's time for that beer - *Farmer*, isn't it?" said Lewis.

"You go ahead," Rosy said, "you *deserve* a beer after my mind-numbing instruction. Since you *don't* smoke, you need *something* to settle the nerves. I'll be upstairs when you finish, but *don't* take all night." He reached into his pocket and pulled out a wad of bills. "Here are a few pounds of sterling. Don't spend it all in one place."

Valentin nodded and Lewis said to follow him as he led the way through the dance hall into a private back room where five men played darts.

"These lads are MI6 too," Lewis said. "Lads, this is the American marksman -*what's* your name again?"

"Farmer."

"Yes, *Farmer*," Lewis said laughing now and his friends laughed with him.

Valentin sensed that all five men had been drinking for some time.

Lewis handed Valentin a beer and a pistol equipped with a silencer. "You only hear a slight ping from this .22 when fired with this silencer," he said, now ramming a ten-round clip into the gun.

"I don't shoot pistols," Valentin said.

"What do you bloody mean you *don't* shoot pistols? You were in the ruddy military *weren't you?* This pistol *is* state-of-the-art. Now Farmer…is it *dirt farmer, pig farmer*, or just plain *sheep-shit farmer?*" Lewis asked, chuckling and glancing at his buddies, looking puckish.

Valentin sensed he could take Lewis and perhaps two of the other men, but he wasn't sure about all five. Yes, they were drunk and their reactions would be slowed but…

"Ruddy Americans," Lewis said, "are *supposed* to be superior to Brits in marksmanship." He looked back at the other four men and nodded to them. One by one they exited a back door.

"Thomas, be a good lad and be our spotter for bloody military police, will you?" said Lewis as one of the men then went outside.

Good, Valentin thought - that leaves four - much more manageable.

Lewis held the door open for Valentin. "After you," he said.

They all stepped into an alley and Lewis found a switch for a light into the alley, walked to the end of the alley some ten yards away, placed six bottles on trash cans, and then ran back to Valentin.

"Okay," Lewis said, "you first, *sheep farmer*. Shoot those *mucking* bottles down."

"I'd rather *not*," said Valentin.

"Typical bloody American," one of the four men said, "when under pressure, they *always* wilt." He then stepped toward Valentin. "Hell, I'll volunteer," he said and grabbed the gun and shot at the bottles, hitting only one.

"My turn," another man said as he took the gun with a new clip and shot and hit two more bottles. "Your turn American," this man said.

"I'm done."

"What's the matter, clod-hopper," Lewis said, "be a bloody man."

Then a third man grabbed the gun with a new clip and shot and missed the remaining three bottles.

Lewis put three more bottles on the trash cans, stuck another clip in the gun and handed it to Valentin. "Your turn, *dirt farmer* - I *know* you'll shoot *all* six down," he said, laughing with malice.

"I've got *no* truck with you blokes," Valentin said.

"*Truck?*" said Lewis. "Over here, a truck is a lorry, and over here all you Americans are overpaid…"

"I know," said Valentin, rolling his eyes. "And we're oversexed and over here and..."

"And **overmatched** - and that's why you're a **ruddy coward**. You're a **ruddy, bloody coward**!!" Lewis hollered. "You're a **coward** and know **nothing** about being a secret agent!"

The other three men stared at Valentin, moved closer to him, raised their arms slightly at their sides and rolled their hands into fists.

"Take a course with MI6 and perhaps you'll *start* to feel like a man," Lewis said as the other men inched closer. "After all, are you a *man* or a *mouse*?"

"*Squeak, squeak*," Valentin said softly.

"Hey lads," Lewis hollered. "Perhaps we can teach this *mucking mouse* some MI6 fighting tactics."

"Okay," Valentin said, "I'll *shoot*."

He looked at the four men, tested the heaviness of the gun, lifted it, twirled it - and, with his left hand, felt for a flashlight in his pocket.

"Come on, *dirt farmer*," Lewis said.

Valentin lifted the gun, fired it, hit five bottles, and, with a final shot, hit the alley light. He pulled a flashlight from his pocket, shone its light into the eyes of the man closest to him, punched him, dropped him cold, and then dropped the gun. He rushed back through the alley door - back into the back room, and stood and waited just inside the door.

"Bloody coward!" one of the men hollered as he and the others rushed back inside the alley door.

Valentin tripped the first two men, grabbed the third by his shirt collar, and smashed his jaw with a hard left jab.

Okay, two Brits down - one in the alley, one at my feet, and three to go, Valentin thought.

The other two men on the floor rolled to get up and Valentin smacked the jaw of the closest man with an overhead roundhouse right, and the man dropped and lay still.

The next man, the biggest next to Lewis, was too far away for a solid punch and so Valentin stepped forward with his left leg, dropped his right foot back, raised his right leg, bent it back, snapped it forward - smooth and sudden, a high-kick, front kick, not fully extended, knee still bent - and delivered a blow with the top of his foot to the side of the man's head. The man fell, wobbled up, and Valentin readjusted his guard, stood in fight stance, swung his right leg in a semicircular motion, landed the side of his foot to the man's jaw, and the man's eyes rolled back and his body went limp.

Valentin put his foot on this man's chest, folded his arms and waited for Lewis, who now rushed in, stopped, and stared at his buddies motionless on the floor.

"Bloody good show, *sheep farmer*," Lewis, said. "Let's see *how* you do when they come a bit bigger and better." And he inched his way forward with a comical bobbing and weaving motion while sporting a maniacal smirk. "You know what Winnie says, '*I like a man who grins when he fights.*'"

Valentin flashed forward with a left jab that hit Lewis's nose and knocked him flat to the ground. "Like Winnie, I too like a man who *grins as he fights - as he falls*," said Valentin as he grinned.

Lewis rolled and rushed at Valentin, who stepped aside and held out his right foot. Lewis tripped, fell, and rolled twice.

"Yeah, I like Winnie's quote *more and more*," Valentin said as he grinned, spit twice on his knuckles, rolled them like a taffy machine, and stood southpaw style.

Lewis looked around at his friends still lying still on the floor. He stood and wiped at his nose, which now dripped blood. "Let's see if you can knock me out, *dirt farmer*," he said and moved in fast with his fists held high.

Valentin stood still, his arms now to his side.

Lewis moved inside and threw a right uppercut that Valentin swayed away from before spinning back with an overhand right that caught Lewis on the temple, toppling him toward the pool table, which he leaned on as the cobwebs cleared. He then stood straight and moved fast toward Valentin, throwing a left hook and a right jab, which both missed as Valentin bobbed his head, side to side.

"Well, if you're not going to *fight* me, you'll *wrestle* me," Lewis said, driving the full force of his body toward Valentin's waist. Valentin moved aside, grabbed the back of Lewis's shirt, and shoved his body forward and rammed his head into the wall.

Lewis bounced back and staggered.

Valentin lifted Lewis's head up by grabbing the top of his hair.

"Thanks for the beer and the *good* time, Lewis," Valentin said, "Nighty-night, now." And he swung hard with an overhand right hook as Lewis's face twisted and his body dropped.

Valentin walked to where his beer sat on a wall ledge, grabbed it, sipped it and looked at his handiwork still motionless on the floor. "Poor buggers," he murmured.

Just then, the Brit that was watching for military police walked in and stared at his unconscious buddies and at Valentin sipping his beer and grinning.

"Care for a dance?" Valentin said. "Your buddies just couldn't keep up with my Jitterbug moves, I guess."

"No, sir. I don't know these blokes that well - besides, I have to get up early. Have a lovely evening, Mister Farmer."

Valentin lifted his beer. "You as well, my fine chap - cheers!"

Valentin walked back through the dance hall and up the stairs, back to Rosy's office.

Rosy looked up as Valentin knocked and then walked into the room.

"Did you have fun?" asked Rosy.

"Yeah, I *did* have fun."

"You get into any trouble down there?"

"Nah," said Valentin. "I was a good-time Charley."

"I don't know Lewis well," said Rosy, "but I know I *don't* want to mess with him. Word is he's a bare-knuckle boxing champion in his unit."

"Yeah, we seemed to *hit it off swell*," said Valentin.

"I'm glad to hear that," said Rosy. "So far, most OSS agents are **not** favored by the hardcore military establishment, like MI6. For the most part, they see us as unconventional rogues."

"Something we *should* rectify," Valentin said as he rubbed his fist.

"Something wrong with your fist?" Rosy asked.

Valentin shook his head. "Must be the humid London weather."

"Run into any dames down in the dancehall?"

"Yeah - I **definitely** saw some knockouts down there . . ."

"...This is a War of the Unknown Warriors."

— Winston Churchill

London, England
Northumberland Hotel
May 1943

Chapter 9

"OSS instructors may ask you if you have *the guts to kill.*"

"I have the guts *not* to kill," said Valentin.

"Well" said Rosy, "this is better than being so gung-ho that an agent's emotions endanger the lives of comrades. Our manual states, and I quote, '...a man...should not have too many ideals, should work with his intellect rather than his heart.'"

"Trust me, it's my heart that regulates my intellect - and both operate on one ideal - the 'Golden Rule,'" said Valentin.

"Just be warned, Farmer, the time may come when it is *kill or be killed. You are one of only a few skilled marksmen OSS has for dire missions.* Remember, many are risking their lives *for you.*"

"Yes, sir," Valentin said quietly, looking down.

"I'm not going to try to glean as to why you're a pacifist and we're not going to wangle you into doing something you resist," said Rosy.

Valentin nodded.

"Emotions, principles, and ideals aside, let's look at facts. A World War I study showed soldiers used six thousand bullets to kill one enemy soldier. It takes a sniper one bullet. Most snipers don't delight in killing - its duty. The quicker a soldier cements that in his head, the easier duty becomes. Any questions?"

"No."

"Finally, let's talk about Paris. Last year, twenty thousand suspected partisans were arrested in Paris. Of these, many were shot due to involvement in Gaullist groups or communist groups, otherwise known to the enemy as terrorist groups. The moment you walk into Paris, you'll be suspect - *until* the moment you leave. To make you *less* suspect, know the following list like the back of your hand:

1) Like America, rationing includes sugar, meat, cigarettes, petrol, and nylon stockings. So don't make the mistake of inquiring for any of these items, especially in Paris.

2) Acohol is rationed on certain days. Just stay sober and you don't have to worry. At a restaurant, ask for the simplest things: tea, coffee - no cream, no sugar."

3) Milk is restricted to children and pregnant women.

4) Chocolate and flour are unavailable - so don't ask.

5) Avoid black market dealers - even if you must eat cat or crow. Black market is dirty business and the enemy monitors them closely.

6) Keep abreast - always - of the latest and upcoming events in the city, especially for your newspaper.

7) France is divided into seven zones. To cross the zones, you must have a pass card, or Ausweis as the Germans call it, which we'll get into.

8) There is no Paris night life for civilians because of a curfew from 2300 till 0500.

9) The enemy is in command of everything: food, police, bookshops, clothing stores, cafes. They censor all entertainment - and all newspapers.

10) Know that not every Frenchman is against your enemy. Some are against the Brits. Due to the enemy's propaganda machine, some Frenchmen even think we got France into the war and left when times got scary. Some have even started vendettas against the Brits for persecuting Joan of Arc.

11) As a radio man or 'pianist,' you'll transmit from Paris on even-numbered days and suburbs on odd-numbered days.

12) Know which days allow you certain rations."

"Yes sir."

"Farmer, you will have logistical needs to locate your grandfather. We'll do our best to help. If you have no luck and you want to return to London, notify us. We'll debrief you and send you back to America. But if you simply break off from your assigned Resistance cell, you'll be considered a quisling and a dangerous man and you'll be hunted by both sides. Your choice to come here and your choice to leave are your inalienable rights, but we require notification if you leave."

"I understand."

"Okay, Farmer, *make no mistake*, you're putting your life in danger. Article X of the Vichy armistice prohibits all French citizens to fight for the Allies against the enemy under penalty of death. To be caught with so much as this code book means execution - or worse - torture. From this day forward, you **must** accept the idea of death. ***Do you accept that?***"

"I accept."

"At the hangar, before takeoff, I'll perform a last-minute security check. You'll be taken to a private room where another officer will perform another inspection. Next, another officer will examine your false IDs, work cards, and ration books. Finally, you'll be given pills: knockout drops - effective for six hours; Benzedrine sulfate to battle fatigue; and cyanide for suicide. Any questions?"

"No."

Rosy stood up and held out a folder. "Here's your Alien's Registration Certificate from Metro Police. Captain Piquet-Wicks authorized it, showing that your current profession is with the Royal Air Force. Here's a key to your room. Good night and good luck."

A good night and good luck waits for me only at Shelby's Creek, Valentin thought - *where **all** nights are good and luck comes as prolifically and perennially as the garden shamrocks by the house on the hill.*

*"...if we fail, then the whole world, including the United States...
will sink into the dark abyss of a new Dark Age..."*

— Winston Churchill

London, England
OSS Research Lab
May 1943

Chapter 10

A man in a white lab coat escorted Valentin into a large basement factory that smelled of oil and paint.

Other men in white lab coats stood around tables working on gadgets. The man escorting Valentin pointed to them. "Most of these men are chemists, some ballistics experts, a few physicists and physicians."

Valentin watched one of these men who looked to be in his late fifties with long graying hair and unblinking bug-eyes come forward and extend his hand. "Hello, I'm research scientist Pauley," he said, low and slow, without expression.

"Hello."

"Here's a pen and paper," said Pauley. "Take notes. Say, 'check,' after each point *I* make so I know *you're* making notes."

"Check."

"I'm with OSS Documentation, Camouflage, and Special Assistants Division. We provide everything you need to appear as a normal citizen in France. For example, your toothbrush, dental work, razor, shoes, and traveling bag must be microscopically accurate and will either be replicated from Lille or come from Lille".

"Check."

"You'll be with me today until 1100, at which time you'll go here to this house at Grosvenor Street headquarters - our OSS printing plant that produces false documents. They'll give you updated documentation you'll need up till the day you leave England; things like changes in curfew, changes in rations, etc.... Also, you should watch every spy movie they have to pick up things like eating like a European, not..."

"Not...like an American - who eats with a pitchfork," said Valentin, grinning.

"I take it someone has already been over this?"

"At least once."

"Just say, 'check,'" said Pauley, matter-of-fact, his bug-eyes unmoving.

"Check."

"Here's a list of information to get you updated on slang. For example, the French call Hitler 'Hit' or 'Big Julius'; they call the enemy 'Boches,' 'Fritz,' 'Jerries,' 'Krauts,' 'Verdigris,' 'Beetles,' and 'String Beans.'"

"'Beetles'? 'String beans'?"

"String Beans because of their uniform color, Beetles because beetles eat vegetables and leave nothing, like the enemy."

"Why is Hitler 'Big Julius?'"

"I guess in reference to Julius Caesar, I'm not sure. I *am* sure that they should simply call him Corporal since that is his highest military rank. Even de Gaulle looks more impressive as a *temporary Brigadier* General than *Corporal* Hitler."

From corporal to fuhrer, Valentin thought – but then guessed it took a *corporal's* mentality to start a war with a great nation like America - *and* a *corporal's* mentality to start a war on more than two fronts -*and* a *corporal's* mentality to start a war he couldn't finish - *not* with 'bullies' instead of 'brains' as colleagues.

"Now," said Pauley, "among other things, you'll be a wireless operator. When operating the radio you see here, you **must** be aware of dangers: one, your enemy has wireless interception that traces Morse transmissions; two, your enemy may send a signal on the same frequency, jamming yours; three, your enemy has direction-finding vans all over Paris and each van has a homing device that pinpoints radio sources."

"Check."

"Your codebook is your bible. **Don't** lose it."

"Check."

"Every Morse signaler's key stroke is different. Home station will know the difference by recording on tape your 'fist,' unique to your stroke. Now, what is your fist?"

"*My* fist is my unique Morse-code key-stroke."

"Why does London want to record it?"

"London wants to record my fist style for a verification check that it's me and not some enemy forger."

Pauley raised his eyebrows and stared at Valentin. "I must say, we finally have an agent with an attention span longer than a kindergartner. I'm **duly** impressed."

"Check."

"Now, if you can last *longer than six months* in the field, I believe you'll be an asset for OSS."

"Check ...I think."

"Now, you'll be sent coded messages carried in the heel of liaisons shoes. And here are your shoes. As you can see, the heel spins to the side to hide a coded message that you decipher with the code book."

"Check."

Pauley moved down the table. "This is a microdot camera. It allows you to photograph an image the size of a letter and save it on microfilm the size of a dot on a lady bug. We prefer this over invisible inks, which are unreliable. Plus, you hide microfilm inside your shoe, your ear, your nose, your butt - any retrievable orifice."

"Check."

"And these are *special* matchsticks, so when you smoke, *don't* confuse *these* for *real* ones."

"I don't smoke."

"I don't think I know anyone who doesn't smoke... Anyway, these matches are special. They're hollow to hold microfilm. Here's a pack of cigarettes to act as a decoy in case you're caught with the matches. Now it doesn't matter if you smoke or not, you'll have to carry a tobacco card and you must carry tobacco or your enemy will be suspicious..."

"Check."

"*This* pack of cigarettes is a *special* pack. The safest way to carry a dangerous message is to have the message written on cigarette paper like so, wrap the cigarette paper around this needle like so, and insert the needle into a cigarette like so."

"Check."

"Here are ranked military badges - in case you're captured, feign you've been shot down."

"It seems dishonorable to wear fake military badges."

"How honorable of you," Pauley whispered, "stupid, but honorable."

"What?"

"Oh, I was just commenting on these stupid flies, must be all this English food," he said batting the flies.

They walked to a doorway that said, 'Clothing warehouse.'

"We've second-hand materials confiscated straight from French refugees and from flea markets of rue Mouffetard. We've shaving brushes, vests, valises, trousers, coats, and even belts. Wear these clothes beneath your drop suit and wear them into Paris. The pants are one size bigger, the shirt two sizes bigger so you look more like the underfed Parisians."

"Check."

"Tomorrow, you have a mock interrogation to check automatic response of identity. Fail and you don't go to France."

"Check."

"Word is you *won't* kill," said Pauley.

"Word is correct."

"Word is you *won't* break under interrogation."

"Word is correct."

"So, you're tough when it comes to a grilling - *not so tough* when it comes to a killing...?"

"Check."

"How are you so sure you *won't* break when they put the screws to you?"

"I'm a farmer."

"Being a farmer makes you sure?"

"Sure as God made little green apples."

"Nevertheless, you'll have a series of interrogation tests. One night you'll be wakened to ask your cover's grandmother's maiden name, another time you'll do the Station S tests in Fairfax, another time you'll drink liquor and then be interrogated."

"Do I *have* to drink *gin?*"

"When in Rome… This is England, remember?"

"Okey dokey, but if I sprout a W.C. Fields nose, I'm suing . . . ."

Pauley laughed and for the first time Valentin saw life spark in his bug-eyes.

"Here are illustrations of the enemy's uniforms - not a lot of Gestapo in Paris - a lot of Wehrmacht and SS in Paris."

"Check."

"Hitler's secret intelligence is the SS. The SS wears a black uniform with a 'death's head' upon it - a symbol they're out to kill the Reich's political foes - that's *you!*"

"Check."

"Here are illustrations of the enemy's planes, tanks, autos, motorbikes, trucks, half-tracks - know their engines, their armaments, their colors, their speeds…"

"Check."

Pauley walked over to a suit. "This is an extra-large size SOE jumpsuit, a camouflage coverall with two body-length zippers and several pockets. You'll wear several layers of clothing beneath this suit, stuff it with several layers of newspaper for filling - the homeless are not stupid - they know great insulation when they see it."

"Check."

"Now, we've lost too many agents baited by fake letters. We've devised a false French stamp - notice how the false one shows a light streak below the chin?"

"There's no color difference?"

"Why?"

"I'm blind to green."

"Your color-blindness is good for me to know. Any other abnormalities we should know?"

"I fear the dark. I need flashlights on my person all the time."

"Flashlights are banned in occupied France. Fresh batteries are rare to come by -get over your fear."

"Easier said than done."

"Then carry a candle and matches, but **don't** let your fears jeopardize a mission."

"Check."

"To date, SOE has sent in three hundred agents: one hundred have been executed; only a dozen that were captured escaped."

"Check."

"Okay, I see that 'Fearless' Dan Fairbairn is your instructor - he's known for intense training, prepares a man to kill another man before he knows what he's doing."

"Check."

"Finally, special operations requires special tools. So your next stop - Research and Development. They've created state-of-the-art equipment for you - most of these materials, especially the weapons and poisons are fresh and straight from 'Professor Moriarty's' research and development headquarters in Washington."

"Check."

"I believe we're through here, Agent Farmer."

"Check."

"Difficulties mastered are opportunities won."

— Winston Churchill

London, England
OSS/SOE Research and Development Branch Laboratory
May 1943

Chapter 11

A man in a white lab coat escorted Valentin into a large basement, not unlike the day before - except this basement smelled *more* of gun powder and metal - *less* of cigar smoke and paint.

A thirty-ish, stick of a man in a dirty sweater approached. His face showed ruddy, his hair reddish and curly, brows busy and thick over hollows of eyes so deep it seemed he'd no need to squint in the sun. "I'm Henry Johnson. How is training at Bletchley?"

"Fine," Valentin said, "reminded me of military training in Louis..."

"Speaking of Louis," said Johnson, "this Penetrometer is also called a Joe Louis -a rubberized weapon used as a catapult to toss mortar shells or grenades farther than what you can throw them by hand. This item," he said, pointing to a suitcase, "has a combination lock you must remember. If you don't remember, *never* pry it open - the contents inside will automatically be destroyed with a chemical that releases whenever there's extreme pressure on these hinges. Inside is the radio - the Type A MK III - on a clear day, she works up to fifteen hundred kilometers."

'Yes sir."

"Here's a study sheet that explains our homing pigeons."

"Pigeons?"

"There may be times when you use pigeons to send messages back to us."

"Good, I may get tired of rationed food . . ."

"Here's a pack of cigarettes," said Johnson. "Inside this pack are five cigarettes. Four are actual cigarettes, one is a Welfag - a single-shot weapon inserted in a cigarette, which shoots a 40-grain bullet. You'll notice it's heavier, so *don't* smoke it and *don't lend it to be smoked.*"

"Ingenius - a cigarette that kills *sooner* than *later?*"

Johnson gave him a dirty look and stuck a cigarette in his mouth. "You don't smoke?"

"I don't smoke."

"You'll start soon - you can always stop - I have dozens of times. Now, you've only one chance for the cigarette pistolette to work - since it has a short barrel, your victim must be at close range - beyond one meter, it's useless. But a well-aimed shot has the muzzle velocity to inflict a fatal or serious wound."

"Yes, sir."

"Now, this High Standard Model B .22 caliber silencer pistol is highly recommended. I advise you to use it as your cannon."

"My what?"

"Your cannon - your assassin's pistol."

"I'm no assassin . . ."

"Our own Research and Development Branch made it - it's virtually silent with little muzzle flash. It comes with a ten-round ammunition clip and is essential for close-range assassinations."

"Yes sir."

"We're sending your rifle with these cleaning patches, cleaning rods, extra firing pins, extractors, and ammo clips. You'll **never** worry about rifle maintenance - the **only** time you'll see your rifle is when you shoot it. It'll be maintained and cleaned by contacts. Rest assured, it'll be in the best of care."

"Yes sir."

"We've prepared a Parker Hale silencer to fit your rifle. With this silencer, the enemy neither pinpoints your location nor, in turn, knows how many snipers are out there. Even at night, there's no muzzle flash to be seen."

"Yes, sir."

"Finally, this is our latest night-vision scope prototype. The Germans actually introduced the 'Vampir' man-portable night vision technology four years ago with this scope for their Sturmgewehr 44 rifle. In turn, we've developed our own night-vision version, soon to be introduced to the army, but we have it first, of course."

"Of course."

"This scope allows you to aim at targets at night with the aid of this infrared light. You simply aim at your target like so, the target becomes magnified, your accuracy increases."

"Yes, sir."

"This is insecticide powder that…"

"No, thanks, I'd rather be killed by *bugs* than *chemicals*," said Valentin.

"These are water purification tablets, which you probably don't want either."

"No."

"One more thing - *if* caught as a sniper, you may **not** want to be caught *alive* as snipers are the most *hated* of all soldiers. *Enemy* and *ally* go to great lengths to remove them *immediately*."

"Why?"

"When a sniper zeros in on an unsuspecting target, war changes from *business* to *personal* - unnerves every man in the vicinity. Ticks them off, not being able to fight back against an expert shooter they see as a *coward* and *yet* greatly *fear*."

"Yes sir."

"But when you have a target in your crosshairs and your finger on the trigger, don't hesitate. Don't question if your target is a *good man* or a *young man* or a man *like your brother*. **Don't** look at his face when you shoot - it *might* spook your sleep. And *never, ever* tell anyone what you do. You'll be like the prized fox in a fox hunt - to traitors, collaborators, and anybody who needs retirement reward money. *Only* your cell leader *will know **you're*** a sniper."

"Yes sir."

"If injured, here is a tincture of Laudanum, opium, and morphine. Instructions for the Trueta method are included for fracture. You'll find a new anti-coagulant called dicoumarin, a derivative of coumarin - prevents blood clots. Here is sulfa powder and Carlisle bandages to prevent lesion infections. And here is Vitamin P, isolated per oxidation from lemon seeds, effective in managing certain hemorrhaging. Medical services may be hard to procure."

"Ye sir."

"These packets contain K, TD, and L tablets. Remember the differences."

"Yes, sir."

"And *here's* my gift to you."

"A ring?"

"It's a signet ring. Open the cap."

"A Sherlock Holmes ring?"

"A ring with the 'L' cyanide pill. If captured, we suggest you use it. The pill is encapsulated in this rubber membrane so you may keep it in your mouth until you choose your fate. Choose to live - spit it out - choose to die - bite hard."

"Yes, sir."

"As you know, spies are tortured and killed. We don't want a spy to weaken - to denounce his cell. If you take the 'L' pill, you'll not feel your next heart beat."

"Yes, sir."

"We prefer one life lost versus many."

Valentin nodded and put the ring on his finger.

"If captured, we demand you deny everything. If captured and you don't take the pill, stall as long as possible - thirty-six hours if possible - *before* revealing secrets. This allows time for fellow agents to be alerted."

"Yes sir."

"That's it Farmer - in the morning, meet here to finalize weapons and supplies."

Valentin looked at the 'L' cyanide pill ring on his finger and wondered if Nanny and Katie had been milked.

"This generation of Americans has a rendezvous with destiny."

— Franklin Roosevelt

London, England
May 1943

Chapter 12

The evening was pleasant with a slight, warm breeze.

The sky showed clear of all clouds and a low, waxing crescent, three-quarter moon now rose fully on the horizon.

"This time is called the 'moon time' - when Resistance drops *always* take place - no wind, no clouds, no trouble," the driver said to Valentin as their jeep whisked down London's streets toward the airport.

Valentin said nothing. His mind weighed heavy on his immediate future - an uncertain future filled with certain change - more change than I've ever dealt with in all my years and now that I'm deep in this pickle, I hope I make another year, hell, another 6 months . . . .

He rummaged through his rucksack and felt for his flashlights and batteries. He'd already put the blue lenses on the flashlights - like cataracts on eyes - and didn't like it one bit. When he needed light, he wanted light, not some darkened imposter. Fortunately, there was no lens for the pencil flashlight, which gave off so little light anyway - if he kept it covered beneath a hat or jacket, he'd be fine. He felt the pencil flashlight now, stuck it in his front pocket and then found the hard aluminum one, the waterproof one, and the plastic bags with the batteries. Since batteries were hard to come by in occupied France, he'd loaded up on them, leaving rations in exchange for their weight. Yes, he was warned time and again of getting caught in occupied France with flashlights, time and time again. "It could be a matter of life and death," they'd say. Yeah, well, when darkness feels like death, he preferred getting caught with flashlights.

He checked his pocket watch - 11 p.m. That's 4 p.m., Iowa time - yes, the crops are planted by now; hell they're shooting sprouts already. It'd be too early in the day for a second milking of the goats and he imagined Nanny and Katie beneath the thick shade of the cottonwoods in the upper grove where it was always cool, the brome and bluegrass always high, always lush. Yes, in three, maybe four hours, Mrs. Rasmussen would rattle the grain buckets and the goats would run into the yard up to the stall. Nanny, of course, would step right up into her stall and look back, her head held high, as if to preen herself for what she was about to offer. But if Mrs. Rasmussen milks Katie first, that'd be okay with Nanny. Even though Katie is less aggressive getting into her stall, she's more aggressive getting to her food. And Nanny the Nubian would wait like the patient animal she is. Yes, there was something to be said about a patient animal, he thought as he synchronized his watch for Paris time, which was Berlin time.

"Tally ho, we've arrived," the driver said as he slammed on the brakes and pointed. "Just head to the hangar and chin up, ole chap."

"Thank you," said Valentin as he jumped from the jeep and hoisted his heavy rucksack onto his back.

In the distant hangar, he saw Rosy, who waved for him to come over to a large table.

"Ready?" Rosy hollered.

"Ready as I'm going to be."

"Let's discuss your operational orders again - pull out your French silk map. As you see, your map is highlighted with precise signposts, from your drop with the Resistance reception committee to your rendezvous with the SOAM boat. Now, this 'X' is where you'll be dropped, on the eastern fringes of Area 2 in the countryside between Gisors and Mantes-a-Jolie. The location is remote, miles from any town, miles from an enemy outpost, miles from the Seine in case a boat patrol is out that night. The reception committee leader, 'Camembert,' takes you to a remote barn to rest for three hours just in case an enemy patrol is wise to our drop. After rest, you'll dress in civilian clothes and hike for approximately three hours. You'll stay near this dirt road till you come to the Seine, near the Saint Cloud Bridge for your boat pick-up."

"Check."

"'Camembert' and his partisans radioed in that there's enemy patrols everywhere tonight. We'll be sending a Spitfire or two to clear some of them. Be careful not to be caught by the strafing - or the patrols."

"Check."

"In exchange for your work, you'll receive help to connect with your Paris grandparents. If, at any time, you feel the exchange is not on par, you may abort. Captain Kraus made me promise this to you. But you must return here to debrief. Are we clear?"

"Check."

"OSS has neither way nor means presently to rescue your grandfather. Your cell will attempt to discover his whereabouts. Your cell will attempt to assist you to contact your grandmother. Are we clear?"

"Check."

"Security is your key to success and survival. Know your fictitious identity like your A, B, C's."

"Check."

"You're the only American agent parachuting into northern France tonight along with a Brit. We've another American agent, Tom Rodgers, who's training now. His background is quite similar to yours and he knows Paris well . . . ."

"When is Rodgers dropping? Maybe we can coordinate . . . ?"

"No. Few people know about you. You're a secret for many reasons. Donovan's not *fully* aware of you - Dansey's *definitely* not aware of you."

"Donovan wouldn't approve of me if he knew the truth?"

"It's not that he *wouldn't* approve. He's for any tactic for the win column. It's just that you're *the* assassin. To authority figures, you *don't* exist. They *don't want to know* you exist. You're someone more expert and precise, but someone who *doesn't exist.* Remember, to the OSS, to your Resistance cell, to the Allies - you *don't* exist. If you are captured or interrogated, we all disavow *any* knowledge of you. There will **never** be any records of you - **never** any medals, honors, or awards for you — **never** even be a three volley funeral, or a one volley funeral if you **don't** survive. When this is over and you *do* survive, that's that - you *survive.* You go back to what you were doing, whatever you were doing, I don't want to know. That's the role of an assassin. No matter if you don't regard yourself as such — that's **what** brought you over here — that's **why** we help you with your matter. You're an extremely valuable commodity, *nearly* **irreplaceable** in fact. The *more* we hide that fact, the *more* secure you are and the longer your valuable role lasts. Do you understand?"

"I...check."

"We're already working on important assignments for you that may save many, many lives. Who knows? If things work out in Paris, we may even employ you to help take out Hit and Mus. You'd have the backing of every Ally and even some Axis that are also trying to take them out. But that's down the road."

"Let's get to Paris."

"Farmer, I know you're *not* a killer. I'm not asking you to compromise yourself - *stop* the enemy - that may be enough."

Valentin nodded.

"I sense you're a survivor. Your instincts seem honed. Within a short time in Paris, you'll develop a sort of innate radar, a sort of angst, a sort of heightened sense - like prey. Nevertheless, I want to update you on some things in Paris:

1) There are thirty-five thousand enemy security troops and administrative officers in Paris and as many, if not more French collaborators.

2) Even though there are more Wehrmacht, the Geheimestaatspolizei is also ubiquitous in Paris. They dress well - in suits and long coats - and may be found in public parks, dark alleys, doorways, museums, the opera, the theater, bars, cafes, and the metro. Develop a *sixth sense* for their presence. They're looking for *anyone* that seems *out of place*. They've *no* restrictions of authority and *know* it. Their arrests are followed immediately by interrogation *and* torture. Gestapo Chief Heinrich Muller is in charge: He has his eye on OSS and SOE agents."

3) As I mentioned, the French Gestapo is called PPF. They're dregs of society - criminals, thugs, misfits, and deviants with motives ranging from revenge on society - to revenge for a lost lover - to revenge on a bossy boss before the occupation - to revenge for being born. They work hand in hand with Gestapo and SS. All are known for torture techniques including solitary confinement, starvation, sleep deprivation, forced-fluids, water-boarding, regulated beatings, pulling out nails by heated pliers, and exhaustion exercises. Any questions?"

"Yeah, **when's** the next plane back to **Iowa**?"

"We'll win this war. Do you want to know why?"

"Why?"

"Marlene Dietrich's on our side. That's right. We're working with the singer/actress to record American propaganda songs on Soldatensender West radio, which reaches Hitlerland to affect their soldier's morale. And in France, America's most popular expatriate - queen of Danse Sauvage - Josephine Baker, helps smuggle information written in invisible ink on paper she pins to her underwear. She crosses the borders and relays it to us. Enemy checkpoints are so impressed by her they don't think to check her panties."

"So she's an underhanded, undercover, underwear runner smuggler?" Valentin said.

Rosy's seriousness finally broke and he doubled over. "Your Resistance cell's going to love your tract captions, Farmer."

"Hope so sir."

"Well, the saying around here is, first stuff your belly and then stuff your suit. Have you scoffed plenty of big eats from the British Army Aldershot Cement Company cooks?"

"Yes sir; all the hot corned beef, boiled potatoes, rubber heels eggs, and pea soup I can muster."

"You know you'll go from cool to cold to freezing, from troposphere to stratosphere."

"Yes, sir."

"And don't forget your 'Mae West' in case you're shot down by ack-ack over the Channel."

"A life jacket is a Mae West, but what is ack-ack?"

"You'll know soon enough. Just duck and hang on when you see the pretty little colorful cottonball puffs that go ack-ack, which is anti-aircraft fire you'll see and feel as you go over the Channel."

"Yes, sir."

"Oh, by the way, what's your lucky charm?"

"I beg your pardon?"

"Well every soldier seems to have something lucky on them when they jump - a lucky coin, a lucky rock, rabbit's foot, picture of your girl."

Valentin pulled out his pocket watch, opened it, and showed the photo of his mom when she was his age. "That's a picture of my girl."

"She's beautiful. I'm sure she'll bring you good luck."

"She always has - she's the reason I'm alive," said Valentin, now smiling and looking for some time at the photo until it blurred.

"We have learned that...our well-being is dependent on the well-being of other nations..."

— *President Franklin Roosevelt*

Croydon Airfield
London, England
May, 1943

Chapter 13

Valentin watched the shadowed shape of a plane, probably his plane, as it taxied on the airstrip.

Yes, he thought - you can still back out of this - you can back out and be on the farm next week greasing the hay sickle for cutting clover.

No... You have a mission, even if you don't succeed, you tried. Yes, you will have tried. That's *who* you are, that's *how* you were raised. So, live with it or die with it.

Now he tasted the same tired English menu of the last few days: old bacon, stale biscuits, pungent tea. Good Lord, he'd been spoiled with farm-fresh food - and Earl Grey tea forever failed to Columbian coffee.

He walked out of the hangar onto the tarmac, sucked in fresh air, walked around the hangar.

He tried to clear his mind, but no use - each step took him closer to the war - further - farther - from home.

Too bad, he told himself; you've made your decision, for better or for worse. "Family's the most important thing in life; all else ties for last," Grandpa Schmitz said time and again.

He returned to the hangar entrance, stood by the door, and jolted back, startled suddenly as Rosy came up beside him to adjust his parachute harness and pat him twice on the shoulder.

Valentin nodded but looked down for he didn't want Rosy to see how he felt - didn't want anyone to see his fear - but God he was scared -scared merde-less.

He listened to Rosy's footsteps as he walked away - Rosy, his last link with Captain Kraus, his last link with anything familiar with home.

God, he missed home.

A short man in full parachute gear came up and stood beside him. "Top of the evening to you sport, I'm Castle."

"I'm Farmer."

"How many drops for you?"

"My first."

"No worries old boy - once you've jumped, its automatic as getting back on a bike."

"I haven't ridden a bike in a while."

"Just remember that Andrews, our dispatch, will holler, 'Jump'. When he does, straighten your body to avoid getting tangled in the parachute chords as he gently pushes you. If he pushes you too hard, you might break your face on the far end of the hatch. But no worries ole boy, you'll do fine. Andrews and the pilot are top-notch. Did at least a dozen drops with them already, I did, *unscathed*."

"*Unscathed* in **your** *mind*," Valentin thought, now annoyed at the man's exuberance.

"The pilot's from the renowned 'Moon Squadron,'" said Castle. "…*almost* no failures…last month I flew with one of your comrades, Serreulles, I believe. Anyway, flak hit the plane and we barely made it back to London. I mean we were sputtering on the runway."

"At least the failure ratio's no longer ripe."

"Bloody flak, that's our biggest worry," said Castle. "By the way, 'ave you seen *Casablanca*?"

Valentin nodded.

"You know the song 'As Time Goes By' from *Casablanca*?"

Valentin nodded.

"Well, we plane jumpers 'ave our own version," Castle said as another English soldier sidled up beside him and they put arms around each other and began to sing. 'You must remember this - Flak don't always miss - and one of you may die - The fundamental thing *applies* - As flak *goes* by. And when the fighters come - You hope you're not the one - To tumble from the sky - The odds are always too damned high - As flak goes by. It's still the same old story - A tale that's too damned gory - Some brave men have to die - The odds are always high - As flak *goes* by..."

"Catchy," said Valentin with a frown as he looked away and thought about where he stashed his cigarettes.

"But it's not always flak that gets us," said Castle. "Sometimes we're our own worst enemy, like when dispatchers pack the parachute wrong or forget to hook up the static line, as was the case with Gary Cross last year. Lucky bugger would have landed horizontal or shish-ke-babbed on a Poplar but ended up swinging vertically and safely from a lone tree. Not particularly overburdened with brains, that one."

"MmNnnn...yes...considerably," said Valentin, trying to sound Brit-obvious. "And how's your failure rate with packed parachutes?"

"Well, yes, we have some fatalities. Mind you bloke, there's nothing worse for a jumper than a 'streamer' - when your canopy fails to open and you're falling to mother earth like a rock and looking up to see just a stream of silk above you. Oh yeah...like Dr. Bruhn, who died from a flawed parachute...and Felix...and..."

"That'll do, Agent Castle," said Valentin grinning without grinning.

"Nowadays," Castle said, "our young female teams at STS 33 Altrincham fold parachutes that have a failure rate of only a few in a thousand - quite an improvement from the beginning . . ."

"MmmNnnn...yes...considerably," Valentin said.

"It's the bloody gremlins you gotta be ready for, bloke."

"The what?"

"The bloody gremlins; the imps, sprites, and air pixies; they're the plague of the RAF; like Murphy's Law - if it can go wrong, it blimey might. 'Bout half of all drops are aborted due to problems, whether in the air or on the ground - with the moon, with navigation, flak, fighters, reception committees scared off by police, with clouds, with rain, with wind, with - who knows *what*? And *what* is sometimes when the bloody navigator can't spot the bloody drop zone. That Resistance bloke Moulin dropped way off course in a Seine marshland last year, never did find his bloody radio operative that jumped with him."

Valentin suddenly wished he'd worn a St. Christopher medal. It was St. Christopher, wasn't it? Or was it Jude? Maybe it was...ah, he didn't remember. Too many saints, too long since he'd prayed to them; perhaps they wouldn't even listen anymore. Perhaps no one listened. Katie and Nanny listened. So did Mrs. Rasmussen. And Randy, and Shelby Creek's birds when he played flute, and the cows when he called them for corn, and the frogs and crickets in late summer when he hushed them in late evening when he lay in bed in the cabin with the south window open and the flora-perfumed breezes blowing light. Gosh, he missed all this. Yes, he was missing all of this immensely now. And if you miss something, shouldn't you rejoin it? What more is there? Shelby's Creek, here I come...*soon*, he said to himself...*soon*.

"We make a living by what we get, but we make a life by what we give."

— *Winston Churchill*

Croydon Airfield
London, England
May 1943

Chapter 14

*V*alentin felt for his flashlights in his pockets.

"I did have to drop 'blind' once though," Castle said.

"Blind?"

"Drop blind, drop cold - it's when you drop *without* a reception committee for the pilot or parachutist - the pilot has no one to help guide correct location and altitude, which increases risk of injury for the parachutist -don't know if you're landing in a bloody grove of trees or the Seine River. Plus, if the moon light *isn't right* - your count to the ground may *not be right*. Plus, you might land plop down in the wrong hands, like a shot of Bushmills in a bloody Beck beer instead of a Guinness, if you get my meaning, chap."

"The *French* Resistance reception committee drinks *Guinness?*" Valentin asked under his breath.

"Cigarette?" asked Castle.

"I don't smoke."

"How do you control your nerves?"

"Prayer."

"We had an agent once assigned to parachute over Brittany - he succumbed to a sudden case of nerves, refused to jump. But, **you** look like you've got a hold of your jewels."

"So this is **not** a blind drop tonight?"

"No."

"So we're the only agents for the ride tonight?"

"Yep . . . Tally ho, there's our Halifax now," Castle said as a plane rolled down the tarmac and taxied for take off.

From the shadows of the runway, a short stocky man approached, his facial features mostly hidden by a heavy helmet and goggles. "Hello gents, I'm Andrews. Castle, you're a bloody veteran already. Farmer, this is your virgin run, I presume."

"Yes, sir."

Andrews looked at his watch. "We're a bit late as there's a bit of cloud cover. If it worsens over the Channel, we abort. You both know your MO?"

"Yes, sir," they said.

"Be aware - we recently flew two new agents over northern France - after a heavy barrage of flak, they went scared, wouldn't jump. This is your last chance to abort before take off."

"Yes, sir," they said.

"Proceed on the tarmac," said Andrews. "I'll meet you on the plane."

Moments later, Valentin peeked inside the open door of the plane and hesitated.

"Step aboard, lad. It won't bite you," said Castle.

"Yeah but I might bite you, ya bloody bloke," Valentin said under his breath.

Soon, everyone was aboard and the hatch slammed shut.

Andrews walked past the hatch with a sealed can.

"He's going to get ice cream out of that," Castle said.

"How's that?"

"We got the idea from American bomber crews that mixed ingredients for ice cream in sealed cans and placed the cans in rear compartments. The plane's vibrations churn the ice cream and the high altitude chills it. When the crew arrives home safely, their reward is the finished ice cream. Sometimes we don't fly high enough for the ice cream to chill but still slurp it down like a milkshake."

A man suddenly showed before them in the shadows. "Hello, I'm your pilot. I never give my name - I never ask your name - bad luck." He knelt down, blessed himself, pointed to a map. "The marks in black show where we expect the heaviest flak concentrations. For you virgin jumpers, flak, known as ack-ack, are the metal bomb fragments the enemy hurls at us from anti-aircraft guns. We'll follow these blue marks, which take us on a winding corridor course that may divert most of the flak, unless enemy positions have changed the last forty-eight hours."

"How likely is that sir?" asked Valentin.

"Quite bloody likely."

Andrews returned and handed the pilot documentation. "Here are the stats of winds, temps, and barometric pressure from the main tower."

"Looks good. Let's all synchronize our watches for the drop. Set 1330. Expected drop time - Agent Castle set 1400. Expected drop time - Agent Farmer set 1405. Good show, men. Keep your chins up."

Valentin felt sick of the 'chins up' crap. Just *once*, just *now*, he wished to hear a simple, *'good luck'* from an American voice. Surrounded by foreign people on a foreign mission - a mission of life and death - *wasn't* his idea of *comfort*. Come on, get **hold** of yourself. You'll be in France soon, with Grandma Lambert soon after that. Get hold of yourself; think about your jump, your hike to the Seine, your ride to Paris. Once in Paris, things will feel familiar, something like home. Just stay focused, stay healthy, stay sane - at least till Paris.

"Oh, one more thing," said the pilot, "other than no names, no smoking on my plane. Knowing that flak can blow my bloody bum back to the Isle of Wight, I don't need to worry about a Player's Navy Cut doing the same."

"Yes, sir," they said.

Then the pilot pulled out a pack of Players and offered one to each agent. "This is for good luck once you land."

"No thanks," said Valentin.

"Don't tell me you like those American C-ration Camels better?"

"I don't smoke."

"Who doesn't bloody smoke in this war? It's bloody bad luck if you don't take a cigarette I offer," said the pilot, his face stone serious.

Valentin took the cigarette, stuck it in his front pocket.

The pilot nodded, walked back to the blacked-out cockpit, set the altimeter, took a deep breath, closed his eyes, murmured a prayer, exhaled, opened his eyes, and looked down the runway.

Andrews sat next to Valentin. "This is an RAF Halifax bomber, a stalwart and sturdy machine but I don't think they're made with your height in mind.

Chances are you'll be knockin' your noggin' as you find your way to the bomb bay…"

"Tally hoe," hollered the pilot. "We have clearance."

Valentin pointed outside to where several men climbed into fighter planes. "Are those RAF pilots?"

"No," Andrews said. "Trainees of the Fighting French Air Corps, just came back from school in London."

"And they're fighting already?"

"Let's hope they're ready," said Andrews. "The Luftwaffe's pretty bloody experienced - two of their best aces have *already* accrued three hundred kills apiece. You **won't** find me in one of those bloody fighter planes."

"Nor I," said Castle. "So what if those fighters have warehouses full of barrels of French wine outside London at their disposal? I'd rather drink motor oil than fight Luftwaffe aces."

Just then the Halifax shook and roared to life as the pilot revved the plane's engines and rpm's and temperature increased: 1000 rpm's, 100 hundred degrees; 2000 rpm's, 120 degrees. The pilot lifted the cross medallion around his neck and kissed it.

Valentin felt the plane's tail yank and the fuselage pulsate with the power of the engines.

He thought about Florine - yes, she'd be finishing evening chores about now - perhaps weeding flowers, bedding barns, cleaning sheds, milking Nanny and Katie. And, within a few hours the Iowa sun would set. And then, Shelby's Creek would be about the *most* peaceful place on earth.

Then the intense shaking of the plane seemed to jar his thoughts like a slap to the face.

And now he felt every bone in his body vibrate as the plane shivered and rolled down the runway.

What *am* I doing? What the **heck** am I doing?

Now the plane's flaps lifted, its body lifted, and the deafening noise of the engines raced and revved in sync with the pounding of his heart.

"The best way out is always through."

– Robert Frost

Flight over Isle of Wight/English Channel
London, England
May 1943

Chapter 15

Clear skies over London changed to thick fog over the Channel.

Valentin watched out a plane window as stars gave way to the murk, and the inside of the plane darkened even more.

He reached into his rucksack and opened the ends of each flashlight, rotated the batteries, clicked each one on and held his hand over the light to avoid attention.

He checked his parachute harness over and over, adjusted the straps again and again.

Now he shivered as the plane's panels leaked in frigid air.

A musical whistling poured in with the air from unseen holes of the hatches and he focused on the whistling as his flute - the plane's roaring engines as a full orchestra.

His stomach hurt.

His lips were dry from licking so often and he wiped away a thin film of spit.

He adjusted the strap around his chest, adjusted his goggles again and again.

He shrugged his shoulders in the tight-wrapped flying suit, which felt like a straitjacket must feel - clear your mind or claustrophobia will set in, he told himself.

No one in the plane said a word - perhaps due to the extreme noise, perhaps due to focus on the mission, perhaps due to the ack-ack surely to come.

Andrews came back from the front of the plane with a lit pocket flashlight in his mouth and a rucksack in his arms. He leaned down before Valentin and Castle with the rucksack open and the flashlight showing into the rucksack of English biscuits. Valentin shook his head. Castle shook his head. Andrews then offered each a thermos of tea and both shook their head. Yeah, hot liquid sounded good, Valentin thought, but having a screaming bladder beneath this stuffed suit didn't and he didn't think they'd open the hatch for a pee.

"All right, boys," Andrews hollered. "We're changing course to a more westerly approach in hopes of steering clear of ack-ack."

Both men nodded.

"Your password at drop zone is, 'I prefer *Internationale* over *Marseillaise*,'" said Andrews. "Say it in French and repeat it to me."

Both men hollered, in turn, "I prefer *Internationale* over *Marseillaise*."

"Again," Andrews hollered. They repeated the code and Andrews raised both thumbs. "Forget your password, forget your luck."

Suddenly, the plane dropped low and Valentin stared wide-eyed at Andrews.

"It's to avoid radar detection," Andrews said. "No worries, boys. We're heading west as far as feasible to avoid the flak. Flying anywhere near Calais is like flying over a hornet's nest these days as Jerry's nervous about the invasion."

Andrews patted Valentin on the back. "Our pilot's good. He studies maps for the drop zone a good hour before every flight."

Then the plane jerked and Andrews grabbed tight to a girder, sat and buckled in.

Valentin checked his pencil flashlight and covered its light in the palm of his hand.

"Okay, boys," Andrews said, "we're near the Normandy Coast, close to the Bay of the Seine. If it's going to get rough, **this** is where it's going to get rough. Buckle tight, bless your flak jackets, say your prayers, and keep your fingers crossed."

"Because of ack-ack?" Valentin asked.

"Ack-ack **and** enemy fighters. If **they** start coming in, **we** start sweating bullets. But no need to make heavy weather of any of this until it happens, ole boy."

A few thousand feet below, a searchlight crew scanned the skies. The sound locator connected to the searchlight now picked up the clatter from the engines of a plane. Then the searchlight and the ack-ack battery picked up the plane.

Just then a shaft of light flashed through the sky followed by a shower of ack-ack tracers, now arcing in the direction of the plane.

Then a torrent of flak lit the sky.

Valentin looked out a window to see the grimy, grainy splotches that looked like vibrant balls of cotton. Suddenly the cotton blazed so bright he closed his eyes, looked away, opened his eyes and saw the cotton images explode into a black mushroom cloud of smoke.

"Welcome to Fortress Europe," hollered Castle. "Looks like the bloody Moonlight Cavalry below is awake tonight!"

Valentin looked back out the window as flashes of flak stabbed at the sky and tiny pink puffs burst all around.

Then the flak puffs showed white and red and some other colors and looked like a rainbow wall climbing to the sky.

"Pretty, isn't it?" hollered Andrews. "Not so pretty if they hit us though. Then it's bloody balls up."

"Already, thousands of Allied airmen have been shot down due to those harmless-looking puffs of powder," Castle hollered. "But you're right - colors like the settin' sun - blazin' up at ya like streamers on New Year's Eve - till they reach a point and poof out like sweet cotton candy. *Nothing* sweet about it *then*. If just *one* of them puff beauties hits us, the next puff you'll see'll be the cloud you're sittin' on in 'eavan."

"Where?" Valentin hollered.

"Eaven, you know, that place above 'ell."

"I take it you grew up near the Cockney bells, Castle?" Valentin asked.

"My Cockney accent *always* comes back when I'm nervous, like ***now***."

"Yeah, well I'll take the colored flak over the heavy black puffs of flak any day," said Andrews.

"Why's that?" Valentin asked.

"Black flak comes from larger shells, 22-pound shells. They hurl those buggers six miles high or more from 88mm batteries. If they pinpoint our altitude with those big black babies, you see only one color when they explode - fire orange."

The plane jerked hard now, throttled harder and began to corkscrew higher.

A puffy grey-black cloud erupted just outside a window and the pilot jerked the plane and rolled away from the concussion.

Another puffy cloud exploded and shrapnel pelted the hide of the plane, which sounded like hail hammering an aluminum roof.

"Bloody buggers!" Andrews hollered, "got these new radio-electric eyes and radar direction tower batteries to pick up planes. If they send the Luftwaffe, we've **had** it."

Now the plane jerked and Valentin felt as if he were in a fifty-gallon drum rolling down a rocky mountain.

Through his window, he watched the sky explode as the enemy fired round after round from 20 mm anti-aircraft and DCA guns from a tower roof directly below the plane.

Then, searchlights zigzagged in a crazy web design like thousands of light beacons at some tiny airport.

Seconds later, several pink puff clouds blasted on either side of the plane, and the men bumped into each other and the fuselage.

"Avoid flying near Lille, they told us," Andrews hollered. "*That's* where they said the concentration of searchlights and anti-aircraft batteries are set up, but hell, they have them *everywhere* these days. I don't know, chaps - the fog -the flak - two out of three things against us."

"What's the third?" hollered Valentin.

"*We're alive*."

"If you don't know a Hail Mary, you better bloody invent one!" hollered Castle.

Valentin stared at the pencil flashlight that showed faint light in the palm of his hand - and thought how he'd shot many bull's eyes, but never felt like one till now.

Just then the plane rocked to the side from a flak blast just ahead in the same air current as the plane.

The pilot maneuvered the plane, climbed - swerved - zigzagged.

"Have you eaten much of a midnight snack, Farmer?" Castle hollered. "You may revisit it shortly. Nothing quite as bloody balls up as mashed-up, upchucked peas."

The plane rocked hard again. The pilot swerved and every man slammed some part of their body against some part of the plane.

"In a few more minutes, we'll know if we get out of this bobbery *just* black and blue or ***mostly*** black ***and*** in flames," Andrews hollered.

"Cheer up, mate," Castle said, elbowing Valentin, "this is my seventh trip already this year and I'm chipper as a jay."

But Valentin saw the fear in his wide eyes and heard the fear in his crackled voice.

The plane rocked again and the sky looked like a Fourth of July fireworks.

"Must be a *large* flak battery!" hollered Castle. "***Never*** seen it last ***this*** long. They must think we're the ***bloody*** Allied invasion."

The plane ascended higher and the whistling, freezing air blew through openings on all sides of the fuselage.

Valentin tasted the frosty air, felt it go down into his lungs and settle there like a punch.

Andrews rushed up front and then returned. "Okay, put your oxygen masks on!" he hollered. "Remember the spit! Remember the pump!" And he saw that his jumpers were nervous as hell and felt obliged to talk - for them - for him. "At fifteen thousand feet, the temperature inside this plane could drop twenty degrees below zero!" Andrews hollered as he folded his arms and then sat down, buckled in and put on his own oxygen mask.

Then flak exploded everywhere.

The plane bounced and jerked and Valentin watched out the window at the layers of fog lighting up, the flak puffs like iridescent thunderheads so thick one could walk upon them.

The pilot ascended, zigzagged, rolled, and reached sixteen thousand feet.

Valentin thought he could see frosty air wafting through every tiny crack and orifice in the plane. Yes, he felt it - worked his oxygen — bladder - which reminded him of his own lungs, and compared the two, and focused and breathed in steady.

He reached for a flashlight and listened intently to the air whistling in the cracks to take his mind off his fears. Yes, now that sounds like soprano - perhaps falsetto, definitely treble. Is that a whole note? Yes, perhaps there are six notes consistent with whole-tone notes on the whole-tone scale . . . .

The plane bucked hard and he listened harder. Now *that* sounds like a counterpoint; definitely more aggressive expressionism. And that forte is *definitely* neoclassical, not nocturne; no, nothing nocturne about it.

The plane shifted and bucked again. Yes, he heard the scale, but couldn't discern the relative pitch, couldn't discern the following and preceding notes. But now he heard the tremolo tempo and sequence, which was successive. No, obviously no serenade. And he listened hard for the tremolo and the tuning. But now came the reprise, hopefully *not* followed by a *requiem*!

The plane bucked so hard he hit his head against the fuselage. No, *no requiem*. And he disallowed *any requiem* from entering his thoughts.

Several more seconds seemed like hours till the plane advanced over Le Havre, over the mouth of the Seine, past the Loire.

And the flak stopped.

Andrews unbuckled himself and rushed up front to the pilot.

With shaky hands, Castle stuck an unlit cigarette in his mouth and it bounced crazily on his lips.

Valentin watched Castle bite down and gnaw on the cigarette. And he listened to his breathing, fast and shallow, like a beaten fighter that'd just gone twelve rounds. Well, *every* fighter gets a little punchy after several twelve-round fights. But not *bad for your debut bout*, he thought as he reached into his rucksack, felt for the waterproof flashlight, flashed it inside the sack twice, and exhaled.

God - this is it - yet *another* **major** milestone that puts you further *and* farther from Shelby's Creek.

He took out the photo locket and looked at his mother.

"Yeah - I've *got* to get back home," he whispered. "I've **got** to get back to Shelby's Creek."

"France has lost the battle, but she has not lost the war."

— *de Gaulle*

Normandy, France
May 1943

Chapter 16

The plane descended, swerved hard east, leveled and the ride turned smooth.

Valentin looked out the window, which showed a moon-lit, star-spotted, silvery night - the most peaceful antithesis to what he'd just experienced with the flak.

He looked below to thick cloud cover.

Moments later, clouds parted, moonlight opened, and the rolling terrain opened too, giving way to flat plains, giving way to perhaps the Loire, then perhaps the Saone and then what he knew to be the serpentine Seine.

He stared at the thin trickle of river snaking smoothly along between tiny bunches of trees he guessed were a bastion of willows, poplars, and pines. He looked at it for what seemed like a short time but was actually a long time.

Then his view was shrouded by sand-sacked clouds so thick it seemed like clusters of smoky black flak surrounding the plane again. And everything seemed dark. Below, it'd be quite dark if the moon were shrouded by clouds - for he knew the enemy below enforced the blackout strictly. Already, he disliked the enemy. Anybody who made his phobic world darker than it already was had to be an enemy. And he wondered if anyone was as afraid of the dark as he, and he shivered.

And then, without knowing it, he relaxed as moonlight opened and shone upon the country below, his mother's motherland, land he liked to think of also as *his* motherland. Yes, France, the other Shelby's Creek, the other land that he loved. Yes, he always felt a soft spot for her and embraced her now in his thoughts.

"Okay," hollered Andrews. "You boys start to think about your drop count if you cannot see the ground."

Valentin nodded, but his mind was not on the jump. His mind was on June 5. One day, when he was ten or eleven, he remembered staring at a calendar. It wasn't a calendar that showed all thirty days of June but the fifth of June only. He was with Dad at a feed store waiting, bored, as the adults bartered and bargained, sniggered, and tittle-tattled, whittled the stick of time as children yawned when they wanted to yawp. The day was pleasant, much more so than the cooler month before or the warmer month after. School was out, playing was in: on the farm, in the yard, with neighbors, with Mom and Dad, Grandpa and Grandma. June 5 - extraordinary in no way - extra ordinary in *his* way: no one's birthday, no holiday or special day of special design in any way except for it being that day, *his* day. Perhaps *everyone* should have a day to and for themselves - and he wondered *how many June fifths remained.*

"Be alert, boys," Andrews yelled. "Drop zone approaches. We make *one* swing to verify the signal, *another* swing to drop containers *and* Agent Castle."

Up in the cockpit, the plane's navigator scanned and rescanned his map, read and reread the coordinates.

The pilot then maneuvered the plane low and slow over the upcoming drop zone, but saw *no* signal lights.

"It's safer against enemy radar to drop at lower altitudes and slower speeds," Andrews said.

"But it also makes plane and parachutist at risk to enemy ground troops," Castle said.

"I have a remedy for that," said Andrews and produced four Sten guns from the floor. He slung two around the neck of each agent, positioning one on their back, one in front. "We look out for you boys – we want to make sure the **right** reception committee is waiting for you - if it's the **wrong** reception committee, you can shoot back."

"How do we bloody shoot back with our hands on the parachute chords?" asked Castle.

"You don't. You use one hand for the chord, one to shoot."

Below, the reception committee finished cloaking their bicycle lamps and flashlights in tin sleeves that only a plane could see as the lights were now hoisted high on poles.

"There they are," said the pilot as he then pushed a button on the panel in front of him and a red signal light flashed back in the fuselage - *drop zone imminent.*

"Okay," said Andrews, "the pilot spotted the ground pattern of the reception committee."

"Yes, there's their light," Castle said, as he looked out the window and down. "But it's *not* a torch."

"*Think* about it," Andrews said. "Normandy gets *lots* of rain this time of year. They probably *couldn't* use torches."

"All right," said Castle, "but if it's a bloody trap, *you* take my turn at latrine duty in a prison camp."

"If we *don't* drop *you and* these supplies, we'll all have latrine duty *at home.*"

The plane dropped low, slowed, pivoted, banked, and circled back.

"The pilot's making a trial run," said Andrews. "This is where he gets nervous."

"Why?" asked Valentin.

"This is where enemy night fighter planes like to engage us, when we're low, slow and our flaps are down . . . ."

"Below, some of the reception committee held their lights high. One flashed the letter 'F' in Morse code. The pilot's light winked in reply as he recognized the Morse code, F-F-F."

"Tally ho, it's the beacon we're looking for," said Andrews. "One more circle for the plane and we hit the silk. Action stations!" he hollered, his voice loud and commanding.

The plane slowed its throttle and descended.

"Three minutes to bailout," Andrews yelled.

Castle stood and Andrews hooked him up onto the anchor cable that ran along the cabin ceiling.

Valentin looked out a window and saw the beacon, about a half kilometer in length in the form of a seven. He looked at the lavender lights on the plane's wing tip and then below to the moonlit, silvery ground.

Andrews knelt on the fuselage floor, just aft of the bomb bay and worked the detachable cover on the floor. He hoisted it open to show a round hole nearly a meter wide. The plane's powerful engines amplified into the opening along with the steady, rushing howl of cool night air. Valentin breathed it in deeply and thought how it smelled moist - like Shelby's Creek in spring.

Men from the back of the fuselage came forward with the metal containers and hooked them to the static line. They pushed the containers to the hatch and dropped eight through the hole.

"I hope those buggers land **before** I do," hollered Castle. "Don't need one bloody splashing on me - they each weigh a tenth of a ton."

Valentin imagined the container parachutes popping open - the containers lifting and drifting willy-nilly, like cottonwood seeds from his grove on a windless day.

"One minute for you, Agent Castle," Andrews hollered.

Castle sat down. "Watch me!" he hollered to Valentin as he dragged his body sideways with his hands, twisted, dropped his legs through the hatch hole, and watched Andrews for the signal with the 'go' light.

Valentin thought of his parachute jumps out a side door at Camp Claiborne when he and his buddies hollered, "Geronimo," but there'd be no "Geronimo" tonight. There'd be only counting silently until his feet hit earth.

The *go* light turned green, Andrews dropped his raised arm, hollered, "Jump!" and gently pushed Castle.

The static line pulled as Castle straightened, dropped through the hole and disappeared into the night.

The plane increased its throttle and quickly ascended.

Valentin checked his chest buckle, his chute harness, his flashlights, and pointed the Sten beneath his armpit, as far away from his body as possible.

"Five minutes to drop," Andrews hollered.

"I cannot see the **green** go light," Valentin said.

"No worries, sport. I'll drop my arm, holler 'go,' and you'll go."

Valentin searched his coverall, counted two flashlights - one in a front chest pocket, one in a leg pocket. He reached into his rucksack and felt the large aluminum flashlight at the bottom.

Andrews held out his hand to Valentin. "I better put your rucksack into your backpack now," he said. Then he tightened his straps and patted him on the back. "Tally ho," he said and then rushed back up to the cockpit.

Moments later, the ground pilot pointed to a half-mile-long beacon below and spotted the F-F-F designated code of the reception committee. The pilot returned a signal and the landing strip lit up with a half-dozen more lights.

The ground pilot turned to Andrews and raised his thumb, which meant ground signals positive, wind acceptable, the plane will circle and make a second run over drop point.

Valentin looked out his window and saw the reversed capital L formation of the reception committee lights. My first new friends, he thought.

The plane dropped lower, banked smoothly, circled, banked sharply, and dropped lower.

Andrews rushed back from the cockpit and knelt before Valentin. "Your drop's from around seven hundred feet so count around twelve seconds."

Valentin nodded.

"Now, when I say 'go,' you go - a one-second delay may throw you off track below."

Valentin nodded.

"One minute!" said Andrews.

The *longest* **minute** of my life, Valentin thought - one of those **minutes** that can change a *lifetime*.

His hands shook a bit now and his bland, hard gum no longer produced moisture to assuage the dryness of his mouth.

Andrews opened the hatch again and Valentin spit his gum out the hole.

Men from the rear fuselage brought more metal containers, attached them, dropped them into the hole one by one.

Valentin stood, hooked on to the cable static line, stepped near the hole, sat, placed his legs through the hole - and felt - and loved - the cool moist air blowing on his face and throat.

He looked up at Andrews and felt a trickle of sweat roll down his face.

He gripped the hole's edge so hard his hands turned white.

He thought again about Camp Claiborne. Yes, he remembered jumping at Claiborne - but didn't remember his knees shaking as they did now. And he considered again about hollering "Geronimo" to possibly relieve some stress, then said it quietly as his heart thumped hard in his chest.

"No worries," Andrews hollered, "the partisans will care for you. It's in the bag!"

"Merci," Valentin said, unaware he'd responded in French as he concentrated on his French password, *I prefer Internationale over Marseillaise.*

"Get set!" Andrews said as he reached up and tugged at the static line to confirm the connection.

Valentin put his knees and feet together and hunched over slightly with his arms to his side.

His hand went automatically for his flashlight as naturally as a gunfighter checks his holster.

And then he concentrated on the parachute chords, which would be *no* problem, and then the Sten gun, which would be a *big* problem.

He stared at the haunting red light that reflected off the face of Andrews, who stood wobbly with his right hand raised high, his left hand bracing the bulkhead.

Valentin focused on his landing - keep knees bent, roll with impact.

He checked Andrews, his fur-gloved hand still raised.

He glanced below to where moonlight glowed bright. Yes, he should be able to steer clear of trees and the river, of course, if off course.

He looked up and stared at the fur-gloved hand as if it were the hand that told an executioner to pull the electrocution switch or gallows handle.

"Go!" Andrews said as he lowered his raised arm in a chop and gently pushed Valentin.

Valentin felt tension from his shoulder cords and a sudden yank as the static line released and he dropped.

His body jerked as the prop blast of the plane opened the chute and yanked him hard, and he lifted into the slipstream.

The slipstream then heaved him back from the plane like a half-cocked slingshot.

He felt the harness buckle bite into his chest and his chute harness pinch under his armpits, then felt his body lift and drift.

Yes, this is it - no turning back now - and he began to count. "One Mississippi, two Mississippi..."

He pulled on the chute's risers to guide away from some trees.

He looked down at the moon-bathed, pearl-colored countryside, saw the containers float down behind him, some already landed. And he watched human stick figures load them onto a hay wagon and cart them into the woods.

He remembered the adrenalin rush of his first jump at Camp Claiborne, but didn't remember this icy, cool air, *not* in Louisiana.

Lord, don't let clouds shroud the moonlight - just a few more seconds. And he remembered how parachutists hated jumping on dark or cloudy nights when they'd depend on a count - a count rarely precise - the impact rarely pleasant.

He felt his front chest pocket for a flashlight while counting the count and pulled on the lift webs to avert the chute chords to a clearing of barren ground, braced, and mumbled, "Six Mississippi, seven Mississippi..."

He leaned forward, *wary* of wandering backward - yes, *too* many stories of *too* many jumpers landing and falling back to a concussion, or worse.

The reception committee flashlights below turned dark and then he pulled on the shrouds to swing and drift in their direction.

Slight winds pushed against his body and he looked up at the billowy white parachute, like a huge umbrella that shifted his body like a puppet.

Below, a meadow showed pale silver and, suddenly, everything seemed silent, and he felt as though floating in a dream. Yes, there was that time in Yellowstone, in the shallow, boiling river with Katherine, who held him by his upper arms as he let his body drift with the current. No, he'd never felt such a tranquil sense of being out of control, letting his body go with the flow. Now he sensed it again - well, except for the harness straps pit-bull-jaw-locked-biting into his groin. Then he pulled at the chute risers to release some of the pressure, but he only glided off course so he pulled back.

The landscape now showed a long line of trees and he felt sandwiched between two meandering landmarks - to his right, the snaking Seine - to his left, a winding road, probably a backcountry dirt road since a main road enabled the enemy quick access to drops.

Bend your knees and roll, he repeated in his head now as his body sped to the ground - bend and roll.

He looked up one final time to the whitish umbrella of his parachute, looked left and right, and pulled at the risers to pass trees coming into sight.

He grimaced as the harness straps gripped tighter, the suit now taut-tight on his groin.

God, let the ground come soon to release the pressure -"Eight Mississippi, Nine Mississippi…"

Now only open pasture showed below.

Now the ground neared as if the earth seemed ready to swallow him up.

He braced, bent his knees, waited for the jolt.

Yes, the pasture grass should be thick, thicker and softer than…the ground met his feet and the impact jolted from his feet to his head. He sprung up, rolled, twisted in the shroud lines, and stopped flat on his back. The chute dragged him until his feet dug in to the moist earth. Behind, the last container dropped to the ground, its parachute deflating as a sheet thrown upon a bed.

He took off the Sten guns, punched at the harness clasp to release it, unfastened it, pulled off his tight sorbo-rubber helmet, lay still and listened to the full-spitting sound of his plane pull up and away and die in the distance as it gained altitude and speed.

Yes, it'd take him *several* hours to get to Paris from this point and the plane would be there - heck, it was above there *now.*

Then there was the crunch of feet on the dry grass and the sounds of several voices and he understood one voice, in French, say, "The English are always late."

He rolled again, unraveled his body, stood up, slipped on a large pile of cow pie, and fell back onto the parachute.

He grinned and lay still, listened to the soft drone of the plane become softer as it flew south.

"Faced with crisis, the man of character...imposes his own stamp of action...makes it his own."

— *Charles de Gaulle*

Normandy, France
May 1943

Chapter 17

Valentin observed silhouettes of cows and human figures move in the distance.

Then he heard hyper-excited French voices, watched their ghostly shadows materialize, move quickly toward him.

One shadow grabbed his parachute, rolled it, and stuffed it into a gunny sack.

Other specter figures now showed.

"Get those canisters to work!" somebody hollered. The same somebody then shone a pencil flashlight in Valentin's face and held out a dark arm to lift him up. Valentin took the arm, was pulled to his feet and then suddenly slapped with a round house hook to his face.

"Yooww!" hollered Valentin.

"Hurt me too," said the man that slapped him as he rubbed his hand, tensed up and shielded himself, waiting to be punched.

"Why'd you slap me?" asked Valentin.

"I wanted to see what language you'd cuss in. If it were a language other than English or French, I'd suspect you to be a spy."

"Did I cuss?"

"No...sometimes *that* is the problem."

"And it's a problem if I'm able to speak the *enemy's* language *fluently* and *happen* to cuss in the *enemy's* language?"

"Well...yes, *mostly* for you," the man said, shaking his finger and head simultaneously, making a quick tisk, tisk, tisk sound with his mouth. "Cussing in the enemy's language would have been *bad* for you...*quite bad* for you. But monsieur, you have honest eyes, so now I trust you. At first, however, I see your bright blue eyes and blond hair like a Prussian. I sensed you not as a Brit and I've never seen an American. I apologize. Slap me if you wish."

Valentin grinned at the small man, his eyes closed tight in expectation of a hit.

"Go ahead, monsieur. Slap me hard before the enemy comes."

Valentin tapped the man's cheek. "I save my slaps for the fascists, not the French."

"Ah, you are a good man, monsieur," the small man said and stretched his arm around Valentin's shoulders. "Now we must move, as the most dangerous phase for a reception committee is **right** after reception. None of us have a doctor's permit to be out after curfew, and police and patrols will hunt us like bloodhounds. Yes, Normandy may be a big place to hunt, even for bloodhounds, but the hounds' noses are well-trained after three years."

He whistled softly then and swirled his arm wildly above his head. "Off the field, into the trees, bury canisters now," he said, just below a shout. "By the way, my name's Pierre."

Valentin shook the man's hand with one hand, and rubbed his own face with the other. "You've got a good slap. I'll bet you don't keep many foreign friends, uh Pierre?"

"I don't keep many teeth either, monsieur," he said as he smiled a gap-toothed smile. "Most agents aren't as forgiving as you. Once again, accept my regret, but a man must do what he must to safeguard himself, and that tactic's the safest way I know. I prefer to lose teeth than to lose life."

"I was told to tell you the secret code - 'I prefer Internationale over 'Marseillaise.'"

"Code schmode," said Pierre. "Who remembers codes other than double agents? If, however, you are a dyed-in-the-wool Frenchman, you remember who penned the Marseillaise."

"Rouget de Lisle."

"Ooh la la," Pierre said and whistled. "We have a *real* Francophile here, boys!"

"I could ask you lots of American questions - who won the World Series, which songs are on the *Hit Parade*, which movie won Best Picture? And your answers might make you appear as American as John Wayne. I could ask where you come from, where you're going, who you are, all that bullshit, but it takes too long. I'm a little man with little patience."

"So you simply slap an agent and if they cuss in *any* language *other* than French, American-French, British-French, British-English, or American English, they're *probably* a spy?"

"Oui, monsieur."

"I still like the password, I prefer '*Internationale* over *Marseillaise*,' as prearranged."

"Aaaah, my hearing's not so good either," said Pierre. "And an agent's going to talk a lot louder if I slap him."

"Perhaps your hearing's not so good because agents return your slap on your ears."

"Perhaps," said Pierre as he gave a Gallic shrug and then lit and sucked on a cigarette until the end glowed and lit his beard-stubbled, pencil-mustached face. "Cigarette, monsieur?" he said, now offering a Gauloise.

Valentin rolled his eyes. "No thank you, Pierre," he said, preferring to avoid his response that he *doesn't smoke*, preferring to avoid backlash as to *why* he *doesn't smoke*.

"But now we must move on and be quiet. Enemy patrols are out tonight," said Pierre.

"Do you think they hear the echo of your face slaps?" said Valentin.

"Oh, you are a funny American."

"I am *not* American to you; I am Agent Hot Dog."

Pierre turned to his reception committee and said in a loud whisper, "Unload the canisters and dump the tin in the Seine. And listen for the high-pitched whistles fixed to all the canisters. We can't miss one tonight! Keep the parachutes!"

"What do you do with the parachutes?" said Valentin.

"We cut them into satin panties for our women. My woman and I were thrilled when they started using black parachutes - ooh la la, nothing like noir silk panties, uh, monsieur?"

"Aren't you afraid the enemy will discover remnants of the parachute on your person?"

"Unless the enemy's sleeping with our women, they'll have no way of knowing we use para saboteur-silk parachutes for underwear."

Now Valentin watched partisans throughout the meadow disconnect the parachute harnesses from the containers and lift the containers into a horse-drawn cart. Several men dragged several containers to some brush, threw them in a shallow hole, took out a few items, placed the items in haversacks, and buried the rest.

"Now, hurry with your jump suit, Hot Dog," Pierre said. "Like they say, the first thirty minutes are the most important to avoid capture."

"I thought it was fifteen minutes," said Valentin.

"Hmmm…perhaps that's *why* the last agents were captured," said Pierre, now rubbing his chin before muffling an ornery laugh.

Valentin unzipped his suit and walked out of it. As he did, the stuffed newspapers flew into the wind.

"Ah, next time make sure the newspapers are French underground publications," Pierre said. "You'll be a better propaganda distributor than the couriers. Xavier, take his suit. Now hurry, Hot Dog - we'll take you to a place that has a radio to tell London you've arrived. You may also get a couple hours of rest, but no more since you dropped later than expected and you **must** get to the Seine **before** sunrise."

Valentin watched clouds cover the moon and placed a hand inside his pocket on his flashlight.

"Monsieur," Pierre said. "When I shone the light on your face, your face showed wet with sweat. The night is cool and you sweat? Are you sick?"

"No, monsieur. I'm fine - just a little *flak-frazzled*."

"Oh yes…the enemy along the Channel is as *flak-crazy* as we Normans are *Camembert-crazy*."

"Well…Camembert may not be as colorful, but I prefer *Camembert-crazy*."

Valentin then checked his watch. Yes, he said to himself, I'm duly impressed with these partisans. Less than fifteen minutes passed since the drop and he, the canisters, and the reception committee were all safe and secure. Yes, truly efficient, even with a hand print across my cheek.

Now they walked through heavy woods and Pierre whispered, "It's much safer if the plane just drops supplies and operatives and then takes off again. It's not easy to safeguard a meadow large as a soccer field for a plane to land. So we change coordinates each time. These trees and hedgerows act as our sentinels and…"

"Boches approach, hide," said a partisan as he ran up to them.

The partisans all dropped to the ground.

Pierre kept his hand on Valentin's back.

They remained motionless.

Heavy, tromping boots and dozens of shadows of soldiers some thirty yards away ran past them now and rushed to the drop zone.

"Hurry, Hot Dog," Pierre whispered, "walk this way and think quiet. If I move, you move. If I stop, you stop."

They dashed through the woods on a well-worn trail.

Valentin kept his hand on his flashlight, his eyes on the back of Pierre.

They walked fast for a kilometer and ran fast for two kilometers till they came to a barn. Pierre and some partisans quickly removed a pile of straw bundles from a small cellar door, opened the door, and stepped down several stone stairs. One partisan stayed up on top, covered the door again with the straw bundles, and rushed back to the woods.

"This barn's been a perfect safe house for us so far," Pierre whispered. "It's off the beaten path - it's not used by a farmer — and, because of the thick woods that surround it, it's difficult for the enemy to see from the ground or air. Have a seat," he said pointing to a far corner that showed cots, stools, benches, and straw bales.

"So is it normal for enemy soldiers to find a drop?" said Valentin.

"A drop, yes; droppers, no. If you are not found in the first twenty-four hours, you have a fifty-fifty chance of escape. But the Boches are improving at finding drops. Two months ago, a cell up north was caught. But they were reckless - burned large fires for both pilot and enemy to see - had a large reception committee - had too much movement of partisans in and out of the area."

"What happened to them?"

"A dozen summarily shot. The rest interrogated, *then* shot."

From a far corner pigeons cooed in cages sitting atop a wooden shelf.

"They're homing pigeons," Pierre said. "Each pigeon has a ring around its leg. Messages are twisted into the ring and the bird released to fly back to London or on to Paris. It works well when the radio does not, and is safer, since our enemy has state-of-the-art radio-detection devices."

"How many pigeons do you have?"

"The Resistance uses about thirty thousand. Our most famous pigeon, Roosevelt, has saved hundreds of SOE agents."

Just then, a partisan put a sealed note into a ring on a pigeon's leg and took it upstairs.

"That pigeon will let London know that you and the canisters arrived safely," said Pierre.

"How are you sure the pigeon will make London?"

"Well, if it *didn't* end up in our stew, it'll *probably* make London."

"You eat them?"

"Before OSS financed us, carrier pigeons, *now and then*, became stewing pigeons. But now the birds *and* we are in good hands."

"That reminds me," said Valentin as he reached into his pocket. "I have one hundred thousand francs for you."

"Merci. We deliver half of this along with your rifle and radio to Paris."

Pierre then opened a bottle, poured liquid into a cup and handed it to Valentin. "It's our local apple brandy, Calvados. It'll warm your innards after your flight."

"Thank you. That flight was cold."

"Oui, monsieur - hot flak - cold flight. Colder if hot flak hits you. In fact, that *Channel flight* should be called *flak flight*. Experienced a few myself."

"No wonder you're a slaphappy slapper and have no patience for a password."

Pierre laughed a guttural laugh. "Oh, you are a funny American, Hot Dog! So, why Hot Dog?"

"Just for *this* drop," said Valentin.

"Frankly speaking - for an American frankfurter, you speak *good* French."

"Must be all those American *French* fries."

Pierre laughed heartily. "Ssshhhh," he said as he held a finger to his lips. "Ooh la la…American…you'll turn me over to the enemy yet. You're a *funny* hot dog. I *don't* think I want to be *drunk* with you."

"Vive la France, et les pommes de terre frites! Long live France and her fried potatoes."

Pierre laughed again and put a handkerchief to his mouth to quiet himself. "Where'd you learn that?"

"My…relatives in France."

"Well, Hot Dog, we need to get you into Paris. First things first: for this sector, I'm the leader of SOAM. I organize parachute drops in landing areas - remote, flat, and large as a soccer field - *and* I organize Seine boat pick-ups, discreet and rare to see as your lady's panty."

Valentin grinned and grabbed for Pierre's cup of Calvados. "Enough for you, you crazy, Calvados-cockeyed crapaud."

Pierre laughed so hard, he nearly fell over. "Crazy crapaud? You know French well, Hot Dog. No, no, no…the *problem* is that we don't have *enough* Calvados," he said as he poured both their cups full.

"Okay…" he said, in-between laughter again and again. "Okay…in a few hours, you'll meet Skipper, another leader of SOAM who also organizes maritime operations on the Seine."

Pierre then reached into a haversack, pulled out bread and cheese and offered them to Valentin.

"No thanks, I'm stuffed with food…"

"Let me guess, English peas and potatoes. Don't get me wrong," said Pierre as he bit into the bread, followed by the cheese, followed by a sip of Calvados. "I'm glad the Brits are on our side - *but* I've *never* understood *how* they can stay 'cheeky' by what they eat."

"À votre santé - *cheers*," said Valentin as he clinked his cup with Pierre's and sipped the Calvados.

"I also have some French wine," said Pierre. "All you need are French fries to go with it," he said as he laughed until his eyes were mere slits.

"I think I'd forever give up *our* French fries for *your* French wine and French cheese," said Valentin.

"Ah, you are familiar with our cheese?"

"Familiar enough to know you don't take out the flavor -as we do in America."

"I'll have to visit your America one day and try your fries, hamburgers, **and** hot dogs."

"You may stay on my farm, but I'll ask you to bring French wine and French cheese - and *plenty* for *me*."

Pierre poured another cup of Calvados and then held up the bottle of wine. "Yes, this Burgundy is from the ancient limestone caves of the region, robust and earthy. It'll make you relax and tire so you sleep."

"Umm...the Calvados is already working its magic," said Valentin as he yawned.

"Yes...yes... You must rest now," said Pierre. "Your cot's over there. We're short on blankets, but long on parachutes. Help yourself. I'll wake you and have a fresh change of clothes for you. French civilian clothes **without** Hot Dog labels."

"Thank you."

"Boys, dim your kerosene lantern lower so Hot Dog can sleep," Pierre hollered to partisans on a far table.

"No," Valentin said, "the light doesn't bother me."

"John Wayne's not afraid of the dark, is he?" said Pierre, laughing, poking Valentin in the ribs. Then he left, up the stone stairs and out the cellar door.

From his rucksack, Valentin grabbed his pencil flashlight and put it under his pillow. He grabbed the aluminum flashlight and laid it beside him. He lay on his side, facing the far lantern light.

Yes, he felt lag from the furious flight, felt the Calvados, felt the late night and shortage of sleep.

He closed his eyes, felt the light through his eyelids, and relaxed.

He listened to the cooing of the pigeons and thought of the upper ceiling of the lower barn of his farm where dozens of the birds lived, where they'd built dozens of nests. He'd watch them, in all their assorted colors, blacks and blues, whites, and spots, flying in flocks round and round the barn, their flight dizzying to watch until they'd land, one by one upon the top crest of the of the wood-slatted red roof. And then, as the sun set, they'd fly again into the barn, into the nest roosts, and he'd sneak in and listen to their cooing and watch their breasts ebb and flow with the slowing of their breathing until they dozed in place.

Now he forced open his eyes, closed them again, and listened until he no longer heard the soothing cooing of the pigeons, and fell into a deep sleep.

"Soldiers of France, wherever you may be, arise!"

— Charles de Gaulle

Mantes-a-Jolie, Normandy, France
May 1943

Chapter 18

"Hot Dog, wake up," Pierre said.

Valentin opened his eyes and searched under his pillow for his pencil flashlight.

"It's time," Pierre said. "You want to be to the Seine *before* sunrise. I've prepared some items for you. Here, on this gossamer-thin sliver of silk are your radio codes. The fabric is digestible and liquefies on the tongue immediately if you must swallow it. Hide them in the sliding heel of your boot."

"So, if I must eat them, they'll taste literally like shoe leather."

"Literally like Brit food," Pierre said and laughed a nasal, deep-throated laugh.

Pierre then showed blank travel orders. "Give these to Skipper. Hide them in your underwear - just don't pee on them or wipe your butt with them," he said and whooped with laughter.

Valentin began to laugh but yawned instead, realizing he needed more sleep, less laughter.

"Just so you know," Pierre said, "on moonlit nights like this - *enemy patrols* are on the alert for *drops* - and *our fighter planes* are on the alert for *enemy patrols*. In turn, our radio people called in *recent enemy coordinates* and sent fighter planes to *those coordinates*. In turn, fighter planes may be headed in **your** direction, so **duck and keep low if you hear or see a plane**."

"Yes, sir."

"Remember, Hot Dog, you *are* French Resistance. To our enemy, you *are* traitor *and* terrorist. If captured, there's *no* detention for you, *no* military prison; *only* summary execution."

"I understand."

"Now open your French-silk map for me. Here, near this dirt road is where you'll find a collapsible motorbike. Check your time at this point. If you're late, ride the bike down the road to this point and collapse it here. There are no enemy outposts in the area, but if you sense patrols may be out, leave the bike alone since it has a motor and is noisy."

"I understand."

Pierre knelt down in front of Valentin, his eyes serious. "Victory's in the air. A year ago, there *may* have been a traitor among the reception committee who'd turn you in for money. Now traitors *are rare*. They don't wish to be known as collaborators when we win, even if we win with de Gaulle."

"You have a problem with de Gaulle?"

"Beggars can't be choosers. We can't *turn* to Petain, who's already *turned* to the enemy and is ready to *turn* to a grave anyway. And since Marshall Foch is a bit colder than Petain, we're *stuck* with de Gaulle, who has the charm of a frog and persuasive charisma of King Louis being lead to the guillotine."

Valentin began to yawn, but laughed aloud.

Pierre checked his watch. "Here, Hot Dog, take this doctor's permit to be out after curfew. And here's another silk map of France. It's a special map, shows this region's detailed topography. I've outlined your exact route. With the map and your compass, you'll be fine."

Valentin put the pencil flashlight in his front pocket, the aluminum one in his pants pocket, and checked his rucksack for the third.

"Remember," Pierre said, his face stone serious, his finger swaying like a pendulum, "substantial rewards are offered to collaborators. *Spies* are *everywhere* - I repeat, *spies* **are everywhere**."

"Yes, sir."

"Remember - be *alert for fighter planes and enemy patrols*."

"Yes, sir."

"Bon voyage," Pierre said as he hugged Valentin and kissed him once on each cheek, four times - as the northern French do. "I wish you *merde,* Hot Dog."

"You wish me what?" asked Valentin.

"I was raised in Belgium. When you wish someone luck, you say, 'I wish you *merde,*'" said Pierre, grinning, his eyes mere slits again.

"I think some Belgian's been wishing you far *too* much *merde*," said Valentin. "You're so full of it your eyes are brown."

Pierre howled with laughter and his laugh lines wrinkled deep as if he'd laughed most of his life.

"Nevertheless," said Valentin, "I wish you *lots* of *merde* as well, and *bonne merde* on top of that."

Pierre laughed till tears fell. "Like a true Frenchman, I wish I could offer a bottle of wine for your journey."

"But you're Belgian."

Pierre whooped with laughter again. "Promise me after the war we get drunk together, Hot Dog."

Valentin nodded, picked up his rucksack, stuffed it in his backpack, and walked up the stone steps to the cellar door. Yes, normally on such an early morning at such a time of year, he'd be exiting the cellar door of Shelby Creek's cabin or the house on the hill to feed the cows, milk the goats, or weed the gardens.

Yes, all of *that* seemed so far away now.

And all of *this* made him miss it *all* the more.

"But now, for the first time, I see you are a man like me…we have the same fear of death…how could you be my enemy?"

— *Erich Maria Remarque*

Normandy, France
May 1943

Chapter 19

Within minutes after leaving the barn, Valentin was deep onto a trail into the woods.

He walked briskly - his compass in his left hand - his unlit pencil flashlight in his right.

He shivered from the cold. Grow up, he told himself. So you see your breath in the cool air - at least you see your breath. You've grown soft since Camp Claiborne. Toughen up or get out. This is no place for whiners. The strong survive from this point. Remember what you're doing here. Hone your wits and flush the pathos, or get out.

He heard a noise and knelt, felt for a gun. But there was no gun. You refused all weapons from London, he told himself.

Then the night fell quiet.

He stood and walked faster.

Moonlight shone bright through thick brush, hedges, pines, and Lombardy Poplars, so many Lombardy Poplars. Was it Monet that liked to paint poplars? Or Renoir? Not Degas. Not Monet. Nevertheless, the French seem to love poplars. Ha, *popular poplars*. Yes, poplars are to Paris and France what cottonwoods and oaks are to Shelby's Creek and Iowa.

And it hit him now that soon he'd be in Paris, soon after with Grandma Lambert, and he couldn't stop grinning.

He stopped behind thick bush, knelt and felt for the aluminum flashlight in his pocket, clicked it on, watched the light come on through the fabric, and nodded.

"Thank you Lord for the bright moonlight that allows quick movement through the thick brush and foreign hinterland", he whispered. "Thank you."

Soon, small open fields showed and he thought how parts of this maréca-geuse prairie looked *quite* mushy - from minor floods, major springs, major rains, he didn't know, but he didn't mind. No, at least it was not raining now as it often did this time of year in the Calvados and the Eure.

He thought about just north of here where the boxed-in, ten-foot-tall for-tresses of brush called *bocage* had created jungle-like cover since the days of Caesar - for enemy and ally alike. No, he couldn't imagine fighting in such ter-rain - felt sympathy for the Allies here within the year - felt empathy for Randy who may be included with those Allies.

His head hurt.

His stomach felt hot, empty, nauseated.

Stop being a baby, he told himself. Buck up and put your head right or you'll **never** get through this.

Then he dropped into a sunken roadway, lay flat and still.

Noises came from everywhere.

Dark figures moved across the distant meadow.

On the road before him, a convoy of vehicles rolled past - lorries, half-tracks, ten-ton tractor carriages with recoilless guns.

The ditch he lay in seemed to shake from their weight.

The clank of their metal was deafening.

And their lights flashed just above where he lay.

He didn't move a muscle, kept his face behind high blades of grass.

After the vehicles passed, he heard the thud of boots and the area suddenly seemed surrounded with soldiers.

Just above, a combat patrol marched, their cleated boots echoed on the packed dirt road.

He heard someone speak, but couldn't understand what they said.

He waited several moments until the vehicles and soldiers sounded far away.

He crawled behind the shadow of a hedge, peeked through the branches and waited several minutes, which turned to thirty, which turned to the distant drone of a plane headed his way.

Then, from the open meadow, shadows of more troops ran his way.

And he heard the low drone of a plane grow louder - saw its lights, saw its shadow approach from the north as it dropped lower and lower.

He crawled behind the cover of a pine as the plane passed. Yes, an RAF *spotter* plane.

Then, another plane cruised in at low altitude.

No, it *couldn't* be a Spitfire - too loud - too slow.

He didn't know that it was a British Bristol Type 156 Beaufighter, a long-distance bomber fighter - armed with a half-dozen 7.7mm machineguns and four 20mm cannons - the preferred night fighter for RAF ground operations due to its comprehensive destructiveness.

He heard faint shouting from the patrol in the meadow. "Rabatz! Rabatz! Rabatz!" soldiers shouted, which he knew meant *heavy enemy attack.*

He watched the Beaufighter drop low as its 7.7mm machine guns opened up in a pulsating, staccato burst as bullets blazed from the outer starboard and outer port wings. The running shadows of the troops in the meadow dropped. A couple shadows knelt and shot up at the plane.

The plane circled and fired two shots each from its 20mm fuselage cannons.

There were no more shots from the shadows.

The Beau flew south, he guessed toward the larger patrol convoys that just passed him. Soon, the air filled with echoes of the Beau machineguns and cannons again, and the horizon in that direction sparked with flashes of fire.

Then all sounds died away save for the droning of the plane, which weakened as it flew south.

Valentin lay stone still and listened.

Where the soldiers' shadows lay, some twenty or thirty meters away, he heard muffled sounds.

He remained still.

He smelled the blooms of primrose and violets beside him.

More muffled sounds.

Then silence.

He stood, looked around.

Silence.

Now he remembered the Iowa winter of '39 when, after a great blizzard, he and Dad went to the barn to check the livestock. Even before they got to the barn, he somehow sensed an odor and a bitter gloom. And the gloom persisted as they entered the barn where they found dozens of snow-covered, smothered, lifeless, cattle carcasses -freshly dead, but partly stiff.

Now, in the pit of his stomach, he sensed a bitter gloom again.

He walked to where he'd last seen the soldier shadows.

Soon, he smelled fresh blood and saw still bodies - bodies like human pretzels - joined somehow amid light and shadow - like the still bodies of Gericault's Medusa.

All the bodies were in uniforms and helmets - all looked comatose.

Some of the faces were only visible in silhouette - some gray with death - some pink with life - some pale as dough from drained blood - some dark where blood had spilled.

The first soldier looked as though he'd been hit in the chest with large shrapnel - his eyes bugged out of his head like hot dogs. In moonlight that flooded his face, he looked more grotesquely animated than real, almost like a mannequin if it weren't for his puffed, rubbery skin. Valentin turned the soldier over to hide his face, only for the soldier's brains to roll out of a large hole in the back of his head and spill onto the lush grass. Valentin fell to the ground, felt blood rush away from his head, tasted bile, and gagged over and over, as if exhaling his insides.

Suddenly, there was moaning, low and irregular.

Valentin crawled to the source and looked away immediately from the young soldier below him lying on his stomach with his arm and leg shot away, his face contorted. "Charley! Charley! Charley!" he hollered, referring to enemy aircraft. Then his voice softened. "Mutter! Mutter! Mutter!" he moaned, referring to his mom. Valentin turned the soldier over. "Advise Patrol Commander," the soldier said "...Advise Command Center . . . Advise . . . Mother . . . Mother . . . Mother," he said and then stopped.

Valentin felt for the soldier's pulse, but it was now still as his face, drained of all blood, gray as stone.

Then, almost unconsciously, Valentin touched the soldier's face to stop the tears, but the tears had already stopped, already dried with blood and mud. The soldier's thick, curly black hair was matted with mud, and Valentin began to pull the mud out of it. He couldn't understand the mud. It hadn't rained - no puddles - and then he understood. The moist, sticky dirt had worked up from the plane's bullets and bombs. Now he noticed the shallow craters. And suddenly - *for the first time in his life* - he *hated* the *smell* of fresh soil.

He felt queasy again, felt the nausea wrench his throat and gut, tasted the bile.

He wiped quickly at the blood now also caked on his arms, on his neck, on his cheek.

He stood and stepped back.

And he stopped suddenly – listened - looked - confirmed - that he was the only man standing in the vicinity.

Silence.

"Knochen-sammlung! Knochen-sammlung!" a voice cried from among the bodies on the ground. "Knochen-sammlung!" the voice repeated and Valentin knew these words meant to hunt for wounded on a battlefield. And he looked desperately for the voice, but then it quieted.

Now clouds cleared completely and moonlight shone so intensely, the night seemed bright as early dawn.

He looked again at the bodies to his left and right, most warped in twisted positions like a car in a bad wreck.

Some lay flat on their backs - some lay curled on their sides in the fetal position - some looked peaceful - as though asleep - as though able to wake for revelry —as though able to say good morning to family and friends, to sip on a coffee, to sing a Sunday hymn. But he knew their lips were already cold - knew they'd never speak, sip, or sing *anything* again.

He stumbled over a body and landed on another, rolled fast and stood.

One dead soldier showed his hands folded upon his chest - a final act of prayer - a final act of loss - he didn't know.

He knelt now and looked inside the soldier's coat for ID papers, accidentally touched the man's neck, already the texture of cooled wax, and he shivered.

He found the ID papers, wiped blood from them so the blood would not cake and obscure the man's name, and then tucked the papers back inside the coat.

His stomach churned and he began to dry heave again.

He stood, jumped over the bodies, rushed back to the forest and back down the trail, and ran and ran...and then stopped.

He gasped for air, held his breath, and listened.

Yes, a moan, then silence, then another moan.

He looked back to where the bodies lay and his mind said move down the trail...but his body led him back to the bodies of the soldiers.

Then the moan again and he rushed to its source, to where, beneath a heavy helmet, a young face winced in pain.

"Listen," Valentin said, speaking the soldier's language and kneeling. "I'm going to help you." And he pulled off his backpack, looked inside it with the pencil flashlight, and found the toothpaste-tube-shaped morphine syrette. He punched the syrette with the needle, punctured the seal, injected the soldier with the 1/2 grain morphine. He attached the syrette to the soldier's collar so a medic would not overdose him. He took his own jacket off, pulled the soldier's helmet off, and laid the soldier's head gently upon the jacket. He saw blood oozing from the soldier's arm and leg. "I'll put tourniquets on your upper arm and leg," he whispered to the soldier.

"Kiste! Kiste!" the soldier said, referring to the Beaufighter. "Dunnschibkanone! Dunnschibkanone!" the soldier said, referring to the Beaufighter's guns. "Kattun! Kattun!" the soldier said, referring to the Beaufighter's overwhelming firepower. And the soldier tried to lift his body and fell back down. "Jabo! Jabo!" he said, referring to a fighter bomber as he propped his torso on an elbow and then fell back down. He grabbed at his dog tags. "Hundemarke, hundemarke," he said and tore at the bottom half of the tags.

Valentin rushed and tied the tourniquets.

"Kumpel," the soldier said, referring to Valentin as his friend as he grasped Valentin's arm.

Then the soldier's body lifted and stiffened as if struck by a massive cramp and, just as quickly, he lay still. "Ich bin dran," the soldier whispered, which Valentin knew meant 'It's my turn.'

127

Valentin then lifted the soldier's head and cradled it in his lap.

"Water," the soldier pleaded as his voice rattled. "Water, please."

Valentin lifted the flask from his backpack, held the soldier's head up, and helped him to drink. In the moonlight he observed the soldier's decorations that gleamed and glittered: his Knight Commander of the Iron Cross stuck in a buttonhole - his eagle emblem - his many medals of unknown origin - maybe a lieutenant, maybe second lieutenant.

With his pencil flashlight in his mouth, Valentin looked over the soldier for more wounds. He sprinkled sulfa powder on each wound he found and applied Carlisle bandages. Then he sighed as he saw, below the shiny medals, several shrapnel punctures where blood pumped out with each heartbeat. He looked into the soldier's face and thought how much he resembled Randy Rasmussen.

Leave, his mind repeated, leave now.

The soldier's eyes stared into his eyes, imploring.

"This damned wool's so itchy," the soldier said, "help me pull this collar from my throat."

Then, with a sudden burst of effort, the soldier tore at the medals and decorations upon his coat, ripping them off, throwing them aside, and grunting loudly with each movement. "Damn lametta!" he said, referring to the adornments. And he kept ripping at his coat, grunting wildly, ripping off more and more of the tinsel upon his chest and neck. "Help me, kumpel, help me!" he said. "Take it off me."

And Valentin pulled off the rest of the decorations.

"That's it," said Valentin. "That's…all of them."

"Thank you, kumpel," said the soldier, exhaling loudly.

"I miss home," the soldier whispered. And he began to sing "Lili Marleen," then stopped. "Please sing with me," he said to Valentin and Valentin did.

Together they nearly finished the lyrics when suddenly, the soldier stopped and began to cough violently.

Valentin lifted his head and the coughing soon brought up blood. The soldier grabbed Valentin's hand and placed a dog tag inside of it. Valentin saw the name - 'Blum.' - the same name as a distant neighbor in Lincoln Township.

"Kumpel," said the soldier… "Kumpel," he repeated as he grasped Valentin's arm tight. "Stand me up, please," his voice now a broken whisper, "I'll **not** meet my Maker…on my butt."

Then the soldier hiccoughed more blood, held his throat, shut his eyes, and went limp.

Valentin felt the soldier's pulse slow and then felt the last of the soldier's life leave - as simply, as swiftly, as one blows out the flame of a matchstick.

He watched the soldier's face until the soldier's tears dried.

He placed the soldier's head back gently on the ground and placed the dog tag upon the soldier's chest.

All fell quiet except for the moo of a cow and the clang of its bell far, far away.

Valentin turned to another still soldier, his face blood-caked save for the webbed streaks down his cheeks where tears flowed. Valentin gently closed the young man's sightless eyes, felt the day's bristly whiskers on his face, and shivered. He pushed aside the soldier's Iron Cross First Class medal, looked inside a front pocket of a spreading-red-stained shirt, and pulled out a photo of a young lady and baby - perhaps his wife and child. Is this soldier a city kid? Is he a farm kid? Did he have siblings? Grandparents? Well, now he had *nothing* - and *none* of it mattered. He opened the soldier's wallet, stared at his name - 'Zimmerman.' – and thought about Henry Zimmerman and his family, members of his hometown Iowa church.

Valentin went to the next lifeless body – 'Schaeffer' and the next – 'Schwery' – the next – 'Musich', 'Kaufman', 'Kloewer', 'Dotzler', 'Henscheid', 'Leuschen', 'Arkfeld', 'Schomers', 'Schechinger', 'Schulte' - all names of people he knew in his Iowa county who hailed from Panama, Portsmouth, Defiance, Westphalia and Earling. Then he came across three names he didn't know and one he knew well – 'Schumacher' - a cousin's name back home. Perhaps *that* cousin's cousin - now lying silent before him wearing a *Swastika pin* on his lapel.

He imagined how each of these young men - only moments ago – had perhaps felt the infinity of life that a young person expects - stretching far ahead. Yes, my body could be lying here beside them. If Grandpa hadn't sailed for the promised terra incognita of America - where dreamers of

Prussia and Bavaria...yes...yes...I *might* be stiff on the cold ground in an ugly uniform riddled with bullet holes through eagle emblems and Swastika insignias. Only if *their* grandfathers had migrated - *they* might be wearing a uniform that resembled *life* - and now maybe *they'd* resemble *life*. All that separates *them* from *me* is *time* and *space* - the *right* or *wrong* place... How many of these boys condoned fascism? Hell, most were under twenty-one; most barely men. How could they understand anything other than duty and dreams? How did it go? Dreams for young boys and old men... True...**only** if young boys **become** old men. How *sad* to die...*with dreams*. Hell, any of these soldiers could've been a buddy back home. Now they were bodies awaiting bones, awaiting wind and worms, awaiting the plow like husks...no, not husks - husks were leftovers of the reaping business. Here, there was *no* reaping and *business* looked *bankrupt*. Damn Hitler, damn the Versailles Treaty that created Hitler, damn the elected mucks that put together all...broken Black Hills promises. Damn the faceless treaties, the game hunters, fickle kings on cushy thrones that relish in spoils - that swat butterfly and mosquito the same - a boy with a toy he won't share - holding it is power - holding it so long it becomes useless, even to him.

And he wondered if the pilots of the planes that shot these boys realized these boys were *more* than *just* toy-soldier *targets*. Did the *killers* realize they *killed souls*?

He knelt and prayed in a whisper. "Lord, please welcome these boys into your heavenly kingdom. Grant them the goodness they deserve, grant their families the solace they need."

And he sat back and shook his head. Is this how this war will end - one young soldier at a time? One boy - barely turned man - at a time? One innocent civilian - young and old - at a time? Must modern civil civilians turn blood-thirsty barbarians to stop the madness?

Suddenly an arm went around his neck.

The arm throttled a hand-locked forearm into his throat and knees thrust into his kidneys.

He felt his breath leave his lungs - felt light-headed as blood constricted to his brain.

With quick motion, he pushed slightly left and rolled right, brought the man behind him to the ground, drove an elbow hard into the man's gut until he released his hold.

He threw an elbow into the man's jaw, grabbed the man's coat with his left hand, jabbed him with his right, and felt the coat go heavy and body go limp.

All right - see what you get, Valentin told himself. Look what happens. You were caught off guard in enemy territory. Yeah, you're *weak* from lack of sleep, *weak* from all this death, but out here *that's* going to earn you a *plot of ground* on *foreign land*.

He looked down at the man he just punched - noticed much blood - dark upon the soldier's coat - and realized he was already near death - near death and *still* fighting the good fight. You're *alive* and *can't even* fight the good fight.

He stood still.

There was no sound; no chirping insect, no mooing cow, no bleating goat, no singing night bird, not even a breeze to rouse the dead air - dead as the day of the blizzard in the barn. And he remembered how someone once said how only the dead know the end of war and how...*how what*?

Now *move*, he said to himself.

He placed the soldier's coat over his face, moved around the other bodies, and ran east toward the forest and the trail.

Now *wake up*, he told himself, or *you'll* end up like your cousins back there. This is *war*; the sooner you convince yourself death *doesn't matter*, the sooner you . . . .

Remember *why* you're *here.* And you *are here,* *not* back *there* - on the farm. These soldier's deaths and the deaths of many to come just *do not* matter.

Move your butt - put your mind right - or - you'll be just as dead as these soldiers.

And *then* what good are you to Grandpa and Grandma?

Still, he stopped and looked back at the bodies, thought of the persons within the bodies - yes, more like cousins, less like enemies.

He ran, but then stopped, dug in his pocket for the vial of suicide poison from London and placed it under a rock.

He drank from the canteen and thought of the soldier who called him 'friend,' who had last drunk from the canteen. And the water had no taste - not tasteless-sweet like his spring or Yellowstone's upper Pebble Creek - but taste-less where there *should* be taste - canteen-fusty, canteen-fetid. It was like his taste buds went numb as he now felt numb...in many places.

And now his nausea was gone and his stomach settled - whatever that meant.

"Only the dead have seen the end of war."

— Plato

Normandy, France
May 1943

Chapter 20

Valentin ran through open fields and hoped for the bright moon to stay bright, clear of clouds, especially now, because somehow, the dark now seemed darker.

No . . . God, no - I can't risk hyperventilating from the dark now, he told himself. Okay . . . I'll simply kneel with my coat over my head to mask the pencil flashlight and stay that way until moonlight shows again.

He ran at a steady pace, alert for patrols, cows, and cow pies - imagined how the latter might end his assignment - imagined the headline: "OSS Operative Slips in Poop: *American agent found in Normandy pasture unconscious with broken leg, concussion and shoe soaked in cow manure.*"

After half an hour, he stopped, knelt, laid the silk map on the ground, covered his head with his coat, studied the map with the pencil flashlight. Okay, he'd started out between Évreux and Vernon, and now must be near Pointe de la Grave, where a monument commemorated American soldiers in the Great War of 1917. And directly east one hundred kilometers was the American cemetery at Château Thierry where row after row of white crosses represented graves of American soldiers. Yes, he and his parents once visited this site - Dad laid a wreath for his close friends that died here – where part of Dad died too – for he remembered how he walked away from the cemetery and cried – rememberd how he'd never seen Dad cry before. Yes . . . Dad fought in this area, fought in uniform with a flag. Well, for me, there's neither *uniform* nor *flag*. But *I'm* expected to fight, to kill. And *none* of it is doing *any good* or *ever did any good*.

But now's not a time to think *or* to cry - that comes *after* all is *said* - and *done*.

He folded the map and noticed the northern Normandy town of Bayeux, where Grandpa and Grandma Lambert took him often. Yes, they all loved

Bayeux - its quiet charm, its eleventh-century cathedral, its Queen Matilda tapestry. And, from Bayeux, they'd travel west to Brittany - and thought about Brittany's Mont St. Michel — how they'd stayed its fortress walls overnight - how they'd looked over the walls - watched the tide flats of the Gulf of St. Malo, Europe's most powerful tide - how the waters rushed in like a feral flood and smashed into the castle walls. No, he'd never been afraid of water before, but was afraid then and didn't sleep well that night. But when he did sleep, a dream turned to nightmare as the tides rushed in, again and again, and he woke and gasped for air. And Grandma woke and came to him and asked him what was wrong.

"The water. I can't breathe," he'd said.

"You're okay," she'd said and held him.

Yes, he remembered her warm embrace, remembered how she'd lain beside him until his breath returned and he relaxed and they both fell asleep.

He grinned now, glad he'd come to France now, glad he'd soon be with her again. Yes, he owed her so much - including his breath.

Now he pulled out his compass and compared it to the map. Yes, twenty - maybe thirty more minutes.

He took his last swallow from his canteen, spotted the blood spatter from the soldiers on it and rubbed the canteen in the dirt again and again. Think about Mont St. Michel again, he told himself, and he did and remembered how, early one morning, he, Grandpa and Grandma walked out from the castle walls to the wet shores where the tide recently receded and dug mollusks that spat up tiny spouts of water just beneath a thin crust of sand.

"You see," Grandma Lambert had said, "the water's *not* so bad now. It brings in mollusks for us." And she'd smiled and he'd felt safe, happy, and at home.

He remembered repeating this trip with them - repeating plucking mollusks - and later, they'd boil the full bucket of mollusks - as Grandpa poured him his first Chardonnay. Gosh, that was good - salty mollusks and sweet wine - a combo that warmed him as no meal ever had. And after that first glass of wine, he'd *never* refused another, especially in France, where, unlike Prohibition America of the time, *never* frowned on its citizens taking a drink -young or old — for, in moderation, all is *joie de vivre*.

Now he felt anger for his grandparents' conditions: Grandpa in a camp - Grandma hiding in a strange flat.

He picked up his pace, wishing to be on the bank of the Seine waiting for the boat - not the other way around.

Fifteen minutes later, he stopped again - his last rest, he hoped.

He listened to the woods humming with the life of nocturnal creatures.

Suddenly crows fluttered, their black silhouettes flapping into the sky until they landed on poplars close by.

Somewhere in a bramble thicket came the tinny ringing call of a pheasant.

In the distance - the lowing of cattle.

Further on – the thumping of bombs.

He inhaled deeply and smelled fragrant wet foliage and blooms.

In the distance, he spotted apple trees, but it was still too dark to see their pink and white petals.

He picked up a handful of moist soil - doubted if any of this soil ever tasted a plow - wondered how his hybrid corn would do here. He put the soil to his nose, smelled the savage and fecund fragrance, and then dropped it as he remembered the fresh soil blown up by bombs by the boy-soldiers' bodies. ***Damnit . . . damnit . . . don't*** do that.... He inhaled deeply and tasted something awful from the back of his throat that tasted...like...hominy...lye-soaked hominy. God...I hate hominy, he said to himself and spit.

Then he heard day's first songbird, possibly a sedge warbler - possibly the European songbird equivalent to the American cowbird. Equivalent hell, he corrected himself - this warbler belts out over sixty notes and *never* sings the same song twice, for he's constantly improvising -yes, he's the *jazz* king - he's Louis Armstrong, Nat King Cole, Billie Holliday, Sarah Vaughan and Duke Ellington rolled into *one ball of feathers*.

Speaking of which...yes...about now...Shelby's Creek songbird babies should be hatching and chirping in full chorus - what a *wonderful* sound *that* would be - what a *wonderful* sight *that* would be.

God - he missed home.

"Man can will nothing unless he has first understood that he must count on no one but himself; that he is alone...without help, with no other aim than the one he sets himself..."

— *Sartre*

Normandy, France
May 1943
0545 Hours

Chapter 21

*D*awn turned milky grey.

Valentin suddenly felt lonely.

On the farm he'd rarely felt lonely. But here he was alone with no one to care for as far as he could see - like that snowy day long ago when he killed the chickadee - the last living thing he'd killed.

Yes, maybe that's *why* he felt lonely, for, even though he hadn't killed since, something inside died *with* those German boys in that meadow. Even though *his* hands were clean, they *felt* horribly dirty.

He looked to the sky, pale now with soft silver light.

To the west, the moon began to set and he imagined how its light shone on those poor, dead, boy-soldiers - now bloodless, pale, and board-stiff with rigor mortis.

No...moonlight should show only upon a supple stream like Shelby's Creek, upon a serene river like the Seine, upon a raging river like the Yellowstone, or, perhaps, upon the face of a loved one before you kiss her.

And now a thin cloud formed a colorful corona around the moon and he loved the diffraction of light by the cloud droplets. He told himself *this* was the moon's way of making up for the horrors he'd seen - and that *it* still had much, much beauty to offer.

He sat, unscrewed the heel of his shoe and took out the photo that Pierre had placed inside.

Because of the dim light he couldn't see the photo well, but well enough to recognize and confirm the boat captain, Skipper.

He placed the photo under a rock, screwed the heel back into place, and rushed down the trail.

He came to a small clearing.

Below and beyond a clump of thick foliage was a larger clearing.

Then, on a breeze, he smelled brine and listened and heard the rippling of water.

He moved the dew-glinted weeds to see, just ahead, the first light of day shining clean on the River Seine.

For a moment he stared at its placid beauty and at the ghostly morning mist rising from its silver, fluid surface.

Along the Seine's forested shoulders were lush groves of shadowy pines and poplars.

On its shores and sandbars, birds flitted and trotted in quick steps.

A heron squawked, which was the wake-up call he needed as he looked back to the map. He checked the coordinates, spotted the large sandbar and the lone, tall poplar signpost just down river, which he walked to, and then looked across the river to where a clump of poplars bunched up like a Monet - which further verified his position.

He looked down river.

No boat in sight.

He looked east to where sunlight burst through fading clouds. God, he loved a spring sun - loved how its light felt warm; loved how it felt like the birth of some new, exceptional world; loved how it resembled the most colorific of all Impressionist paintings. And he watched now how it suffused, in various shades, the landscape - the rolling hills, the treetops, the water, the shore. Yes, he said to himself, eight hours ago, this *same* light was dying over *my* farm. And he imagined the brightest orange and purple tints left in *that* Iowa sky, and the enriching silence that came with *that* afterglow.

And now he wondered *where* he'd be when this *very* sun would set.

He didn't know.

He did know that as *it* would set, his farm's songbirds would *rise*, the larks belting out madrigals, the house wrens tweeting effervescent, bubbly sopranos, robins chirping in harmony - all relaxing - after weeks of migration. And he remembered how the male robin arrived *before* the female, in spring, and wondered if he left *before* her in autumn. No, he didn't know, but he sure as *hell* wished to be back in time to find out.

Suddenly, his peripheral vision caught sight of a boat.

Yes, he guessed it was the French-style fishing boat he was to board, but other than a barge or a ship, he didn't know one boat from the other. And he remembered how Grandpa Lambert once tried to educate him on the boats of the Seine but he never paid much mind - he was all about terra firma, not terra infirma - all about land, not water - all about tractors, not boats.

Still, this boat coming toward him now was an impressive one - perhaps because it reminded him of ones Monet painted - perhaps because it would take him back to Paris - back to Grandma.

He listened in the woods and waited until the boat neared the shore and its engines fell silent.

A lone man in a captain's cap stepped out on the boat deck. He looked up and down river now for offshore enemy patrols.

Valentin remembered how Rosy said this *Skipper* knew the bend of the Seine like the back of his hand - knew how long it'd take an enemy patrol to round the bends *after* he heard their boats - how *he'd* be ready if *they* stopped him - how this *Skipper* had passes, license, fuel controls - how this *Skipper* obeyed *every* Reich restriction except *one*: transporting secret agents.

Now Skipper tossed two fishing lines into the water, each with a bright red float, each with a lead sinker and hook. He looked around and waited a couple more minutes then waved to the shore.

Valentin kept low; rushed onto the shore; tossed his shoes, shirt, pants, and backpack onto the boat deck.

He jumped into the water and swam the few yards to the boat's ladder, climbed aboard, rushed into the cabin to dry off and dress.

Skipper now showed with his back to the cabin door, his head turned to watch for patrols. "I'm the SOAM skipper. You call me Skipper," he said, his voice raspy, his tone devil may care.

"I'm Farmer."

Skipper then bent down and picked up three fishing poles and a gaff hook and kept them angled from the stern. "We want all patrol boats to think that fishing is the *actual* priority of this boat, and so, to back up the pretense, my cargo hold is *always* full of fish caught near La Havre to be delivered to Paris."

Valentin looked around at the stockpiles of barrels of apples, bushels of potatoes, and boxes of Calvados.

"Be ready to hide in case of a spot inspection," said Skipper.

"Does that happen often?"

"Not as much. Now they mostly know me, know I'll provide all the liquor they want. So they mostly just wave me on unless they need liquor. In case they don't wave me on, and want to ransack my boat, there's your hiding place - in that space beneath the floorboards, beneath a casket-length gear locker."

Skipper bent down to a small radio on a small table, relayed a message to London, and heard a reply.

Then he used a fish-gutting knife to lift a floorboard and hid the radio in a space beneath the floorboards. He wound the radio aerial strung outside the cabin, hid it beneath another floorboard. "Voila - earned my keep for the day," he said, smiling a gap-toothed smile.

He then reached into a gear locker, pulled out a bottle of Vodka, chugged a big swallow and offered the bottle to Valentin.

"No thanks, I only drink beer and wine."

"I *can't* drink wine - wine's like fruit - vodka's like steak - and I'm a meat lover."

Valentin forced an awkward grin.

"Come topside when you're ready," Skipper said as he lit and puffed deep on a Gauloise.

Valentin peeked into the space beneath the floorboards and saw bedding and a pillow, and there was nothing he wanted more than to lie down in it. Yes - too much training - too much plane lag - too much war - already made him feel like he could sleep for a week. He finished dressing, took a deep breath from the fresh smell of the Seine and thought how this river, being too far from the sea, sees no salt, no seagull, no ship - only small vessels, barges, boats and bateau mouches that meander up and down its comatose course.

He walked up the cabin's steps to the bridge, heard the squishing sound of wet rubber boots and looked behind him to see Skipper, who looked much different than his photo in the dim, pre-dawn light - as diffent as night and day in the bright, post-dawn light. And darn, what a sight - cadaverous, scrawny, wild winged hair, mutton-chop sideburns that bushed over his ears - sideburns that seemed to say, "I no longer listen," as if he'd already heard it all and wished to hear *no more* – but, any lack of listening seemed compensated by studious eyes - no, not studious – more mad, like a hyena – no, more savage like…he didn't know - but killer-capable, he knew. Yes, predator - *with* fangs – yes, *this* he knew. Atop Skipper's head a mangled mop of steely, salt-and-pepper hair sprouted like tangled ivy. Its length touched the collar of an oversized, tattered sweater that bulged from a bloated belly. His nose was webbed with busted vessels - possibly booze telltale - possibly brawls telltale - probably both. A scraggly, blue-black moustache looked littered with food and fermented with drink beneath a crooked, hooked beak. His skin showed dark-splotched like a clochard's and he scratched constantly at his cheeks - pitted and scarred - mapped with deep wrinkles.

"Damnit," hollered Skipper as he kicked off his rubber boots, put on his sabots, reached into his pants pocket and pulled out a cigarette stub. "Damnit," he repeated, "I hate when I squash my stubs - happens when I'm oiling engines or packing fish."

Then he found one not squashed, lit it, grimaced, spit it, and then reached into a front pocket, tapped the top of a pack, and lit a Gauloise.

Valentin observed, in his matchstick flame, Skipper's hands and nails - grimy, dirty, gear-greased, tobacco-tarred, and probably smelling of fish or substances he didn't know - substances other than hands dirtied with clean soil - he knew.

The end of Skipper's cigarette now sprouted fiery red as he sucked in a breath and let it out slow as the smoke curled sluggish in the damp and heavy air. He shook the match out fiercely, sat on a rail and stared at Valentin with an arched, disdainful brow.

Valentin looked back at him - realized how much you can tell about a person in the way they smoke a cigarette: easy pulls, then squinty eyes through the smoke while holding the cigarette aslant like the Brit secretary - seductress mode; quick pulls, holding the cigarette nonchalantly as if it were just another finger, with ashes falling everywhere like Rosy - business mode; long, slow pulls, holding the cigarette as if it were the sixth of a six pack like Skipper - don't give a flying muck about muck mode.

"See that scar on my brow?" Skipper asked. "It's from a bullet from the Great War when I was French Foreign Legion. Then, the entire world seemed before me. Now, it all seems behind me." And he turned and spit into the Seine.

Valentin grimaced as he watched Skipper suck the remaining swallows from the Vodka bottle and flash a heroic grin as if finishing bottles was a great victory.

Yes, if Skipper was in the Great War as a young man, he couldn't be much more than in his late forties, though he looked in his late sixties as his back showed bent, his eyes fleshy with scar tissue, his face cracked with deep lines like dirty scars. Yes, he guessed Skipper had seen *many* days and nights of fighting, drinking, smoking, and severe Seine winds. And he guessed John Barleycorn had been Skipper's chum for some time - evident in his red nose, red-rimmed eyes, pasty face and crow's-feet-lined eyes one gets from too much fret, too many bogeys, too much booze. . . .

Skipper turned and lifted the sails. "I feel a north wind kicking. Have to get every ounce out of the damned fuel rations."

Then he turned back and stared with the mad eyes. "This boat's a felucca, an upgrade from a flette," he said, flashing a devilish smile. "This boat was used for sardines *before* the war - used for fancy fish for fancy restaurants *during* the war - *this* war. I've got a trawler too, but it's along Brittany's coasts being filled with even fancier fish for even fancier restaurants. The trawler's faster, the felucca's slower. Both are old and rusted - like me. Both have *minor* engine and *major* piston problems - like me."

His maddened eyes then softened and his mouth opened in a tooth-gapped, scarecrow-scary grin. "And both boats are brightly colored from bow to stern with eternal moss stains, as if anchored with Giverny pond's lilly pads since christening. But both are mine *and* I am theirs."

Valentin nodded.

Skipper took a long swig of a fresh bottle, winked, and grinned through tight lips and eyes that stayed hard and mad. "We'll be in Paris before noon. Rest till then. I'll let you know when we pass Poissy so you can prep."

"Yes, sir."

"Oh, just so you know, my boat currently has *no* flowers. Many boats have flowers - geraniums mostly - in cabin windows and flower boxes. Geraniums bring spiders. I hate spiders. I don't hate flowers but I don't allow flowers on my boat. Flowers are for land, boats are for water. Bars and brothels are for land, neither for my boat. My boat is for my bottle, my bottle for my boat."

He stood then, lifted the bottle, chugged, and smiled, but didn't smile - as if to say he was as ready for life as for death. "Remember, there's only two things worthwhile in life," he said, now lifting his bottle high, "*...orchids and morphine* - on your death bed."

"I thought you didn't care for flowers."

"No...I just don't allow them on my boat," said Skipper, his singsong voice mushy.

"Perhaps you should get orchids on your boat and your life would be nicer."

"My life will be nicer when this damned war ends and my boat docks in the remotest corner of the Seine and becomes - like me - permanent bateaux lavoir versus bateaux mouches."

"You use your boat as bateaux mouches?"

"Just what the muck do you think *you* are?" said Skipper, his singsong voice as unsteady as his stance. "*You're* an Allied agent - Allied agent - tourists - same thing... Yes . . . orchids...and morphine...well...rest well," he said and Valentin watched his demeanor mutate that way drunks mutate on a dime – from love to hate – from hate to love.

Then Skipper sang in an energetic baritone with a version of "Le Figaro" and winked and waddled away, pulling up a red sash around his thin waist that held up pants rolled up to his knees. And as he walked to the bow, Skipper thought how he normally never winked at anyone unless he sensed he was being read - correctly. Yes, he knew this young man on his boat could read him, and no, he didn't like it, but he respected it.

Valentin smelled the booze on Skipper's breath as it seemed to carry downwind, bow to stern, and knew the man believed in booze for breakfast, lunch, dinner, midnight snack, whenever interminable thirst called for it. Yes, of all vices, drinking was deadliest; the one he respected least. Its not that he didn't believe in booze; heck, he suffered *plenty* of unscheduled hangovers after *plenty* of unscheduled bottles of superior wine. But not everyday - heck not more than once a month or even every two months - and then certainly *not* when operating *something* that could kill *someone*. "Better a quick gun to your head than a slow bottle to your mouth," old man O'Halloran said at his parents' funeral.

He went below deck and lay on the thin mattress beneath the floorboards.

The smell of fish was within nose range and becoming overwhelming. In fact, if he thought about it too much, he might even gag - so he thought about his creek; about the minnows that swam like schools of mighty mini-dolphins; how if you dropped a pebble in the water, they'd gather and you'd scoop them up, use them for fishing in larger lakes for largemouth and smallmouth bass, in larger rivers for catfish. And how, in his mind, catfish was the only truly good Midwestern fish to eat, sprinkled with basil and garlic, baked with olive oil and butter.

Now he placed the false planking over the top of him. Yes, there was plenty of room between his face and the floorboards, plenty of air and air holes in the space.

Still, he grabbed the large aluminum flashlight and held it tight in his left hand - the pencil flashlight in his right.

Before he closed his eyes, he sensed how confident he felt about Paris.

Finally, he thought about Skipper again. No, he wasn't afraid of him; heck, he'd handle him easily face to face. But it wasn't face to face that bothered him - it was the potential backstab. Like Rosy said, **trust no one**. Would Skipper turn him over for a case of vodka? Would Skipper wake him with a fish-gutting knife at his throat? He shook off these thoughts.

Still, he couldn't sleep.

He sat up and went back on deck to breathe in the salty air that brought on fatigue.

For the first time since daylight, he looked at his hands - his fingernails still stained dark with dried blood from the soldiers.

He felt queasy, went belly down to the edge of the boat to scoop up water to scrub his hands.

Instead, he gagged and vomited into the water, which he couldn't reach with his hands to clean them.

He crawled to the cargo hold, lifted the lid, held his breath, and rubbed his hands amongst the flopping fish until his fingers pulsated and the cuticle skin felt raw and he nearly bled fresh blood.

He stood, inhaled, dropped to his knees, gagged, dropped to the deck, and vomited again.

He lay still now and inhaled slow and deep.

So much for sea air having a medicinal effect for all maladies — but then, some maladies may *not* have a cure.

And he regretted that he'd already acquired nightmares that may forever haunt his perfect world - by his perfect bed - by his perfect open window on a perfect early spring eve - by the perfect creek - at once-perfect Shelby's Creek.

He inhaled the river air deeply, which still seemed night-stagnant, still smelled slightly of bitter brine and foul fish.

And, with this odor in his nose and lungs, he thought again of the dead soldiers. No, keep this memory at bay now, *at least* until you get home - at least until this France business is done.

But he *knew* he'd carry those boys in his head like a scar unhealed, ready to bleed with the slightest scratch.

And he *knew* there'd be *more* scratches and scars *before* this business was done - knew he'd *never* see a sunrise, a sunset, or Shelby's Creek the *same* way.

His body called for him to lie down - perhaps his mind would as well.

He went back to bed, pulled the planking over his body, rubbed his whiskered face, rubbed his bleary eyes.

He slept hard and dreamed much - dreams that had been dormant since Iowa - since the last night in the cabin. But in the cabin, the dreams were peaceful and pleasant and these dreams now were not - these dreams seemed in a race to catch up with recent trauma - the flight with the flak - the hike with the Reich - the dead and dying - the blood that soaked upon his fingers, into his cuticles, into and under his nails. And *these* dreams/nightmares spoke *always* of last breaths - of Grandpa's and Grandma's - of Mom's and Dad's - Grandpa's and Grandma's - peaceful and paced as if an engine is simply shut down - Dad's and Mom's anything *but* peaceful and paced - but tense and traumatic.

That *last* breath.

We *all* have one *last* breath.

Yes, we, all of us are renters, **not** owners - never as **obvious** as in that **last** breath.

He jumped up and hit his head hard on the floor planking.

He tossed the floorboards off to the side and sat upright.

He breathed hard.

Beads of sweat rolled off his forehead and he peeled his sweat-wet shirt from his back.

He lay back down, more exhausted than he could ever remember.

He looked at the stars that showed at the top of the stairs and wanted only to watch them, wanted only to feel the coolness of the night air that drifted down the stairs.

No, there was *no way* he was going to place those floorboards atop of him now - Skipper could if he was so inclined but that was *his* choice if trouble lurked.

His eyes closed.

Now even the dreams/ nightmares and recent memories seemed exhausted.

Perhaps now I can sleep soundly, he said to himself.

He listened to the boat engines throb softly in time with the beat of his heart.

He felt tired as an eve following a day of making hay.

Then his eyes shut and he felt at home, knowing he was on the Seine, knowing the Seine was as close to Shelby's Creek as he might be for some time.

And now he would sleep the sleep of a newborn.

"On these 15,000 acres more has been thought, spoken, and written than anywhere else in the world. Here are the accumulated stratifications of wit, reasoning, and good taste. Here is the planet's freest, most elegant, and at least hypocritical crossroads."

— *Anonymous*

Paris, France
Seine River
May 1943
0800 Hours

Chapter 22

Valentin stepped up and out from the cabin of the boat as it wound round a Seine bend.

He squinted into the bright sun and watched with wonder as the first pallid patina portico homes came into view with their slated roofs, cast-iron balconies, French windows, and slatted jalousie shutters found neither in Shelby County, nor Iowa, nor in America other than perhaps New Orleans.

His heart beat faster.

His mouth moistened.

Yes, he'd been away too long.

And he felt immediately the essential affinity he'd always felt about Paris, felt it in his attachment and affection for the river that runs through it, for the architecture and art that tempers it, for the wafting scents of its gardens and foods, for its alluring sounds of operas and orchestras - that all define the city as much as corn, clover, cattle, and creek define Shelby's Creek.

Now he grinned as he remembered his first visit to Paris - where he received his first wide-eyed impressions of a big city - his first narrow-eyed impressions of a big city's people.

And he thought how he had the *best* of the New World in Shelby's Creek - the *best* of the Old World in Paris — therefore *best* of *both* worlds.

And yes, Selby's Creek will *always* be home in his heart of hearts - but when away - when it was time to be away - Paris was home - yes, Paris was *always* home away from home.

Heck, American composer John Payne agreed: "Home, Sweet Home", right *here* in *Paris* -"Be it ever so humble...there's no place like home" And many *other* Americans felt the same - Benjamin of Franklin fame; Thomas Pain;

Thomas Jefferson; Maceo Jefferson; Nathanial Willis; Nathaniel Hawthorne; Oliver Wendell Holmes; Henry Wadsworth Longfellow; Whitman; Henry James; Hemingway; Eliot; Flanner; Fitzgerald; Ellington; Armstrong; Barnes; Barnum; Beecher; Baker; Bulitt; Blackwell - all expatriate patriots of Paris - bona fide Francophiles, especially the likes of Josephine Baker — who sang of her love for two tricolors: America's and France's - the latter's love expressed to her blindly and she back, especially with "J'ai deux amours, mon pays et Paris."

Yes, Paris birthed revolution, enlightenment, was the cultivated capital of the world - now a capital in chains, he thought - as the first signs of the occupied city showed with a flag that waved - *not* with tricolors of red, white and liberty blue - *but* tricolors of red, white, and swastika black.

Yes, if character is stolen from personality, what's left - a skeleton - a shell - a dementia victim - to the pains of loved ones who remembered their loved one *before* . . . .

And no, its not like Paris *hadn't* fallen victim to occupation before: by Norsemen, by English, by Austrians, by Russians, by Prussians, by Romans, by Danes, by Franks, by Greeks, by Gauls - by golly, what a *popular* place.

But something told him this *current* occupation darkened and would darken the City of Light in ways *longer* and *uglier* than ever.

When would the next la belle époque happen? *Not* soon enough.

He took deep breaths now as the city moved before him.

Yes, Paris, the Seine's mother city - a city lovingly sung Paname by Piaf - a city called *champ* over all other Western European cities - for renaissance, for revolution, for haute couture, for joie de vivre - a city whose recipe included romance, gastronomy, history, amusement, religion *and* sin, opulent architecture, opulent art - blended, basted, baked, and consumed as part *and* parcel of the passionate people. And, once a person samples her, once inside your soul, you *always taste, always prefer* her over other cities as you *prefer refined* demi-glace to a *rube,* beef-bullion cube.

Yes - whether you pick corn in Iowa or mumble mantras in Mirzapur, you'll *always* savor the flavor of Paris - for Paris *spoils* its offspring *all* its mortal days.

Yes, Paris is Sleeping Beauty and it's up to the prince in each person to waken her.

Yes, God made poets, Impressionists, and Paris - and saw that *each* of these made the other - and *behold*, it was *all* good.

So, why'd he love Paris more than any other city...no, why was it the *only* city he loved? After all, Paris's climate could be akin to damp London - its people could be akin to aloof New Yorkers.

And he grinned as he remembered that provincial French say, "If it weren't for the fortiori - the mucking, grumbling Parisians - *Paris* would be *perfect*."

Yes, just as his farm would *always* be the place he'd *never* leave, Paris would *always* be the place he'd *always* come back to — and if he likened Shelby's Creek to a newborn, he likened Paris to what brings a newborn to essential life - love, art, passion. No, there was no place that rooted life as the farm - no place which inspired life like Paris. Yes, Paris had a way of acclimating man to his own evolution - Paris humanized humans. And perhaps that would be the city's salvation, to help it survive where Warsaw died.

Yes, may Shelby's Creek *always* survive and may he be there to survive with it - through flood and drought - through blizzard and heat - through pestilence - through chemicals...through Cains. Yes...the Cains...I *should* be at Shelby's Creek *right now* to fend off the Cains *and* their chemicals, which may one day steer the essence of Shelby's Creek the way of Warsaw.

Gosh, I wish I could drink some of the creek's cold, clear water right now. I am so thirsty.

"...The enemy rests in the shadows. We learn this evening of the sur-render of Paris. I will never forget the lilacs and the roses. Nor the two loves we lost."

— *"Les Lilas et les roses," Aragon*

Paris, France
Seine River
May 1943

Chapter 23

Skipper walked up from starboard.

He looked at Valentin and grinned, his remaining teeth looking more like a mix of pinto beans and dark chickpeas than teeth.

He offered a ceramic jug to Valentin.

"No, thank you."

"Its Normandy Calvados applejack - cider brandy. Trust me, you need a swig."

Valentin took the jug by the thumb handle, lifted it, sipped the sweet apple ferment and felt it warm his body. "You're right, Skipper, it's what I needed."

Skipper grinned again, his eyes like a knight's helmet slits. "You think I'm a drunk, don't you?"

"It doesn't *matter* what I think," said Valentin as he took another swig to show no aversion to a drink.

"I'm *asking* you what you think."

"As long as a man's vice puts no one in the grave but himself, I have no problem."

"I drink carefully, but copiously . . . I like you . . . you don't judge. Except for the Resisatance leader I work with, the same man *you'll* work with, I *hate* judges."

"Only one judge can judge," said Valentin, pointing to the sky.

"Yes, thank *your* God we have a society of laws to decode right from wrong."

Now Valentin thought of his parents and how neither they *nor* the drunk driver who'd killed them received the *right* sentence and took another swig.

"It was about a year ago," Skipper said, "when Allied planes bombed the Suresnes lock over yonder and the Seine drained completely. Fish flopped in the mud, boats docked stuck in the muck."

"Allied bombings in Paris?"

"Yes, last month a bunch of B-17 bombers hit the Renault plant."

"Renault makes *French* cars."

"These days it makes *enemy tanks* and the Allies *knew* it, *thanks* to the Resistance."

"Was the bombing successful?"

Skipper shrugged. "Usually Allied bombers are as accurate as a drunk playing ice hockey but the plant was hit somehow, delayed for sometime."

"How many were killed?"

"I don't count deaths, only my own, and then I'll let you know," he said and grimaced in a comical Gallic manner.

He handed Valentin a cloth with some oil. "Clean and polish your shoes. Dirty shoes *from the woods* alert SS to a partisan *from the woods*."

"Yes sir."

"Now, if you're going to act French, look French. Here's a black Basque beret - I ordered extra large - when they told me you were American, I figured you possessed a *big* head."

Valentin smirked and tried it on.

"There, now you look like you belong in the fifth, sixth or seventh, not the first, second, or third - those arrondissements *still* belong to the rich and to the Reich."

"Go figure."

"You're educated, aren't you?"

Valentin nodded.

"You were raised by good parents. My ma always said parents shouldn't produce progeny unless that progeny can be put through college at conception. Pa always said to hell with what Ma said. So, you can see, I never went to college. But you, you're educated. Educated and *with* a conscience, I can tell. Your face isn't effeminate, but your feelings are. You'll have a hard time in war-torn Europe."

Valentin took another swig of Calvados and handed it to Skipper. "And if *I* were to guess, *I'd* say you are your *own* boss, always have been, always will be."

Skipper grinned, took a swig, wiped at the ferment dribbling down his chin. "I'm a libertine, meaning a man of liberty, through and through."

Valentin grinned.

"Now, if you're going to speak French, speak French, not American French."

"I learned French in France," said Valentin. "My mouth, nose, and tongue are forever shaped to speak French the way it *must* be spoken."

"Let me familiarize you with French terms that *may* not be in your vocabulary since the war: couvre-feu is curfew, planque is safe house, refractaire is objector of the compulsory labor service . . . . And when you cuss, don't say, 'nom de Dieu,' or 'son of a bitch,' or whatever you call your preacher, patrician, or politician. Simply say, 'merde.' 'Merde' is uttered much more than even the 'Marseillaise.' By the way, the Marseillaise...by the way, the Marseillaise... by the way the Marseillaise...catchy tune, uh?" he said, his head moving in sync with his long, poinard-like forefinger, his body swaying ineptly, more from applejack than from the choppy river current.

Then he steadied himself against a boat railing, grinning big, his eyes helmet slits again. "Like I was saying, by the way, the 'Marseillaise' is banned in Paris, along with the tricolore, along with alcohol on certain days. But *every* day, *alcohol, the tricolore and the 'Marseillaise,'* are allowed on *my* boat - every day, every hour, every minute."

And he took another swig as he waved a small tricolore hidden inside his shirt and sang, *'Aux armes, citoyens'* of the *'Marseillaise'*

Then, for several seconds, Skipper stared at Valentin with the maddened eyes that seemed to madden more and more. And then his eyes changed to helmet slits again as he whooped with laughter. "Yes, American, I like you. We need to drink together more often."

And he handed Valentin the Calvados and Valentin took another swig.

Then Skipper's mushy liquor voice changed to clear and serious. "I'll update you on current events: there are thirty thousand enemy soldiers in Paris - that's a sea of uniforms - brown, black, green, gray. They dine in the finest restaurants, visit the museums, walk the gardens and the quais, attend the operas, and generally do as tourists do, only in uniform. You'll see military vehicles, but not as many as you'd think. You'll see processions of staff cars and Gestapo Citroens, more than you'd think. Otherwise, the streets are busy with velo-taxis, pedicabs, bicycles, a periodic smoky gazogene, a horse-drawn cab, a soap-box-derby-style cycle-car, or French transport trucks."

Valentin nodded.

"No, Paris is no longer the Paris you knew – it's no longer the City of Light, but the city of furloughs, curfews, and controls. Do you know the song, '*The Last Time I Saw Paris*,' by Jerome Kern, lyrics by Hammerstein?"

Valentin nodded.

Skipper took a long swig and began to sing another Hammerstein song. "'*A lady known as Paris, romantic and charming, has left her old companions and faded from view. Lonely men with lonely eyes are seeking her in vain, her streets are where they were, but there's no sign of her...*'"

Valentin took another swig of applejack and felt a confidence not felt since leaving Iowa. "What's a pedicab? A velotaxi?"

"Bicycle-powered rickshaws, covered and uncovered."

Valentin nodded.

Then Skipper tilted his head to the sky and sang Hammerstein again, "'*The last time I saw Paris, her heart was warm and gay. I heard the laughter of her heart in every street café. The last time I saw Paris, her trees were dressed for spring. And lovers walked beneath those trees and birds found songs to sing. The last time I saw Paris, her heart was warm and gay, no matter how they change her, I'll remember her that way.*'"

Valentin suddenly felt glad he'd soon leave Skipper. Yeah, he liked him okay - trusted him okay - but he seemed so indifferent about life - and such blasé cynicism wears a man down – especially when you're already down.

"And do *not* ask for milk, lemonade, iced tea, or water with meals as Americans do. Do *not* whistle *or sing* - as you *might* be whistling or singing *American* tunes. Keep your hands out of your pockets while walking, and, while walking, wear your beret, drag your feet, droop your shoulders. Remember - you're a Frenchman, *not* an American - you're a shuffling Parisian, *not* a strutting soldier.

"Yes, sir."

"Oh, and here's a pack of French Gauloise cigarettes."

"I don't smoke."

Skipper acted like he'd just been punched and fell backwards. "Don't smoke?"

"No, sir."

"Don't smoke...okay, but you shoot. And two of these bogies are Welfags loaded with bullets. This one and this one. Keep them apart from the others - keep them in this steel cigarette case to keep them dry and straight. Just remember the difference between the Gauloises and the loaded cigarettes in case a young lady asks you for a cigarette - you don't want to kill her before you sleep with her!" he said with a strong French nasal chuckle.

"I already have one Welfag..."

"And keep these real Gauloises as well. Gauloises are gold compared to the 'national tobacco' dried grass Parisians are forced to smoke."

Valentin examined the bullet-loaded Gauloise. "Yeah, I always sensed cigarettes *dangerous* to your health."

"Now, more than half of our agents that dropped into France have been killed or deported to death camps. I'll not mince words - your life expectancy is, *at best*, six months."

"I...think I'm *ready* to start *smoking*."

"We dock in thirty minutes," said Skipper as he began to hum another song.

Valentin watched Skipper wobble back starboard and wondered why he hadn't fallen into the Seine along with his many empty bottles of vodka and gin - and no - I *won't* suggest that rhyming line as a new song to sing or hymn to hum.

Then Skipper glanced back as Valentin took another swig from the jug.

"That a boy," hollered Skipper. "You'll graduate from my class yet," and then mumbled, "I don't think I know anyone who *doesn't smoke*."

"In Paris one can lose one's time most delightfully; but one can never lose one's way."

— *Oscar Wilde*

Paris, France
Seine River
May 1943

Chapter 24

$\mathscr{V}$alentin looked into the Seine - into its waters reflecting puffy-white cumulus clouds - and thought of similar clouds in his farm's creek - and of the time of day there - no, the time of night there.

He imagined the falls splashing down its seven tiers - the soft bellow of the cattle in the blue-grass pasture, now lush, dewy - the quiet creek - and the creek's not-so-quiet whippoorwill - imagined Nanny and Katie inside the brome-perfumed barn in fresh straw, their legs folded neatly beneath them, their agate-Netherworld eyes closed, their milk bags heavy - and up high in the corner rafters the sleeping mama swallows in their feather mattress mud nests, their wings spread wide to keep chicks warm while their breasts moved like tiny balloons, slow, in perfect rhythm with their breathing.

And of all these images and sounds, the one he missed most was the one he thought he'd miss least - the whippoorwill - imagined the bird planting its plump, round, feathery form in the cattails, cooing its glum, but soothing song. Maybe he missed it most because its melancholy tune reflected most how he now felt. Instead, he wished for the waterfall to be sight and sound he missed most - imagined *its* musical splash - could see *its* long journey down stream - down river - down sea - to here - where it'd rotate back -to there - just like he would soon - he hoped.

In the far distance, he spotted the Île de Cité - birthplace of Paris - where Gallic fishermen, Parisii, landed around 3 B.C. and called this wetland island Luteia - which became a popular port. And since Parisii were a fighting species, many skirmishes with many other tribes occurred here. Yes, many died - much blood spilled - same old taxed yarn - battles and blood - for riches - for real estate - however *real*. Yeah, here, same as everywhere, millions die for riches and land *never* theirs - *forever* losing everything never theirs with a last breath.

Yes, within the river's image of these white clouds - *much* blood has flowed - from conflicts, from disease - from Wars of Religion to Wars of Land - to siege after siege - clash after clash - virus after virus - from 1832's cholera and 1871's Commune - to Siegfried's bloodthirsty Norsemen - to Black Death a hundred years later with a hundred deaths per day over three hundred fifty days. And there was the bombardment of Big Bertha that killed hundreds - but hundreds fewer than the bugs of typhus and dysentery - and the countless plagues and poverty of the Medieval - countless crimes from the Burgundians - from the Inquisition - from the "Battle of Paris" - from the "Week of Blood" - from the 1832 revolt - from the June Revolution - the July Revolution - the Fronde Revolution - the Bogus Revolution - the February Revolution - the "ugly" revolution - the "beautiful revolution" - and the French Revolution - including 2800 guillotined heads - *not* including trial sheep heads - Huguenots and Huns - the Massacre of the Innocents - the Bartholomew Massacre, when Protestant cadavers filled the Seine along with French Admiral Coligny's headless and ball-less body - the cordons of 1590 and 1870 - the aftershock industry of the 1830, '48, '51, and '71 revolutions - the Cabochiens - the Bonapartists and republicans, and the countless, uncounted suicides and homicides finding final rest in a river. Hell, instead of 'The Seine,' it should be called 'The End,'- or - 'The Dead Sea.'

Heck, even Antoine Gros - that great composer of Napoleon paintings - failed to learn *how* to *live* when technique turned *tepid* and the open arms of the Seine inspired him *more* than critical critics.

Heck, even Monet tried death in these waters, but when bad luck turned good - omega turned alpha - and he regarded the Seine as the 'cradle of his work.'

And even Saint-Gaudens tasted death here when he thirsted for the river's roiling, glistening waters and then had an "Ebenezer Scrooge" moment, went back to his studio, back to Boston, back home.

Still, the Seine was *his* Shelby's Creek away from Shelby's Creek. And yes, both seemed reliable, inspiring, artful, appealing, embraceable, and, mostly feminine - like a maiden with changing, but steady ways.

He took an aggressive swig of Calvados and then looked over to where sleepy fishermen sat settled upon the quais ledges.

The fishermen held steady to Lodgepole-long, cane-jointed poles arcing to the water and upon the water, their quill bobs swayed over the deepest and calmest part of the river where the best fish crowded outside the current within backwater pools.

Then he looked in a full circle - saw no enemy soldiers - but felt them - the way you feel rain before it storms.

"Lead, Kindly Light, amid the encircling gloom... The night is dark, and I am far from home."

— *Cardinal Newman*

Paris, France
Seine River
May 1943

Chapter 25

"*Goujon*," said Skipper as he waved to the fishermen. "Those fishermen are catching *Goujon*. *Goujon* is *merde*! But then I'd prefer Paris *Goujon merde* over Paris cat or rat du jour."

"Cat or rat?"

"You'll soon learn that starving Parisians can't be choosers in occupied Paris," said Skipper as he took another swig from the jug and then cradled it against his shoulder as a mother cradles her baby.

"Cat or rat?"

"Today, and for the next few days, blend into people of Paris - all Parisians are aware of Jean Texcier's unofficial dictum: '*Ignore your occupier. Don't look at him, don't listen to him, don't talk to him, don't light his cigarette when asked.*' **My** dictum says: '*Light his cigarette, be civil, not silly. Never stand too still too long in one spot — like coffee with a croissant, fit in - enemy security looks for anyone that doesn't fit in. Be seen, be recognized, be known, be polite, be a flaneur. Dine in the cafes. Ride the metro. Attend concerts. Stroll from Notre Dame to the Tomb of the Unknown Soldier, and be known. Just because they occupy us, they don't oppress us - at least not the best of us. Your papers will be checked. The more they're checked now, the less they're checked later when you're readily recognized and readily involved in underground. And know that your papers may be checked just as often, if not more, by a French gendarme as by an enemy soldier. Never look sly, angry, or scared; never glance back over your shoulder; never shilly-shally about getting on the metro or crossing a boulevard; never hide behind building corners. If you sense a tail, check window reflections or bend down and tie yours shoes. Never act suspicious, for suspicious is what suspicious does. Don't feel nervous, don't look nervous. The more confident you look, the less conspicuous you look. Trust me - you'll develop a schemer's sixth sense. Remember, your enemy wears a uniform, but your enemy also wears*

street clothes and he may be French. There are many, many spies today - men and women
that betray the Republic, that denounce fellow Frenchman.'"

"Why do French collaborate?"

"Prestige, fear, money - mostly money - some collaborate in subtle ways to
survive - some take factory jobs for the Reich to feed their family - some sleep
with the enemy to feed their family - some collaborate in hard-core ways for
profit."

"Hard core?"

"There's a quarter million hard-core French collaborators in France -
Frenchmen connected with Petain's puppet government - Frenchmen who
join enemy forces - Frenchmen who print in their papers the *advantages* of the
Reich for their own *advantages* - Frenchmen who denounce Resistance neighbors
- Frenchmen who use their talents in the media for the enemy's propaganda
machine. So, **trust no one** - dubito ergo sum, **trust no one**. Never voice your
opinion in public- never voice your opinion to your waiter, your milkman, your
neighbor, your butcher. Friends turn in friends to protect themselves, to get
themselves a load of coal or extra rations. Collaboration motives are many -
Resistance allies few. The time of the Terror *has* returned to Paris - the time of
paranoia and suspicion - the time where a once-trusted neighbor can no longer
be trusted."

"Yes, sir."

"Know that over twenty thousand partisans have already been shot."

"Yes sir."

"Know that another fifty thousand have disappeared."

"Yes sir."

"*Trust no one.*"

"Yes, sir."

"Let me see your papers. This affiche is worthless here," Skipper said, ripping up the railway pass. "We no longer travel by train - to travel by train is to
walk into a lion's den - the enemy checks all civil papers of anyone leaving Paris
by the Gare d'Austerlitz or the Gare de Lyon. *You'll* travel by transport truck or
by boat - both with an appropriate hiding place or an appropriate travel permit."

"Yes, sir."

"Now, take your last swig of Calvados, get your mind right and *prepare* to be a *French Resistance agent* **in Reich-occupied Paris**."

"Yes, sir," said Valentin as he put the cork in the Calvados and looked to the quais and noticed that the bateau-bains, the floating pods used as one uses a beach, were mostly gone now and remembered when he once joined other young Parisians upon them for summer sunbathing – remembered the Renoir-like scene of river, bathers, beach umbrellas, colorful canvas chairs - all gone now. But maybe it was still early in the day. Maybe there'd be sunbathers later. But he doubted if they would be as populous or as young - for the war surely stole both.

He looked to the trees, leafless, denuded - every horse chestnut, plane, poplar, and oak strangely stark and skeletal.

"What happened to the leaves?" he asked.

"Parisians strip them for heat."

Beneath one of the bare poplars, a little girl sat alone, fishing with a piece of string. Behind her, a couple pigeons came trotting down the quais. Behind them, several clochards came tip-toeing behind the pigeons and tossed crumbs.

"They hand-hunt them," Skipper said. "Watch!"

The clochards then tossed a net over a pigeon as the rest fluttered away. One clochard grabbed the pigeon's neck, twisted it, and the little girl screamed, jumped up, and ran away, leaving her fishing pole behind.

"Tough times breed tough measures," said Skipper. "The pigeons of Paris are - like cat and rat - plat du jour these days."

"That poor little girl looked more shocked than when Esmeralda first saw Quasimodo . . . ."

"Know that this Paris is *not* the Paris Victor Hugo penned – his Paris was a demure *beauty* to today's Reich *beast*."

"I prefer Balzac over Hugo," said Valentin.

"I prefer Baudelaire – 'get smashed and stay smashed' – not vice - virtue!"

"I prefer Balzac over Baudelaire."

"You *would* prefer Balzac, as *I* once preferred Balzac, but you see, he's not as easy to stomach with the bottle as Baudelaire. And you probably prefer Monet over Manet since the latter suffered syphilis, just like my Baudelaire."

"I *do* prefer Monet, *not* due to a lack of lesions, but due to a lack of forte to Manet. I even prefer de Maupassant over Baudelaire, not because *his* syphilis was *less* severe, but because his words are *more* severe."

Skipper grinned at Valentin, his eyes like helmet slits. "You don't mince words, American. I respect that. *Perhaps* you'll be stronger in worn-torn Europe than I guessed."

"Perhaps," said Valentin as walked to the front of the boat - listened to ducks quack - listened to waters splash - and, for a moment, it seemed like he could open his eyes and there'd be *no* occupation.

Then Notre Dame Cathedral came into full view and he stared at her - at her ship-like structure - her Daddy-Long-Leg buttresses connected to her apse as oars jut from a vessel. He remembered how Hugo called her a *"vast symphony in stone"* and liked the ship analogy better - for ships - unlike stone - *breathe life*. And Notre Dame *breathes life* - from her pipe organs — choir - her vespers - masses - and *only people* can make stone a symphony - the canonization of Joan of Arc -crowning of Henry the Fourth - marriage of 'Napoleon the Little' - marriage of the Duphin — self-murder of Antonieta with a pistol owned by her lover - temp-home of the Crown of Thorns . . . Yes...*all* these sufferings - tributes, devotions, marriages, coronations, canonizations - that *breathed life* into Hugo's *symphony*.

Then he saw silhouettes of soldiers in her courtyard, and the cathedral suddenly seemed part of the occupation as her sepulcher seemed bound beneath gray clouds; her ark hollow; her winged, bow-shaped legs skeletal.

Yes, he'd tried to picture enemy soldiers milling around his favorite city - a city severely cultured - now a city severely colonized. But the picture never materialized, **not** from Shelby's Creek - perhaps the beauty of Shelby's Creek was a shield against an ugly Paris.

Now, as he looked at those soldier silhouettes, he missed Shelby's Creek as *never* before.

"Religions change; beer and wine remain."

— Hervey Allen

Paris, France
Seine River
May 1943

Chapter 26

"Are you religious?" Skipper asked, nodding to the Cathedral.

Valentin shrugged.

"Each self-righteous religious man I've known makes *his* god *his* own *personal* property - claims God is on his side when there are so many sides."

Valentin grinned.

"Now there's a big difference between religious and spiritual - the latter, automatic, natural; the former, manual, forced."

"Do *you* believe?"

"Everybody should believe in *something* - I believe *I'll* have another drink."

Valentin looked back to the cathedral - imagined the island once being marshy and pastoral when cows and Celts ruled the first hours of civilized Paris - how Caesar routed them - how Vikings routed them - how King Charles routed them - paying pounds and pounds of silver for their exit - how later, more Vikings returned, stole more treasures, killed more clergy - *more* severances paid. Too bad the *current* enemy won't leave for a severance - Parisians might pay whatever meager severance remained.

Just then, parishioners filed out of the cathedral.

Valentin thought it odd to see Bible-toting civilians in colorful clothes mixing with rifle-toting soldiers in grey uniforms and shook his head - mass inside the cathedral - gun-wielding soldiers outside. Well, as with everything, time changes things, for better or worse, as Grandpa Schmitz's favorite scripture says - "The race is neither to the swift nor the battle to the strong, but *time* and *chance* happen to them *all*." So, *time* is *now* for the occupier - but *chance* is, they'll *last less* than the cows and the Celts.

"She needs a bath," Skipper said as he pointed to the cathedral. "City soot darkens her the way occupation darkens the city."

Valentin looked away to the far quais where the Seine's waters splashed wildly from the widest parts of the river and then back to the prefecture to where a swastika flag flew upon brownstone walls.

He glanced to the tower of Eiffel - thought how it made its grand entrance to Paris's stage over fifty years ago already - how within those fifty years, its city nearly lost all its loves - just like you losing nearly all your loves — but in much, much less time. Yeah, who'd have guessed that you'd be the sole soul at Shelby's Creek so soon; and who'd have guessed that ole Eiffel would sport a foreign fascist flag instead of its true red, white, and blue?

He looked to the twin towers of the Conciergerie - thought of its many stories - the revolution - where several of some two thousand and one *terror victims* were imprisoned - two thousand *unknown* aristocrats - one *well-known* queen. And, at the bottom of the twin towers, in an alcove below a wrought-iron fence, was an ancient paving that puffed up like mini-baseball plates - in the middle of this paving was a Y-shaped gutter meant to catch rain - but it also caught Royalist guillotined blood - which drained to the Seine. And just north stands a gold statue that stands atop a tall pedestal, wings unfolded, arms holding two wreaths stretching to the sky. As a child, he wondered if the Royalists saw this statue before placing their head beneath the guillotine blade. Or did the Royalists hear the song of a lark before placing their head beneath the guillotine blade? Or did the Royalists see the clearness of a blue river before placing their head beneath the guillotine blade? Whichever they may have experienced last, he hoped the Royalists experienced a sunny day - for - in full sun - the statute shines a brilliant gold — in full sun, a lark is more apt to sing - in full sun, the river shows bright blue from a clear sky. Yes . . . he'd hoped the Royalists were given a songful, sunny, clear, final day.

And he remembered one more thing about that alcove - whenever he looked down to those puffy, paved, baseball-like plates to where the blood drained, he'd see a spider in its web within the wrought iron bars - and, even though it didn't seem like such a likely area to catch prey, that spider and its web was always there: content, prepared, waiting . . . waiting...

"Hey, we dock up here at Port Montebello," Skipper said, nodding to an area opposite the cathedral.

"Yes, sir."

"Remember, until liberation, Paris is the end of laissez-faire, the beginning of unfair. Know that you'll no longer recognize Paris. Gone is her spirit, her light, her soul. All that remains are her structures. But structures always crumble, as do symbols, and symbols are all the enemy brings to *our* Paris."

Yes, now, for the first time since opening Grandma Lambert's letter, he felt *fully assured* he'd made the *right choice* - maybe it was the Calvados - maybe it was the comfort of being in Paris - maybe it was because he was surely within walking distance now of her. And, if he accomplished nothing else, he'd be with her - and *that was half the mission accomplished.*

He looked toward boulevard du Palais where Paris's first public clock - the Clock Tower of the Institut Francais, stood as it had since 1370. He imagined its Gothic gold hands - the time they once told at its beginning in 1370 - and the time they told now, *for him.*

No, there'd be no turning back the hands of *this* time now.

Here he *is* and *here* he'd *remain* until success *or* failure.

He stepped forward to the boat's gate - one step further and farther from Shelby's Creek, he said to himself…one step *further and farther.*

"It is well known that Satan visits Paris often. His appearance always signals disaster. For this reason, he is at home there."

— Rene Benoit, 1568.

Paris, France
Seine River
May 1943

Chapter 27

"Agent Farmer, get your butt over here," Skipper hollered from the wheel of the boat.

"Yes, sir."

"Okay, your first order - after we dock, go to the Latin Quarter. You'll have more than half an hour to casually make your way to Café de la Gare, beside Café St. Michel."

"Yes, sir."

"Be there at 1050 hours - when one of our contacts dressed in a gendarme uniform will ask for your papers - verify it's you - and slip an address into your papers. Go to this address, go upstairs, third floor - meet a man in a grey beret in the hallway. Show him the half of this metro ticket, which matches his half. Tell him the password on this note. Got it?"

"Got it."

"Which café?"

"Café de la Gare."

"What time?"

"1050 hours."

"Where's the meeting place?"

"The gendarme's note will specify."

"Which floor?"

"Third."

"What's the password?"

"Interested in the Museum of Man today?"

"Your response?"

"I prefer evolution."

"His next password?"

"Then you must also like hamburger?"

"Your response?"

"Hot Dog."

Skipper stared at him with the mad eyes. "Without a password, an agent can't even pee in this town. Now say it."

"No password, no pee."

"Again," said Skipper.

"No password, no pee."

"Forget your password, forget your luck," said Skipper. "Now say it."

"Forget your password, forget your luck."

"Again."

"Forget your password, forget your luck."

Skipper crumpled the note with the password and ate it like an apple. "You start to like pulp roughage after a while. After all, it's all *merde* in the end. Oh, and wait no longer than five minutes for a rendezvous. If longer, leave - for there's a problem -perhaps he was arrested - perhaps he sang and you'll soon be arrested. Just leave and go to your safe house. Don't worry; our people will find you. One more thing - you may go under cover as an enemy soldier - with your Germanic looks you don't have far to go. But remember, your enemy is acute to dialects and accents - it's missing merde like this that'll get a bullet in the brain. Be short and sweet with answers to questions like who you are, where you live, where you've been, where you're going . . . . Remember - the less you talk and the less you move - the easier for you to prove. And always check for tails. Until you blend into Paris, you may be watched with scrutiny. As you move, stop, have a cigarette, check for tails, and then move again."

"Yes sir."

Skipper winked, sauntered up to Valentin, kissed his cheeks, twice in turn. "Remember, as a partisan, you'll be nervous and anxious, worn and weary, but with a bit of savvy, with lots of luck, you *might* live."

"I know - six months . . . ."

"Good luck, young man," said Skipper, his mad eyes and lively face now somber as stone. Then, quick as a whiskey shot, a glint of the goblin showed in his eyes and he reached into a tool box, brought out a full bottle of absinthe. "For *that* day when I *dock* with *my* orchids and morphine and dream of *green fairies!*" he said, his gap-toothed grin broader than ever.

Valentin grinned back. "For *that* day, Skipper."

Skipper tossed the boat rope to a soldier sentry who suddenly winked at Skipper, caught the rope, and tied off.

Skipper glanced at the sentry and nodded in familiar acknowledgement.

Valentin caught both of these exchanges and knew immediately that Skipper and the sentry were comrades of some kind, though what kind, he didn't know.

"…the glory of France, an ornament of the world…I love it tender-ly…I am indeed only French through this great city."

— Michel de Montaigne

Paris, France
Quai De Montebello
May, 1943

Chapter 28

*V*alentin jumped onto the cobbled Quai De Montebello bank and Skipper tossed him his luggage.

"Papers, please," the enemy sentry said now in perfect French.

Valentin reached into his inside jacket pocket.

"And open your suitcase," the sentry said. "Why *aren't* you gone from Paris with the Service du Travail Obligatoire? You're certainly between the age of eighteen and fifty. *Perhaps* I should inform Inspector Ritter of your status."

"*Perhaps* you should read my papers," said Valentin, feeling cocky from the Calvados and from the friendly exchange he'd witnessed between the sentry and Skipper.

The sentry turned to Skipper. "What's on your boat *besides* this passenger?"

"The patrols have already checked me, but here, take a look," Skipper said as he went to the boat's cargo hold, pulled up a fish crate, reached down into the crate, and brought up a flopping goujon by its gills. "Do you wish to help me clean it?"

"Get out of here," the sentry said as he winked and Skipper winked back.

This second exchange told Valentin these two *supposed* enemies were not as disagreeable as one might suspect.

"You boys are wearing rifles now, uh?" Skipper said as he pointed to the carbine slung over the sentry's shoulder.

"You never know when you have to go hunting in Paris these days."

Valentin glanced back at Skipper, now joined by four other men that loaded the boat's fish into bushel baskets.

The sentry looked over Valentin's ID papers. "Why *aren't* you working in military service or working in the factories? Do you have a fiche de demobilization exemption?"

"Yes, I'm with a reserved occupation - commissioned to work for *Les Nouveaux Temps*."

"From Lille?" the sentry asked. "I'm glad to see you survived the bombing up there. But *why* didn't you take the *train* to Paris?"

"My friend runs this boat and journeys from Paris to Le Havre often. I opted for a scenic Seine ride versus a crowded train ride."

"You seem annoyed."

Valentin considered speaking his mind after seeing the amiable exchange between this sentry and Skipper - and then he did. "Enough of the baloney."

"Who are *you* to speak to *me* like that? I could have you imprisoned or sent to a work factory."

"I saw your friendly exchanges with Skipper; I'm not obtuse."

The sentry stared.

"Okay, play your role so I can play mine," said Valentin.

"Shut up. Now what's your first assignment with *Les Nouveaux Temps?*"

"I'm hired as a drama/art critic. But I also cover restaurants, nightclubs, special events for the Kommandant von Gross Paris. And I interpret."

"Make sure to give Braque a good review. He's worked with some of my colleagues," said the sentry as he rifled through Valentin's ID, wad of wrinkled francs, ration cards, demobilization cards, and identity cards. "Keep these papers with you at all times, especially in Paris, especially your demobilization cards, especially now that the labor draft is in effect."

Valentin nodded.

The sentry stepped close to him, stuffed his ID papers in his pocket, and whispered, "Stay away from Gestapo. You'll know who they are as easily as you know a priest from a perch. Black leather's a big thing for them. They drive black Citroens. They also carry leather briefcases and shave their necks. You won't see any Parisian shaving his neck or carrying a briefcase these days."

Valentin studied the sentry - a bit like Randy Rasmussen only taller, thicker, eyes more schooled.

"We all have jobs to do in this war," the sentry said. "Some jobs are harder than others."

"Yes, we all have jobs - some born into them - some bore into them."

"I suppose mine is *both*," the sentry said.

"Have you killed?"

The sentry stared, looking Valentin up and down for some time. "No."

"Then you can live with that. A clear conscience is the best sleeping pill. Duty should be in line with conscience, conscience in line with what's right."

"You read too much Montaigne," said the sentry, tongue-in-cheek, as he looked around to ensure their solitude. "If you're a soldier in *this* war, *duty* has *nothing* to do with *conscience or* what's right."

A man in a leather coat walked past them.

"Monsieur," the sentry said to Valentin, his voice rising "what is your name again?"

Valentin opened his mouth, hesitated, caught himself, and said "Phillip Delcourt."

"Yes, Phillip Delcourt," said the sentry and then quieted his voice as the man in the leather coat walked away and up the stone stairs. "My name is Rolf - Rolf Wageman."

Valentin thought of the Wageman family from home and then thought again about the familiar exchange Rolf showed with Skipper. "I sense you know Skipper . . . ."

"Too much fraternization in daylight is unwise," Rolf said. "Today, you cannot be friend *and* foe in France. *You* may be seen as collaborator - *I* as traitor. Spies are everywhere."

Valentin nodded.

"Good luck working for the paper. They need somone of *your* expertise."

Valentin nodded, assuming the sentry referred less to his cover paper, more to his resistance paper.

Rolf looked around again to ensure their solitude and whispered. "Come see me here in two days."

Valentin nodded and walked toward the quay's stone stairs, past the stone bench and grinned - remembering all the times he'd sat there - after Notre

Dame Mass - after brunch on Sunday or lunch any other day with Grandpa and Grandma Lambert - after Paris was asleep and he couldn't sleep - after a concert and all the hoopla had died and he needed to clear his mind. Yes, this stone bench was his *favorite* place to *ponder* in Paris and then noticed the few leaves leftover from winter stuck beneath the bench and thought how similar these dried, grey-browned leaves looked to the Catacomb bones *and* to the enemy's uniforms.

He checked his watch and looked at the cathedral, wondering why the bells in the towers were not ringing for it was top of the hour.

Then he imagined them ringing, imagined them ringing back home in Westphalia's church tower - and thought of John Donne's poem "For Whom The Bell Tolls."

Yeah, it tolls for *thee*, he said to himself.

"Yes, long before the War, France stank of defeat."

— Andre Gide

Paris, France
Fifth Arrondissement, Latin Quarter
May, 1943

Chapter 29

*V*alentin topped the stairs to the street and immediately heard the distant, but heavy synchronized treading of jackboots.

Marching jackboots in the Latin Quarter? Who'd have thought?

Then a withered young woman rode by pedaling a velotaxi. Inside the taxi were stools, and upon the stools sat a stocky soldier, sharply dressed and well focused. Beside him sat a younger woman, also sharply dressed and well focused. And Valentin thought of Florine milking Nanny and Katie and wondered if she looked as funny on her milk stool as this man looked on his stool.

In another velotaxi, a convertible, another heavy soldier sat still on his stool, focused on a newspaper on his lap. This cart was pedaled by a spindly teenager who pedaled it somehow quickly and sharply round boulevard corners. Behind this velotaxi were the words 'Speed, Comfort, Safety.' Poor Paris, Valentin thought - a spindly, occupied citizen enslaved by a fattened, occupier soldier - the poor, peddler's face sweaty and contorted - the fat-jowled soldier's face calm, with a pipe stuffed in his mouth.

He walked past the bouquinistes, glanced over the literature, mostly French pro-Reich propaganda.

"A book, monsieur?" a vendor asked.

"No thanks - no time to read these days."

"Ah, you have an authentic French accent - Parisian, but you are new around here."

"Yes, I come from Lille to work in Paris again, where I used to live."

"Welcome back, monsieur. What do you think of Paris now?"

"As a former Parisian, I miss Paris," he said, careful of his response.

"As do I, said the vendor, as do all Parisians. So are you a fan of de Gaulle or Petain?"

"I am a fan of Paris," Valentin said, still careful of his response.

"Are you here to join the PPF or any organized group?"

"No, I'm simply here to do my job and enjoy what *light* is left."

The vendor laughed. "What *light* of the City of Light, I see. Quite clever. I see you are a true Parisian and so perhaps you are interested in a banned book, which I keep under my shelves for *real* Parisians - the recently-translated *Moby Dick*. It's American and expensive, but it'll go fast."

Just then, a group of young men in dark uniforms began beating on a young man in a fancy suit.

"You'd think the Zazous would learn," said the vendor.

"Zazous?"

"Yeah, the teenage youth of Paris who've created this cult. Their name's inspired by Cab Calloway – the boys wear their oiled hair long – the girls wear their loud skirts short. The males, as you can see, dress up in *zoot* suits: bulky, long suit coats with padded shoulders, drainpipe pants tied at the ankles and shirts with wide upturned collars. Most also wear fancy hats, long-chained pocket watches, and sharp-toed shoes. As you see, they often carry a caned umbrella, or a cane of some kind. And the girls are just as showy in high heels, dark sunglasses, and red-painted lips."

"So they get a beating for wearing odd clothing?"

"No, they get a beating for annoying soldiers, for being individual, and for listening to jazz - all of which go against the grain of the Reich."

"Who's giving the beating?"

"Their arch-rival opposites, the youth of the fascist group Parti Populaire Francaise - young French thugs that do the Reich's dirty work, though the Reich respects them little more than a country respects an illegal immigrant."

"So the Zazous hang out in the Latin Quarter?"

"They used to gather at Hot Club de France but who knows if its still open due to the Reich's hatred of jazz?"

Valentin looked with confusion at a list of names on a poster and asked the vendor about them.

"Lists are hung in each arrondissement that show names of Parisian hostages executed in revenge for sabotage. In Paris alone, more than sixty thousand such prisoners have already been executed."

Valentin looked toward the river and wondered how long it might take to reconnect with Skipper, with London, with America, with Shelby's Creek. Gosh, it couldn't take *that* long, could it?

"Imagine that someone comes into your home - someone you don't like - he settles down, gives orders... To me that was unbearable."

- Pearl Cornioley

Paris, France
5th Arrondissement, Latin Quarter
Latin Quarter
May 1943

Chapter 30

"Vive Hitler! Vive Hitler!"

Valentin looked to a far street corner where a Quasimodo-slouched man hollered as he held a tin cup in one hand, waved a half-empty bottle of wine in his other.

"Vive Hitler! Vive Hitler!" he repeated and stood tall on a cinder box. "The Allies have abandoned us - British imperialist scum has abandoned us - turncoat American cowards have abandoned us. Delinquent races have destroyed us. Watch the Reich - they attend church, they kneel, humbly ask for blessings. Do our true enemies, the heathen Bolsheviks or the Saxons do this? No!"

The vendor shook his head. "Normally, this drunkard would be cleansed from our streets, but his public speaking proves more powerful than propaganda for the enemy. Every day - in town crier fashion - he condemns the French, praises the Reich, and receives rewards from passing soldiers, punishments from passing Parisians."

"Repent, French citizens! Repent! The Third Republic is dead! The French proved easy to fall, easy to defeat, easy to occupy. Why? Because the French gorged on wine, women, and song while the Reich planned, organized, and executed. Fellow Frenchmen, forget old France. France's old leaders sicken me. Even the women of France are *more* men than the men. The women of France know a *real* man when they meet one. Already the women of France have fifty thousand children fathered from *real* men, men of the *Reich* . . . . "

"It's actually seventy-five thousand illegitimate children," said the vendor. "But what young French men are left? Young men in Paris are mostly enemy soldiers, soldiers with food and money for single women to survive."

"Our country's defeat was best for a state that was effete. Now our country will thrive, not dive into the Maginot hole. France was dead and now lives thanks to the Fuhrer! Long live France! Long live the Fuhrer!"

"Shut the hell up, you stumblebum piece of merde," said a middle aged, stout woman who walked within arm-distance of the drunkard.

He then held his bottle to a propaganda poster showing an enemy soldier holding a French child. "Forsaken Frenchmen, trust in the Reich. The Reich will not abandon you like your French leaders. The Reich will make us right . . . . "

"I said shut the hell up!" the same woman repeated as she swung her purse at the man's head again and again until she hit him, and he fell from the cinder block onto the street.

She raised her purse and hit him again and again, now the force of her weight and gravity on her side. "We lost the battle, but not the war, you traitor trash," she said, still swinging her purse until two soldiers rushed behind her and pulled her away.

Nearby, a sixty-ish, stoop-shouldered Frenchman in a dirty black beret and tattered turtleneck stepped out from an alley, saw no soldier by the drunkard now, rushed up to him, picked him up as if helping him, and then punched him square in the jaw. The drunkard spun to the curb and his body laid still. The Frenchman checked around for soldiers and then grabbed the drunkard's coin-filled cup and ran down the alley he'd come from.

"Happens about every other day," the vendor said, chuckling. "The drunkard collects the coins and Robin Hood there kicks his butt and takes his riches."

Now students gathered behind soldiers, making mocking gestures at them, holding the victory sign with their forefingers above their heads, sticking their tongues out, saluting with their middle fingers while rubbing a fist to a nose.

"Goodbye," Valentin said to the vendor.

"What's your name?"

"I'm...late," Valentin said as he walked to a kiosk pole showed a placard outlined in black with red lettering with a pronouncement of a recent soldier assassination committed by partisans, followed by a list of the partisans summarily executed in retaliation for the assassination: 'Simone Cadet, Georges Honore, Madeline Jardin, Claude Metiers, Marie Morland, Marcel Chappelle...'

He looked back to the Seine quais to see if his boat was still docked even though he knew it was not.

He looked ahead to the Seine to the Port of Paris to see if Skipper was still there, but he was not.

Yes, you can *still* call *all* of this off and be back in Iowa in a week - you have no obligations other than...

"Your work certificates, monsieur?" a stoic voice said.

Valentin turned around to face a gendarme who looked a half-foot shorter and a half-life older than he.

"Your name and address, monsieur?"

"Philippe Delcourt. I'm staying at a hotel tonight until I meet with *Les Nouveaux Temps* tomorrow."

The gendarme looked questioningly at him. Just then, someone hollered for his help, farther down the street.

The gendarme handed Valentin his papers and rushed down the street.

Okay, Valentin thought, stop standing still like you don't belong here. Get a move on. Act like you know what you're doing as Rosy and Skipper warned.

Then he walked as he was told to walk - drooped shoulders, feet dragging with a neutral gait – like Parisians.

Now the scents of Luxembourg's flowers wafted upon the wind until the sweet scents mutated to dismal odors from a public pissoir just ahead. He turned into an open stall of the green-rusted urinal, held his breathe, and relieved himself. On a wall inside the stall a poster showed de Gaulle's photo. For a moment, he felt he might be accused of putting it up but then, just *how* inspiring is it for the Free French general's mug *upon a pissoir that reeked of urine*? And he laughed to himself, knowing the situation would be less funny - minus the Calvados.

He stepped out into the fresh air, released his breath.

Up ahead, citizens formed a line that snaked slowly into a butcher's shop. In their hands were ration cards and an edition of the ration coupon paper. He looked at their thin forms and faces - their eyes - cold and despondent – a mannequin's apathy.

And there were also what looked to be World War I vets – you could always tell the vets - middle age - missing an arm, missing leg - and a *certain* look - yes, that *certain* look. Was it of anger? Shock? Dismay? He didn't know. But it *showed* - in their eyes - in the way they held their mouths - as if to say they'd seen something in those battlefield trenches and 'no man's land' battlefields that changed their lives - something that possibly made eyes less human, more animal. Perhaps they'd viewed horrors that they once believed man incapable of inflicting upon one another. Perhaps some eyes absorb such things as a sponge - hold such things as monuments in their minds - and *that* was exactly what he wished *not* to take back to Shelby's Creek - *that* was exactly what he wished *not* to wake up to in a cold sweat in the cabin at midnight, when only whip-poorwills, owls, or frogs should be guilty of waking you. And he remembered a book by World War I vet, Jean Giono - remembered Giono's words: "I cannot forget the war...I might pass two or three days without thinking of it and then suddenly I see it again, I feel it again... And I feel frightened...I am still afraid, I tremble, I shit in my pants...I prefer to think about my own happiness...there is no glory in being French...there is only one glory, to be alive."

Valentin looked away from the vets, back to the people in the queue - all thin.

But not all Parisians were thin - not all Parisians waited in food lines - up ahead, at the sidewalk café courts, several Parisians seemed to avoid lines and weight loss - yes, the rich - *always* have money for cafés - for black market pur-chases - for comfort for survival.

Up ahead, another sidewalk café looked busy, mostly with officers and soldiers.

He noticed two officers wearing tasseled swords that dangled from scab-bards that pressed against polished knee-high boots. Yes, the swords seemed a bit overdone - after all - unless they fight Marco Polo on horseback - or stab and sever a tough café horse steak - what was the purpose? Why the bravado? Well, he guessed soldiers granted furlough in Paris wished to look their *best* as the Russian front *surely* wasn't making them look their *best*.

An old man, perhaps blind, perhaps not, stuck his walking cane out in front of soldiers, who sidestepped to avert being tripped.

Another old man sat on the corner holding up a bicycle, which looked more alive than he, as he stared straight ahead like some peasant Rodin statue.

Young Parisian women, however, did not seem like statues. They still moved with grace, even if on bell-ringing bicycles. Their shapely legs pumped the pedals and their dresses caught the breezes that blew the dresses up and behind to show more of the lovely legs. Now *that's* a sight I don't see every day on the farm, he thought and forgot for a moment the City of Light turned dark.

More young women passed - elegant, classy-French-gorgeous. Even if that attractive, subtle haughtiness seemed slightly amiss, they were physically perfect - model-slender - because, of course, they were on a model-slender diet - and biked for transportation - as if training for the Olympics - and he sensed he fell in love with every lady that passed.

Yes, it must be the blooming flowers – *baloney* - it was *Paris*.

To be in love in Paris in spring should compel a commitment to a commandment - for *not* to be in love in Paris in spring - was *surely* a sin.

On a side street now, a couple of newlyweds sat on a stool before a background screen. A photographer hid his head beneath the blanket of his camera. Two other couples stood beside the photographer and teased the newlyweds so they'd smile. Yes, Parisians still marry and Parisians still smile - part of Paris's légèreté - even if photos must be taken in daylight - even if the honeymoon might be in a tiny flat *with* rationed food.

Across the street, several women sat out in the sun getting their hair crimped, curled, and set, though the set was precarious due to being outside in the in the wind, due to lack of light, due to lack of electricity inside.

Two men in long leather coats passed him.

He checked his flashlights deep inside his pocket and looked ahead to where he saw the Café St. Michel.

"You see how *well* the SS eat?" said a deep voice.

Valentin turned to the voice: a thirty-ish man, not well-dressed, but newer clothes, clean and pressed.

"Paris starves and the SS has dinner parties," he said.

Valentin said nothing, remembering all the warnings about conversing with strangers, and walked on.

Suddenly, a tremendous racket echoed from across the river as Citroens and Lorries rolled ahead of half-tracks and tanks that came clacking up the street toward the Police Prefecture.

He wished to watch the scene, but remembered it not wise to stand and stare as a Midwesterner stares at Manhattan skyscrapers on a virgin visit - for there was nothing that said prey to muggers like tourists that stared at skyscrapers, and nothing that said prey to Gestapo as strangers that stared at a strange Paris.

He glanced at a kiosk that showed several posters, sliced and ripped, defaced with graffiti.

"That'll cost you ten thousand francs," said an elderly French man, "ten thousand francs for tainting an enemy poster."

Valentin glanced at him.

"Merde," said the man, hunkering down, glancing around, pulling out a marker, drawing a toothbrush moustache and a pair of devil horns on a soldier on a poster, followed by a large "V" across his chest. "I have neither ten thousand francs nor ten thousand hours to live, so I'll do my part for my Third Republic or Fourth Republic, whichever is still here when I'm not."

Valentin grinned as the man walked to another kiosk where he slipped in between two tall soldiers and marked on more posters.

Valentin walked on and thought how, other than the enemy uniforms, the thin Parisians, the bikes in stead of cars, the mostly older men and mostly younger women, the defaced posters, the taped windows, the outdoor salons, the indoor soup stations, the ole red, white, and blue swapped for the new red, white, and black - Paris seemed -*relatively* the *same*. In fact, I feel as though I can safely sit on a table beneath a brassier over there at Café St. Michel and sip an espresso . . . Yeah, well, it's *that* sort of *false sense of security* that's going to get you killed - its *that* sort of *false sense of security* that's going to make your expected lifespan as a spy change from six months to six minutes.

"Papers, please," a gendarme said, as the two men in leather coats he'd seen earlier looked on in the background.

"French resistance is the new French Republic."

— Anonymous Partisan

Paris, France
5th Arrondissement, Latin Quarter
May 1943

Chapter 31

*O*kay, Valentin thought - my papers have been checked three times in thirty minutes - and thus far – approved - with flying colors.

Suddenly, he sensed someone eyeing him across the street.

He looked straight ahead, made a casual beeline for the opposite street, thought casual thoughts.

He glanced up at the Fontaine St-Michel, listened to its splashing waters - thought of Shelby's Creek. Had Florine wondered down to the spring? Had she hoisted the flag? Sat by the oak? Listened to the songbirds? Had she and Mr. Rasmussen spent the night in the cabin as he invited them to?

And he listened intently to the St-Michel fountain - imagined intently sitting on the bank of his Shelby's Creek spring . . . .

Then he heard wooden shoes and saw a gun barrel poking out of a slit of a concrete pillbox at the corner of the boulevard and *knew* he was *nowhere* near his spring.

Then he glanced to where he suspected the tail that followed him.

The coast looked clear.

Still, he leaned against a storefront wall, picked out a Craven cigarette from a front pocket, lit it, inhaled, exhaled, and felt a cough build in his throat as the strong acrid taste made him spit. Gosh, how can people smoke this *merde*?

He put a finger and thumb to his tongue, wiped at a tiny loose tobacco leaf and spit from the side of his mouth to expel another.

Inhaling and blowing, inhaling and blowing - that's what all **this** *smoking stuff's about* - a lungful of dirty smoke - a mouthful of dirty smoke. But he **must** smoke the darned thing now that he lit it - for to throw away an unsmoked cigarette in occupied Paris might arouse more suspicion than wearing an American flag.

As he spit again, he glanced over to Café St. Michel.

At the café, stout officers sat, fatted elbows on marble-top tables, fatted butts on wicker chairs, bloated necks pouring over stiff collars, pumpkin faces wrinkling with laughter.

In his lap, one officer held a mannequin of a woman, her face makeup-heavy, stoic as a statue.

In his lap, another officer held a girl of a woman, her face vibrant with giggles as if on a carnival ride, and he slapped her butt and rocked her back and forth.

No, I've no right to judge these women, Valentin thought - perhaps they were of the 'Travail allemande' department of the French Resistance, working under cover as Rosy mentioned - perhaps they had children at home starving while their husbands were in a prisoner-of-war jail cell - perhaps they had elderly parents at home starving while their husbands were in a factory in forced labor in another country - perhaps...who knew? "Judge not, lest thee be judged," the *good book* says, and that's what makes it a *good book*.

Still, he watched a moment longer and listened to the laughter of the officers, raucous, malicious; laughter that came with pompous power.

He looked at the elderly waiters wearing traditional white aprons and dark horseshoe waistcoats - sporting a mollified mope - as if *they too* took a Café des Deux Magots pledge *not* to smile at patrons. Their mustaches were the same - thick, dark, and weakly waxed as if they shared the same coiffure with the same groom setting. But *there was* an odd comfort in their *iconic presence - somehow* they gave promise that Paris *would return* and occupation *would end.*

And he looked to the unused charcoal brasseries and sensed he'd use them again one day - in peace. And he'd be part of bringing *that* peace, he hoped.

He stopped leaning against the wall - stamped out his cigarette butt - walked down the boulevard - blocked out the café laughter, the soldiers, their moles, Skipper, his boat, and *everything else* behind him.

He walked on, noticed no dogs or cats but plenty of rats - like the French revolution - like the Commune - like the many manifestations that lead from one Republic to the next - and rats *always* came with *each* troubled time - manifestation of rights - manifestation of rats.

And he remembered how Paris once exhibited much manifestation march-ing and thought how indeed, the French are known for having selective seeing as the Germans are known for selective hearing. Well, if revolution was evolution and if man evolved and revolved faster through selective seeing than hearing, so be it.

But now, after three occupied years, he wondered if Parisians even remem-ber *how* to protest - as Reich manipulation replaced civil manifestation.

Yes - yes - *they remember.*

And *they'll* be back.

Yes - the French *will* rise again - their indelible passion *will* lure them back to their political postures where *all* French like to lead - *none* like to follow. That *is* the heart of a republic after all.

"France cannot be France without greatness."

— Charles de Gaulle

Paris, France
5th Arrondissement, Latin Quarter
Boulevard Saint Michel
May 1943

Chapter 32

A truck rolled slowly up the street, loudspeakers blaring - "Surrender your radios - to be caught with a radio is to suffer penalty of punishment. Surrender your radios now."

Valentin watched the truck turn onto Boulevard Saint-Germain and then glanced at a storefront window at the reflection of a car he sensed was a tail.

Then the car turned onto Boulevard Saint-Germain and he sighed with relief.

He checked his pocket watch: 1045 hours.

He walked on.

Gosh, he loved the Left Bank - always preferred it the Right:

Left - open collar.

Right -buttoned collar.

Left - casual cafés.

Right - the ritzy Ritz.

Left - intellectual Café de Magots.

Right - monarchy Meurice.

Yes, give me open air with brassiers and quirky patrons - sober or drunk - loving or hating - but *always* more color than the yin and yang, black and white Right.

Heck, progressive thinking started and stopped on the Left Bank - surely *less* collaborationist than Right - surely *more* resistance than Right.

Heck, if he'd been born on the Right, he'd move to the Left - just out of sheer boredom.

He looked down the street at the three-, four-, and five-story, stone-plastered houses with the damsel-in-distress top-tiered windows and chimney pots jutting up like stone warts.

He walked to a typical twisting Latin Quarter alley, barely wide enough to fit the width of a tractor, sandwiched and shouldered by five-story structures and walked on - rue de l'École-de-Médecine, rue de Médicis, rue Soufflot . . . .

Yes, these streets were his favorites - for intellect, art, jazz, existentialism . . . .

And it was here where Paris became the hub, the crème de la crème of the world's finest artists — freedom for bohemians, for minorities, for females who liked females, for males who liked males, for artsy-fartsy misfits that fit nowhere else. Gosh, he wished he'd been here then to absorb, to partake in the most profound artistic enlightenment by the most profound artists . . . in Montparnasse . . . in Monmarte. Yes, *here* was the heart of art that may never beat the same way again.

He thought of Delacroix's studio nearby, his pencil drawings of panthers on the pane like neon at night with the first glimmer of blue gas street light.

In the same direction, Café Procope on rue de l'Ancienne-Comédie, once *his* café because of its quiet location, its clever waiters, its legendary coffee, its legendary Enlightenment history - ancient and recent - and because it was where artists and intellectuals flocked - away from tourists and tipplers - artists and intellectuals like Voltaire, Balzac, Rousseau, Sand, de Maupassant, Cezanne - even fellow expatriate patriot Benjamin Franklin.

Now he glanced up at Montmarte - thought of Moulin Rouge - and Lautrec. Yes...Lautrec. Well Lautrec was Lautrec as Manet was Pissaro as Seurat was Cezanne as Cezanne was yawn, yawn, yawn . . . Hell, if you must paint cartoons and caricatures, at least put color in like Gauguin and Van Gogh.

He looked to the end of the block where several SS soldiers walked with several plainclothesmen. They all looked steely-eyed over the crowd - heads moving in a slow, wide arc.

Suddenly, the soldiers rushed up to him and he felt his chest freeze until they ran past him toward the quais.

He checked his pocket watch - ten minutes to rendezvous.

He walked back to Café St. Michel.

Now it hit him how street signs changed - how marquees changed - how scores of shops were boarded-up - coiffures, patisseries, boulangeries - doors nailed and locked -windows dark with black cover, shuttered or taped to decrease glass breakage.

Yes, so many other things changed - gone - the civilian bustle of the Latin Quarter - gone - the wafting odors of fruits and vegetables from Les Halles and

Porte de Clignancourt - gone - the days of Parisians carrying a fresh batard, ficelle, saucesson, or baguette, the crisp crust showing above the top of the bag and often bitten into from the top by its owner before he arrives home for dinner - gone - the cremeries with as many assorted cheeses as Sinatra has songs - gone - bustling grand boulevards, parks, museums, markets - gone - the quay along the Seine; the boats; and the amoureux embracing in the silent, stealthy shade of the bridges - gone - the hundreds of bronze statues already sent across the border and liquefied for shell casings - gone - the bulking green and white buses - gone, the bustling fruit, vegetable, meat, and fish stands beneath the sidewalk awnings — gone - the petits métiers, the organ grinders, singers, and painters - gone - the chestnut, kindling, and oyster vendors - gone - the street sweepers, knife grinders, glaziers, flower sellers, umbrella menders, dog washers, self-employed tradesmen, as much a part of Paris as its quay and cobblestones - gone - artists along the quais - gone - locals of the portico homes, busy on their balconies, balconies now with shutters closed, many closed since the dawn of war when their occupants left - gone - café patrons that spent long leisurely hours conversing, dining, quarrelling, Parisian style - gone - fatted-calf days of busy boulangeries, epiceries, charctuceries, patisseries, as fubar as Muscovites in winter without fur hats or a Monet without water - gone - ***everything's gone*** that was ***once Paris***. And what remained in steady quantity - the *only* true plat du jour these days - seemed to be the *same* plat du jour of the last three years - *occupier du jour*.

Just then, a cyclist soared by as if passing the finish line of the Tour de France. Leaflets dropped behind him as he disappeared down an alley. Valentin knew better than to pick up a leaflet. He could see it was an underground tract, and to be caught with one on his person meant big trouble. He could see the headline of one that read "For an eye, both your eyes - for a tooth, your whole mouthful." Yes, probably a communist underground paper - for Rosy said that it was communists that escalated Resistance violence no matter the lopsided enemy reprisals of 'for every officer slain, fifty French hostages slain.'

He checked his pocket watch. Yes, back home it was about 3 a.m... Gosh, it must be peaceful at Shelby's Creek and it must be lonely for the cabin without anyone inside, in the bed, next to the window, with the breezes light and the creek's falls ebbing and flowing - ebbing and flowing in its natural way with its natural world - the way a *good* life *should* be.

"...the voice of the Resistance...the voice of simple people, people without rank, who, without even knowing it, rescued the honor of our country..."

— Henry Frenay

Paris, France
5th Arrondissement, Latin Quarter
Boulevard Saint Michel
May 1943

Chapter 33

Valentin felt his stomach growl now from hunger pangs. Yes, it'd been only three weeks since he'd left the farm, but boy was he ever ready now for farm-fresh food, especially after England - yes, a juicy, barbecue-basted rib-eye on the grill - fifteen minutes one side - five the other - garlic toast - butter-baked potato - corn-on-the cob - peach cobbler - homemade goat's milk ice cream for dessert. . . .

Yes, it's hard to beat farm-fresh food, even harder to beat French-fresh food - a platter of fresh chartucerie followed by a platter of cheeses - brie, camembert, roucqfert - followed by baguettes and foie gras - followed by a platter of patisseries - Napoleans, pecan pie, pommes - followed by…that's enough, he told himself.

Yes, perhaps he'd *change* his mind about this *assassination business* after all - *just* for *French fare* - for, other than dining in the woods while camping, food in France *always* tasted better than *anywhere* else.

He saw a sign that read "Hotel." Yes, you could go into *that* hotel *right now*, order a meal, sleep in a clean bed with clean sheets for twelve hours, wake, contact your network, and tell them you decided to *get out* while the *getting's good*. No, you didn't commit *any* partisan acts, didn't commit *any* crime *for* the Resistance or *against* the Reich.

"Avoid hotels." Rosy's voice echoed in his mind. "French police and Gestapo inspect registers early every morning. They'll knock on your door when you are fresh from sleep and listen for you to respond in English. If you need a safe house that's *not* prearranged, stay at a brothel: the Sphinx on the Left Bank, Le Chabanais, the One-Two-Two on the Right Bank and many, many more. You see, of the one hundred thirty brothels in Paris, only thirty were reserved for the enemy and *most*, if not *all* brothels *hate* the enemy."

He walked by a shop window with a photograph - a ten-by-fourteen bust of the traitor French leader - under his bust a large sign read "COMPLETELY SOLD OUT."

He laughed aloud.

Another window showed a photo of the traitor French Prime Minister Laval, and Petain. Under this photo were copies of Hugo's book, *Les Misérables*.

Valentin laughed again.

Then his mind cleared to the sounds of soldiers' voices - voices foreign in France - like Japanese in L.A. - like German in New York - which, until about a year ago was not so far-fetched, as these two tiny countries - Germany and Japan - neither alone the size of Montana - *nearly* took over the *entire* world.

Then he heard the faint murmur of a sudden crowd marching straight up Boulevard St. Michel - dozens of Sorbonne students carrying posters, some showing Petain with withdrawn empty pockets with the words, "Sold Out" - some showing Hitler hanging from a noose with the words, "Heil Kaput" - some showing a mutilated Mussolini with the words, "Fascist Fettuccini."

Gosh, he felt proud of these students - students that should be checking posted exam results this time of year - *not* checking and acting on the status of the French Republic.

Just then, the students stopped in front of a pro-Fascist bookstore.

For an instant, the scene seemed strangely frozen - students, posters, gendarmes, and batons - still, dull, silent, like a picture-show reel stuck.

Then a sea of blue gendarme uniforms held guns in the air, fired blank rounds, flashed forward and grabbed posters, pulled students to the ground, and beat them with batons.

At first, Valentin looked away. Be a cool hand, he told himself, cool as a cucumber.

Walk away.

Then he heard the screams of the students, the smacks of the batons on heads and bodies.

He rushed to the ruckus, which quickly came his way as a gendarme pulled a young, spindly male student to the sidewalk.

The gendarme's baton came crashing down on the boy's head, making a solid thud like a boiled egg hitting concrete.

Valentin glanced round fast, taking in the perimeter of the street, the high-pitched Mansard roof tops, confident no one was looking.

He stepped back into the recess of a doorway, grabbed the gendarme by his cape, yanked him back into the doorway and, with the same momentum, hurled a hard right overhand hook on the gendarme's chin firmly as a carnival hammer hits a dinger to ring a bell.

The gendarme saw nothing but a blur of buildings above him, then blackness.

Valentin winked at the fallen boy, whose freckle-peppered, pimpled, blood-ied, and tear-filled face changed awkwardly to a grin.

The boy rolled up, looked down at the comatose gendarme, kicked him twice, and then ran toward Rue Saint Séverin and disappeared down a sleepy alley.

Valentin stepped back into the darkness of the recessed doorway to wait for another gendarme cape that might come his way.

"A great flame follows a little spark."

— Dante

Paris, France
5th Arrondissement, Latin Quarter
Boulevard Saint Michel
May 1943

Chapter 34

*V*alentin checked his pocket watch - it was time.

Just then, a gendarme strolled past him from inside the café, stopped, turned to him, and asked for his papers.

The gendarme stared at the papers and then at him, nodded, and left.

Valentin noticed a slip of paper sticking out of his folded carte d'identité that the gendarme must have put inside and looked at the paper and the note on it: "Café St. Michel, left - Rue de la Huchette, left GION."

Well the note wasn't real clear, but he knew that GION was just around the corner on Rue de la Huchette, one of his favorite streets.

He scanned the perimeter for a tail, puffed a Craven, passed Café St. Michel, and rounded the corner onto Rue de la Huchette.

He leaned against the building, puffed his Craven, waited to see if he was tailed.

As he waited, he thought about this street - a medieval maze of tapered passageways, cafés, hotels, and entertainment venues, half the width of a normal boulevard, twice the length of the tower of Eiffel, parallel and just south to the flow of the Seine.

No, he'd not spent much time on Rue de la Huchette, though he'd spent much time nearby: the Sorbonne, Luxembourg, and especially Petit Pont - where a Roman bridge of the Lutece stands near Paris's oldest tree, an acacia, rooted some three hundred years ago - one of Paris's prized possessions - one of his prized visits, thinking of Shelby's Creek oak when he did. But *now* was *no* time to visit trees . . . .

He scanned the perimeter again, tossed the Craven on the walk, stamped it out, turned, and opened the door of GION.

He walked into the foyer, shadowy with two dusty shafts of mid-morning light spilling in through a large side window.

The light landed on the first step, also *his* first step in this *perilous* crossing, he thought.

He looked up the stairs, his eyes now bringing into view the spiraling steps winding up several floors.

He looked back.

Okay, he said to himself - I can either walk back *out* that door and back to Iowa - *or* walk up those stairs and on to . . . Lord only knows . . . .

Then, absentmindedly, he stared at the grayish light seeping in through the glass door upon the curled end of the stairwell banister . . . *but* if I walk back out that door and back to Iowa, there's *no* pardon waiting at Shelby's Creek - *no* amount of time at the creek will assuage the pain I'll bring to myself *if* I *don't* try.

Then the light on the stairwell banister that still transfixed his gaze changed from gray to yellow to grey-yellow and gold - yes, the common color of Iowa's sky at sunrise . . . . .

And he broke his gaze, rushed up the stairs, two by two until he counted three floors.

"Interested in the Museum of Man today?" whispered a man - his back turned in the empty hallway.

Valentin stopped dead at the top of the stairs, stared at the back of the body speaking.

"I prefer evolution."

"Then you must also like hamburger?" said the man, his whispering words whistling through gaps of missing teeth.

"I like hot dogs."

The man then reached up to a wall sconce and unscrewed a light bulb till the light faded and the only light now showed at the opposite end of the hallway.

"Do you have a metro ticket for me?" Valentin asked.

"It's beneath the leg of the desk to your left," the man whispered back.

Valentin checked that the tickets matched and then heard a pistol cocking from the man's direction. "Does it match?" asked the man.

"It matches," said Valentin, wondering if he should dive down the stairs to avoid being shot.

"I prefer you keep your distance," the man whispered as he turned his face to the side. "And I prefer you *do not* talk," he said as he now lit a pipe with a match.

In the flame, Valentin saw the man's silvered goatee hanging stiff from his chin, like an old goat.

The man adjusted his black beret lower to his eyes and buttoned his old tweed coat as his pipe smoke lifted lazily, its smell wafting down the hall, sweet and cherry scented.

"Keep behind me ten meters at all times," the man said. "Look for the back of an old man with a cane if you lose me - but I *don't* expect you to lose me. We arrive at your destination in approximately ten minutes. You will be where you are supposed to be when I sit down. After I sit down, I will get up and leave. Do *not* follow me. The bartender will tend to you. When he asks what you want, you will say Louis Latour Cabernet."

At the far end of the hallway, someone opened their door.

Valentin stepped down the stairs slowly as a person passed him and this person opened the foyer door, closed it, and the hallway fell quiet again.

Valentin stepped back up to the third floor hallway.

"Know we will have a tail follow you to check your description," the man whispered. "If you *don't* check out, I'll *not* lead you where you think I should lead you. Now, go to the end of the hallway with your back to me. Stay there until you hear me close the foyer door below."

"Whatever happens, the flame of French resistance must not and shall not die."

— *de Gaulle*

Paris, France
5th Arrondissement, Latin Quarter
May 1943

Chapter 35

Valentin waited, heard the foyer door close and rushed down the stairs.
He opened the door just in time to see his contact's cane go left around
Rue du Chat Qui Pêche.

He moved casually as to not attract attention, but stepped in large strides as
he wished to close the gap of more than half a block with his contact.

As he passed Hôtel Normandie, he felt eyes on him from a man and woman
standing on the sidewalk stairs. The woman looked to be the same person he'd
suspected eyeing him earlier. He walked by and glanced back. Yes, it was the
same woman - taller than average - stark, white skin - dark hair tied in a bun -
big eyes - hooked nose - thin lips. Earlier, she'd been smoking and watching the
crowd, but now he saw the squint and focus in her eyes when he looked her way
and *knew* she was a tail.

He passed the Bureau de Police, which looked to be open for business but
what kind of business, he didn't know. Whose side were *they* on? Protect and
serve the Third Republic or the Third Reich?

He rounded the corner at Rue du Chat Qui Pêche just as his contact's cane
rounded another corner to the right.

The alley was so narrow that he rushed down it without fear of someone
seeing him and suspecting him.

He came to the end of the block as the cane rounded right, and then the
next block that rounded right again on Rue Des Deux-Ponts.

He saw the cane-wielding man then cross the street and walk left in the
opposite direction he'd started on - Rue de la Huchette.

Yes, it seemed they were going round and round, possibly to shake a tail,
probably for the contact's contacts to verify that Valentin was Valentin or Farmer
was Farmer or Phillipe Delcourt was…whoever *he* was.

Soon, the contact was back on Boulevard Saint-Michel, turned left on Rue Saint Séverin, left on Rue de la Harpe, right on Rue de la Hutchette for the third time. If that looney bird doesn't look suspicious to a tail or Gestapo, I don't know what will, thought Valentin.

The contact then crossed the street again and made a b-line for Number 18, Hôtel Normandie and entered the right-side door of the hotel below a sign that said "BAR."

Valentin waited a few seconds and then walked casually to Hôtel Normandie into the same door.

Inside, the contact sat in the back with a newspaper covering his face, his cane leaning against a table.

"Can I help you?" a bartender asked.

Valentin walked close, spoke softly. "Louis Latour Cabernet."

The bartender, a bald, fifty-ish man with Neanderthal bushy brows, a pencil-thin mustache, and wide, stocky shoulders, looked at Valentin for a full five seconds before placing down the glass he'd polished. "Can I help you?" he asked again.

"I'd like a Louis Latour..."

"I heard you," the bartender said, now whispering.

"That old man brought me here," Valentin whispered.

"What old man?"

Valentin looked back at the contact, as he stood, grinned, straightened his arched back as if a miracle healer touched him, and changed his shuffled gait to a fast trot as he rushed out a back door.

"That's no old man. That's a young man," the bartender said and picked up another glass, polished it. "We're out of earshot of anyone, so we may speak normally. I am Bartender. I don't know your name. I don't want to know your name. You may feel safe here. We have an astute protection squad surrounding the hotel."

"Protection squad?"

"Several lookouts who warn us of trouble - one lookout out front, one out back, one in the alley, four upstairs in each direction on the top floor of the hotel. If anyone enters the hotel or bar looking suspicious, I know, and everyone who needs to know will know."

Valentin nodded.

"Within a few moments, I'll take you to the team - meanwhile - have a seat. What'll you drink?"

Valentin looked up at a painting hanging over the bar that showed a beached whale and a sign below it that read, "Jour sans alcool"- no alcohol served to the French on this day. He remembered that to mistakenly order alcohol on such a day might alert an enemy.

"Well," Valentin said, "I know today is *not* a jour sans alcohol day, *even if* your sign says it is."

Bartender's eyes slanted as he grinned. "Trust no one - *exactly*. You learn well, whatever your name is. You'll do better than those other idiots they've sent us. *Never* order drinks on a *drinkless* day, *never* order meat on a *meatless* day. If you do either, you may get *you* and *I* in trouble and my bar closed. So what'll you have to drink?"

"Not tea!"

"A million Brits can't be wrong."

"Coffee."

Just then, two men and a woman walked into the bar, to the back, and disappeared.

"Have you eaten?" Bartender asked.

"No."

"We have eggs and ham with melted cheese if that suits you."

"That suits me fine."

"Jambone Special," Bartender hollered to the back kitchen.

Just then, a man in the back of the bar motioned for Bartender.

A few minutes later, Bartender came back. "Plans have been delayed one day. Here's a newspaper. Inside, you'll find your itinerary and a password for tomorrow. Read it, memorize it . . . ."

Valentin nodded.

"When you finish eating, check in with your new place of employment, wherever that is - but whatever you do, return here **before** curfew at midnight."

"Yes, sir."

Bartender then slipped an envelope to him. "Inside is a map - remember the lines of Montparnasse and Bienvenue are now one station - remember sometimes curfew sirens sound off - remember gendarmes with loudspeakers sometimes announce the curfew warning. If caught out after curfew, take off your wooden-soled shoes and walk barefoot to your destination and you may not be caught. If caught, you'll be taken to military police headquarters where you'll be *their servant* until curfew lifts and where you'll do lots and lots of praying."

"Praying?"

"Praying an enemy soldier or officer is not killed that night. Then your *servant status* changes to *summary execution status* as reprisal."

"If a soldier is killed and I'm caught out after curfew, I'll be killed?"

Bartender nodded.

Valentin swallowed hard and synchronized his pocket watch thirty minutes earlier than it showed.

"Here's a room key. You'll sleep in an upstairs room this evening. Leave your things with me until then."

"Yes, sir."

"You'll meet your cell tomorrow night."

Valentin nodded, read the paper, ate the cheesy eggs and ham, drank his ersatz acorn coffee, and felt grateful he didn't have to pay, only because it wasn't *worth* pay.

Several people walked into the bar then and Bartender stopped talking.

Valentin memorized his password and itinerary from the newspaper and handed it back to Bartender, who rolled it up and took it to the kitchen.

Valentin exhaled, stood, walked out the front door and rounded the corner of Rue de la Huchette, following his recent route in reverse.

"France was a long despotism tempered by epigrams."

— Thomas Carlyle

Paris, France
5th Arrondissement, Latin Quarter
Jardin de Luxembourg
May 1943

Chapter 36

$\mathcal{V}$alentin turned left on Boulevard St. Michel toward Luxembourg Gardens. In the distance, a queue of Parisians waited in a food line for soup.

Valentin grimaced - soup - soup on a warm day in May?

He looked closer and saw that the soup sat in three huge pots with large ladles with long handles. No, in this heat, he'd rather eat leaves.

Then clouds rolled in, a northwesterly wind rolled in with them and whipped at the huge red flags with black swastikas hung in place - hung out of place where Tricolor flags once hung.

He walked by Montmarte Cemetery and wondered what would happen if *he* were cut down in Paris. Would Grandma ever know? How would they get his body back to the family graveyard in Iowa? They wouldn't. Oh well - if cut down - that would be *that*. Oscar Wilde said something about *that*. How did it go? *Good Americans die in Paris.* Well, if Paris is good enough for Oscar, it's good enough for me.

He remembered how American painter George Catlin brought the Iowa Indians to Paris - to, supposedly, preserve their culture - but proably also to preserve his pockets - with French fees. And how one of those Iowa Indians - Little Wolf, lost his wife - who was then buried here in Montmartre cemetery - where Little Wolf kept vigil beside her grave daily until he and the other Iowans returned to Iowa.

Yes, if I were buried here, I would, in a way, regret that no one from Iowa or anywhere would keep vigil at my grave or place a posy or pansy from time to time . . . But then, I'd be dead . . . but then . . . but then . . . .

And he remembered the two army generals overcome by the newly christened Commune - how they were shot near here - and peed on.

Well, if *I'm* cut down by the enemy, *I* don't want the enemy peeing on me - even if I *am* dead.

Heck, nobody in Iowa would pee on me if I were dead...or would they? Perhaps Claude Cain would . . . .

No...perhaps Paris was *not* a first choice for death, *but* perhaps a first choice to be laid low with the tombstone inscription - "Here lies someone who cared about culture." Yes . . . such a message might mean *more* to the living in Paris than to the living in Westphalia, but then *who* cared, he'd be dead . . . .

Stop talking that way, he told himself, or you'll start living and dying that way.

No . . . talk that way, and make the arrangements, or your OSS corpse will be dumped in the Seine . . . . .

So, what about the 16th's Passy Cemetery as final dwelling where the right-brain, left-wing ghosts of Manet and Debussy haunt? Yes . . . Edouard and Claude would be nifty companions, but Marcel Renault was also there, and there'd be *far* too many arguments about his French auto being superior to the Mercedes, or even the Citroen. And life, even after death, had its limits.

Or what about Picpus Cemetery - home to thirteen hundred headless Revolution victims - including sixteen nuns? Heck, even Lafayette's wife's decapitated family was there as well as the Marquis, whose grave was memorialized by an American flag . . . No . . . Picpus is too gruesome - too many ghosts with too many headaches - perhaps a nice place to visit - but no place - *not* to live.

Well, what about the Pantheon - dust-to-dust bins of Voltaire, Hugo, Curie, Braille . . . ? After all, Grandma Lambert always said "Don't have small ideas, have big ideas." But this one seemed *too* big - unless, of course, he saved de Gaulle's life or penned a successful sequel to *Les Misérables*. Nah...the Pantheon was *far* too grandiose for an Iowa farmer.

So, what about the Cemetery of Dogs? It had history dated back to 1899 - a nice location in the 4th on Pont de Clichy. You're an animal lover and it's got lots of animals: Goats, monkeys, hamsters, horses, cats, dogs, birds . . . .

But then . . . who said you need a *cemetery* in Paris?

Bodies are buried everywhere - beneath Place de la Bastille - beneath Chapelle expiatoire - beneath the shopping feet of Les Halles's bargain hunters

- beneath construction digs - single bodies, groups of bodies, parts of bodies, decapitated bodies, twenty thousand Communard bodies . . . .

Well - within - or without a cemetery - it didn't really matter, he guessed.

Nah…neither cemetery nor sin matter - when you're dead.

Still . . . I'll tell my Resistance cell that I prefer Montmarte - even if Wilde was at Lachaise with his Epstein-styled, Egyptian-winged tombstone adorned with endless kisses from female admirers. Besides, who was going to leave a lipstick kiss on *my* tombstone unless she tripped and landed face first on the marble?

Then a breeze blew flowery fragrances from Luxembourg Gardens and hit him full blast, and he felt happy to be *above ground.*

Now, in the near distance - the eight-domed cupola crown of Luxemburg Palace built by the queen of French cuisine, the Italian Marie de Médicis.

Yes, it was she, Marie, who, missing the Italian ambience of Florence, created this Palais - just *how many Frenchmen* know *how much credit* Marie deserved for *their* fine fare, etiquette, elegance - how many know it was she who brought to a *then* unrefined France - Florentine cooks, sparkling glasses, painted China, musicians, delicacies, Degas-esque dancers - how many know *she* influenced French painters - who mastered art from *Italians* - as they also mastered gastronomy from *Italians.*

But gosh, he'd *never* tell a Frenchman he was enlightened by Italians *before* enlightenment - no, not even as a joke - for it seemed French liked Italians as much as Irish liked English or dogs liked cats.

He stared at the Palais and imagined its ghosts - Marie and Louis - a creator and a king - and, of course, Bonaparte, a creator and king and wife, Josephine. Yes…all four sat down, one time or another, beneath the same chandeliers - and, except for the chandeliers - Marie would recognize little of her original dream home - completed the same year she was kicked out of Paris to live and die later, in exile, in Cologne.

Well, at least she lived her dream, for a while, which he supposed was one of her loves for a while. Besides, Maker doesn't *make* our loves to be permanent - he guessed - that included people, possessions, *and* Shelby's Creek . . . Love is *rent only* - not *rent to own.* You *own* your soul and you *owe* your soul - and *that's that.*

215

He sat on a bench, listened to the splashing fountain, closed his eyes, imagined the waters of Shelby's Creek - let go of your farm - let go of all your losses, past, present, and future - embrace your loves as they last. . . .

Gosh, it was so easy to think it, but did he have the strength to live it?

No . . . not now.

In the distance were two gangster-looking Gestapo wearing rey-green coats, Al Capone hats, patrolling Luxembourg as hungry Yellowstone predators must patrol spring offspring, he thought.

He watched their arrogant air, fueled by power -and gosh, he'd love to take the air out of their power - if given the chance - *if* the chance *didn't* mean killing.

Now he walked left and they walked right and nearly bumped into each other.

"Papers, please," the Bogart-looking one demanded now.

"Children who applauded *Punch and Judy* in the park—and those who danced at night and kept our Paris bright till the town went dark."

— Oscar Hammerstein II.

Paris, France
Jardin de Luxembourg
Latin Quarter
May, 1943

Chapter 37

Valentin looked at both Gestapo agents' jaws - guessed which one owned the weakest - which one would fall with one quick jab.

"I look forward to your compositions in *Les Nouveaux Temps*," the Bogart-looking agent said.

Valentin nodded as both agents left, their heads high, their eyes scanning the garden.

He checked his pocket watch - yes, still time to catch the metro to the Champs-Élysées where the enemy's daily noon parade happened.

He walked down the garden paths - now dusty - well worn - without recent rain and wondered if the paths were dusty the day the thousands of Communards were shot here, here . . . in this peaceful, floral place. He didn't know, but if you must die violently and die for what you believe in, what better place than a peaceful, floral place?

He looked up into the branches of chestnuts, beeches, and poppies bloom-ing, and imagined their austere forms filling out as the stick form of a teen transforms into a budding adult.

He looked over to the fountain, at its sun-sparkling lapping water in the octagonal pond.

Young children sailed toy sailboats and scooped sand into pails.

Moms or nannies read books on the lawn nearby.

Ducks swam and squawked . . . Ducks? Ducks swimming in public in starving occupied Paris when ducks seem much more palatable than pigeon?

Then a protective gendarme appeared near a duck - aha, the duck's own fine feathered, non-fowl friend, he thought, keeping the bird safe as the Crowned Head of Britain's Swans. But surely, there isn't an official French "Act of Ducks," as there was an official Brit, "Act of Swans," - in place surely to protect the birds if Queenie tires of pea soup . . . . .

Now the sky grayed and, in the moist, heavy air he smelled sweet scents: magnolia, honeysuckle, lilac and orange blossoms - and then the earthy scents: wet ferns and shrubs - profound, though most profound when dying with leaves in late autumn - when still-vivid chrysanthemums, asters and dahlias - in purples, plums and ebony - refuse to die with the season - until the season dies with winter winds.

He walked beside a hedge, lush and pruned, persnickety as a poodle.

He walked past Brosse's Baroque-shaded Medici Fountain where Platane trees looked lush, their leaves so large, it seemed you could roll several cigars with just one leaf, he mused.

He walked on to the statues of Stendhal, Flaubert, and George Sand *where* - because of *her* romantic story - *he* wished one day to propose to the woman *he* sought to marry. But at this rate, Sand may still be standing and waiting *long* after he's fallen . . . .

Okay, he said to himself - here you are in Luxembourg Gardens, one of your favorite places on earth, and yet you feel lonely and sad - probably the loneliest and saddest you've *ever* felt here.

No, neither parents nor grandparents are with you.

No, *bad* Katherine is *not* with you - but a *good* Katherine *could* be with you.

Yes . . . that's it . . . Luxembourg is *no* place to be *unless* you're with a loved one - as it is a place to be *especially* with a loved one.

Dark clouds superceded gray clouds.

Soon, the whole sky filled, thunder rumbled, drizzle dropped, and it seemed the atmosphere was mourning - weeping for Paris.

He glanced over at the children's theatre where, years earlier, he'd last watched Punch and Judy - partisans of the puppet world.

He looked for the merry-go-round and its hanging brass rings that allowed free rides if you grabbed one before your ride ended and looked and listened for children but now there were none.

He looked and listened for children anywhere, but now there were none.

Yes, the sights and sounds of children playing were the best medicine when sad and lonely - but now there were none.

He stood and moved quickly out of the garden to the nearest metro.

Parisians fitted in their finest, filed up the metro exit steps with satchels; suitcases; burlap bags; pillowcases; and baskets full of fruits, potatoes, rabbits, chickens, and eggs from regional farmsteads.

No, these people would not starve from Paris's paltry rations - there were ways to subsidize in times of trouble - if you had farm relatives - if you could buy black market - if you were rich - *or* if you were a Cain. Yes, the Cains would fare well for fare in occupied Paris. Even if they didn't have the money they'd collaborate - they'd manipulate - they'd even, as the French say, 'kiss butt - even - if butt poops on head'.

Yes, the likes of the Cains will always have money and food - for money begets money - and money begets food - in all times - good and bad.

He boarded the last car of the metro as he knew the front compartments marked 'Nur fur Wehrmacht' were reserved for the enemy and wished to be as far from them as possible.

The train was packed - hot - smelled of sour sweat, fresh vegetables.

He took an empty seat, but soon gave it up to an old man.

A sign on the ceiling, written in the enemy's language said "no-smoking," but a Resistance act rearranged it to say "Green Race," reference to the enemy's green uniforms.

He looked around - all faces stoic, not speaking, not moving, not typical French - like they were just getting by - not really living.

But *getting by* was surely *better* than *not* - for *not* to get by - due to your *own* doing - **ensured** tenure *with* Mephistopheles - well, according to some faith - and faith seemed the last stop for believers and non-believers - and few were "non" at the *end* - if given time to think about the *end* . . . .

He checked his pocket watch and realized, for the first time, the locket showed no photo of a family member, specifically Grandma or Mom.

Well, when and if he returned to Shelby's Creek, Mom's photo would go back in the locket and things would return to normal - if normal ever returned. But Gosh, normal was so abnormal - as he looked at the armed soldiers on the metro bench, as the train squealed to a stop.

"... the Resistance was a true democracy ..."

— Sartre

Paris, France
Champs-Élysées
May 1943

Chapter 38

Valentin topped the metro stairs and walked down the shady alameda of the Champs-Élysées, which looked more new *farmer's market* than old *Champs-Élysées* as shop owners now turned street vendors - barbers, peddlers, shopkeepers worked *outside* due to lack of electricity *inside* - their stands beneath umbrellas, awnings, sky. And they all looked thin but tan - tantamount to homeless, healthy hobos - *with* shower and shave.

He passed a butcherie with a sign that said "Sorry, Nothing."

Another said, "Our Supplies Exclusively for Soldiers."

He walked on to Le Paris movie house and remembered as a teen, he'd attended many movies at Vendome's on Avenue de l'Opera, especially American movies, especially Westerns, especially when homesick - which happened more often than he let on to Grandpa and Grandma Lambert.

What brought about his homesickness?

Well, he loved Paris in equal parts to his farm but, at times, there was too *much* space on his farm - at times, too *little* space in Paris. Overall, he guessed he preferred too *much* space - easier to breathe.

As he walked, once again, posters seemed everywhere.

Besides the posters, swastikas seemed everywhere - the Louvre, the ministries, the senate public structures, Ministry of the Navy, rue de Rivoli, Hôtel Crillon, Place de la Concorde . . . heck even the Arc de Triomphe showed a colossal banner hung with a monster-size swastika upon it that whipped sharply, constantly.

Some posters showed names of spies - printed on yellow paper - terrorists on red.

Both showed black borders to highlight the names and crimes, detailing terrorist actions, underground printing activities, offenses against the Reich, crimes against the state: 'All terrorists are condemned to death' . . . .

Yes, that's *me* . . . well, *almost* me - I'm not officially a "terrorist" - *yet*. I still *haven't* committed any subversive action - still haven't printed propaganda - still haven't distributed propaganda - and, most importantly - *haven't killed.*

Yes, I can still call it off - I can be back at Shelby's Creek *before* the second cutting of clover.

Suddenly, it struck him how walkways had changed - once littered with cigarette butts and dog feces - as walkways of Omaha's stockyards are littered with cigarette butts and hog feces. Now however, walkways showed few cigarette butts - no sign of dogs. And, with no dogs, there was no chance of stepping on besoin - as besoin is lucky when stepped on with the left foot in accord to French folklore - so, as dogs disappeared from Paris, luck disappeared with them . . . .?

He looked ahead to the Arc de Triomphe.

Gosh, I wished I were on top of the Arc now, he thought.

Yes, I'd happily rush up those three hundred stairs to the top where there's no occupation, no angst, no chains - only fresh air from the chestnut blossoms wafting down the Boulevard . . . .

No, I wouldn't even look down to see the people, the soldiers, the occupation, the war - only up to see the sky, clouds, birds, rain, sun, moon, no war . . . yes, life *could* be *so simple.*

He looked to where many people stood beneath the Arc.

Sandwiched between the people, a sea of gray uniforms ebbed and flowed.

Some soldiers stood erect and pious before the stone slab of the Tomb - an ironic show of respect to the symbol of nameless dead of Verdun - symbol of two million Frenchmen killed.

Still, what sacrilege - for the enemy to have military maneuvers through the Arc - the monument also dedicated to France's independence.

Now the sea of uniforms materialized into a martial parade with a band and battalion of soldiers.

Déjà vu, he thought, knowing how the Guards of Prussia surrounded the Arc in Paris's 1871 defeat and then thought of these two countries - France and Germany - neighbors, brothers - but brothers now more like Abel and Cain - neighbors now more like Hatfield and McCoy.

Darn...that same old, tired, rotten chestnut . . . what's wrong with a *friendly* game of football to settle countries' differences? Or let it be *unfriendly* - especially if it's *European* soccer football. Still, *everybody* would go *home* - winners *and* losers - but they'd go *home* where the heart and heartless dwell best, he guessed

Now, to either side of the band, several soldiers set up machine guns and mortar.

Valentin shook his head - soldiers with instruments of destruction beside soldiers with instruments of song?

Suddenly, a convoy of military cars sped by at top speed, honking their horns at anyone who might consider stepping onto the street.

The cars turned left on a main thoroughfare about the same time the military band turned the corner of a sleepy street called Foch - named after that French military hero - who, like Napoleon, like Lafayette, like Petain or de Gaulle - seemed to mean little to Paris now.

"When words leave off, music begins."

— Heinrich Heine

Paris, France
Champs-Élysées
May 1943

Chapter 39

*V*alentin checked his pocket watch. Noon.

Just then, an elderly lady shuffled out in front of the band, her cane acting as the strongest of legs that moved her hobbled, arched body forward. An annoyed soldier rushed over to her and helped her across the street.

Then, somewhere far behind, he heard an accordion play the Marseillaise. Other soldiers rushed in hot pursuit to find its source.

From beneath the Arc, an elderly man strolled out alongside the band wearing only a beret and dress shoes and carrying a sign saying that the Reich's clothes rationing was making him cold. Two soldiers rushed over to him.

Then someone whistled, "Notre France Vivra." Before soldiers could rush to this source, an officer hollered an order and a drum major raised his baton and twirled it.

Then some three hundred other musicians joined in playing snare drums, brass fifes, Chinese bells, trumpets, and tubas as the band burst into a rousing pomp-and-gravitas rendition of, "Preussens Glorie."

A group of rifle-bearing, goose-stepping soldiers marched in perfect sync behind the band, their hard-stepping jackboots nearly as loud as the instruments.

Yes - he'd heard much about this daily noon parade that started from the Champs-Élysées, ended at Place de la Concorde - and here it is - in full glory - the First Sicherungsregiment - the Kommandant von Gross-Paris's garrison in full swing, playing as they'd played every day for three years.

Suddenly, the band and soldiers stopped for a military review.

Another elderly man shuffled across in front of the review and a gendarme rushed to him and led him in the opposite direction.

From behind a nine-foot wrought-iron-fenced courtyard, veiled within the leafy shade of chestnuts and oaks - someone played the French national anthem low on a harmonica. Two gendarmes rushed in that direction.

Standing on the sidelines, most Parisians watched, some even kept beat with the music as if the band had nothing to do with the occupation.

"Stand up," hollered a gendarme to an old man sitting on a chair beneath a café awning. "I said stand up," the gendarme repeated, but the old man ignored him, adjusted his tie and brushed croissant crumbs from his gray suit.

"What's going on?" Valentin asked a middle-aged lady beside him.

"That old man refuses to stand up for the parade. Everyone must stand up to honor the parade as it passes - Reich-rule."

Just then, the gendarme tossed the remains of a drink in the old man's face. The old man took a napkin, wiped the liquid from his eyes and moustache - three other gendarmes rushed in - two lifted the old man by his arms - the third kicked his chair from beneath him. The old man brushed his suit once more and then walked on.

Now all Parisians up and down the boulevard stopped walking, eating, or drinking as they watched the field-gray uniforms and full military parade march down Champs-Élysées.

In front of him now - clip-clopping, goose-stepping soldiers marched in rhythm in their hobnail-heeled jackboots - a sound he'd *never* heard before - wished to *never* hear again. No…nothing musical about it - robotic - like the sound of some noisy, automated machine that mass-produces cheap parts inclined to break, designed to break.

He stared at the black boots - the root of the annoying echo - the root of these soldiers.

No…he - wasn't sure of the fertilizer used to grow these soldiers, but sure it included *much* fertilizer - wasn't sure of growing conditions, but sure of clouded days of mucked-up ideologies, followed by days of blinding sun that mucked-up all prior, decent ideologies. Yes…the black-boot root that grows stalks that produces leather belts, holsters, oversized, snapping-turtle shell helmets - branches out to stick grenades, rifles, and pistols - leafs out to medals, tassels, iron crosses - chintzy as tinsel on a fake tree - and the *final* plant for harvest - nightshade.

And he looked to those dark faces beneath those snapping-turtle shell helmets - the unseeing, dull, shark eyes - thought how these brainwashed robots stomped on the same stones used many times for many barricades - how the same stones would be used again for barricades to fight again. . . . But he doubted such thoughts ever entered *their* minds - trapped within *those* helmets - trapped since they made *that* pledge to *that* Fuhrer - trapped since programmed *not* to question orders . . . trapped.

But still, it hit him like a slap - goose-stepping enemy soldiers at the Arc of Triomphe - the triumph belonging in *no way* to this enemy - and yet belonging to this enemy - victorious as the easiest of Napoleon's victories.

The parade now tapered off toward Place de la Concorde.

Champs-Elysees fell silent.

"Papers please?" a French voice said to him.

He turned to a fifty-ish gendarme - big bellied -thin legged - similar to a candied apple with two sticks.

"I read *Les Nouveaux Temps*," he said. "I'll look for your name."

Valentin nodded and turned down the boulevard.

He came first to Faubourg Saint-Honore and then to Place Beauvau - the French White House - more sandbag than white - sandbags stacked half-way up the buildings.

"The president's not home," said a boy. "He's probably getting his puppet strings reattached in Vichy."

Valentin grinned but said nothing, knowing not to trust anyone, not even this boy . . . .

"Or, if we're lucky, the Gestapo has him at their Rue des Saussaies torture chambers," the boy said.

"Perhaps," said Valentin as he passed Palais de L'Élysées - wondered when a French leader would again reside there - pondered how Napoleon would have reacted to this mess - perhaps he *wouldn't* have reacted - perhaps he would have acted.

He looked across Pont Marie - once the Seine's most romantic bridge - now littered with gun emplacements and enemy boats beneath.

Yes, he was *now* in the heart of Paris - the aorta of the Seine.

To his right stood the American Embassy - neutral during the occupation until Pearl Harbor - *now* enemy headquarters.

A heavy military truck zoomed by - followed by another and another - their tires making strange rattling sounds on the cobblestones - sounds he'd *never* heard before on Paris's streets - sounds as out of place as *not* hearing the chatter of Parisian voices or *not* seeing baguettes in Parisian arms or *not* smelling the wafting aromas of those Parisian baguettes.

He looked down at the streets, still glistening from the recent rain and knew little remained in those cobblestone cracks that remembered a *free* Paris - no warmth from *that* sun - no perfume from *those* fallen autumn petals - no stem from *those* fallen autumn leaves - no memory for *that* Paris.

He looked to where sunlight glared upon the fountain where King Louis XVI was guillotined in 1793 and wondered if rains still washed Revolution blood in between the stones through the soil, through the limestone, to the Catacombs - to rejoin guillotined bodies buried there like cordons of wood.

And as he stared at the cobblestones, he envisioned the Revolution, the Terror, the the scaffold, arms tied behind victims' bodies, bodies laid upon slabs of wood and tied in place beneath the blade. He imagined bloodthirsty crowds chanting, "A' la guillotine! A' la guillotine!" - the phantom drum beating - rolling in quick, matched rhythm with victims' final heart ticks - then - quick as a raindrop - the Guillotine whooshing down on bared, blue-blooded necks - heads dropping like pop flies into royal-red wicker baskets.

Yeah - 1793 - *another* resistance against *another* tyranny - *another* ministry - *another* trial - *another* blood-letting of evolution rendered *null* and *void*.

He wondered if - during the Terror - these cobble stones glistened beneath clearing skies as they did now - and if - in the second month of 1793 - or the tenth month of 1793 - either the king or his queen felt streams of *sunlight* or drops of *drizzle* in their faces or heard the bubbles of a fountain - *before* being laid upon the chopping board where the fountain now bubbled.

No, he knew not of the sunlight or the drizzle - but guessed the only bubbles then belonged to the champagne *served* at the Chez Meot to executioners following Antoinette's chop - following *her* apology for stepping on *her* executioner's foot - when foie gras was also *served* - cake was not.

Nearby were red, white, and black concrete sentry pillboxes.

He looked at the sentry soldiers and thought of the Communards, the Vikings, the Prussians, the Huns . . . all sackers of cities past, now all dead, their bones now dust, dust for survivors to sweep.

He shook his head - so much violence - so little reward.

He looked to the greening gardens of the Louvre and thought how *this* was the most ancient part of the city, where cobble-stoned Grands Boulevards stood upon fourteenth-century ramparts alongside Renaissance façades . . . .

Yes, *this* all spoke of the *best* that man has built, as farmers feeding nations speak of the *best* man has built, as a son that remembers fondly how a father made him feel speaks of the *best* that man has built, as a world with peace of mind, peace of heart, and living in peace speaks of the *best* that man has built. . . .

He checked his pocket watch.

Yes, it was time get a move on to *Les Nouveaux Temps*.

No . . . just one more moment, he told himself, and closed his eyes, inhaled the sweet garden scents, thought of his farm - of Florine milking Nanny and Katie - of Randy in basic training - of Grandma Lambert in a flat somewhere nearby - of Grandpa in a camp somewhere, *not* nearby...

"Do what you can, with what you have, where you are."

— Theodore Roosevelt

Paris, France
Champs-Élysées
May 1943

Chapter 40

Les Nouveaux Temps welcomed Valentin with open arms - told him he'd write ads and reviews of Paris opera, theatre, and shows - told him he'd interview French and German sculptors, playwrights, actors, maestros, musicians and meet with Palais Garnier director, Jacques Rouche, who he hoped to befriend, which he hoped might earn excellent future tickets for excellent future seats.

"And don't be late for work," *Les Nouveaux Temps* warned him. "Being late is publisher Jean Luchaire's *biggest* pet peeve, other than the French Resistance."

Yeah well, Valentin thought, the day's coming when the likes of Luchaire will step up the proverbial steps of the proverbial scaffold to the proverbial French guillotine - and the likes of the French Resistance will drop the not-so-proverbial blade.

. . . Okay, first things first - my first *Les Nouveaux Temps* assignment - tonight at Palais Garnier, a classical performance. First, *interview* Director Rouche then *review* the concert.

He returned to Hôtel Normandie, checked into his room, napped, woke, exercised - forty pushups, forty sit-ups, three times each - checked his flashlights, checked his personal items from his rucksack, memorized radio codes, memorized his identity again, put on a coat and tie, and went downstairs.

Bartender motioned him over. "You hungry?"

"I have an appointment."

"The cook made a 'Napoleon' pastry for you."

"A 'Napoleon'? How do you get fancy French pastries these days?"

"You *don't*, but she has a crush on you and made it especially for you. Her name's Agathe - thirty-five - a widow with three kids. I'll introduce you."

"Well, I'm not in the market for a woman right now, still getting over one. But I'd like to thank her for the 'Napoleon'."

"Well, when you're in the market, she's in the market," said Bartender.

Valentin nodded, walked to the quais, then along the Seine as a walk along the Seine always added inspiration before a concert and he'd always done it, whether performing or attending.

And Lord, the Seine looked inspirational tonight, as a bright, waning moon glistened in her tranquil waters, its shine staying all the way to Pont Neuf where he crossed the bridge and accessed line one at Palais-Royale to Place De La Concorde, then line nine to Madeleine.

Yes, from Madeleine, he'd walk the final few blocks to Palais Garnier - yes, plenty of time – but - you *mus*t hurry back after the concert to beat curfew for you don't want to bump into trigger-happy soldiers *after* curfew.

He looked around the metro car at the Parisians, who now looked especially tired. He'd heard they stood up in a resistance gesture when the train stopped at the George V station, in recognition of the British Allies. Well, he'd never been a fan of George V, but still might stand.

"Police! Your identity card," said a high-pitched, urgent voice.

Valentin looked around to face two gendarmes, one short, one tall, both staring with vulture eyes.

"Why aren't you in the compulsory service?" asked the short gendarme.

"He works for *Les Nouveaux Temps*," the tall gendarme said, handing back his papers.

"What will you write?" asked the shorter gendarme.

"Reviews - opera, theatre, exhibits."

"Ooh la la, we have another Lucien Rebatet," said the shorter gendarme.

Valentin hated the reference, for he knew Rebatet was a radical racist and fan of the Reich - knew of his famous book, *Les Decombres*, which reflected his pro-fascist, bigoted ways, especially his stance against the painter Pissarro - due only to *his* race.

So, Valentin focused on remembering this short gendarme on liberation day -eyeing where he'd punch his jaw.

"Why would you have to come here from Lille?" asked the short gendarme.

"I write and translate French and German - Sprechen si deutsch?"

Both gendarmes shook their head.

"We hope you remember the Reich side is the right side to be on in Paris," said the short gendarme.

Valentin mumbled in German. "When American Shermans rumble into Paris to roll over your quisling French butt, I hope *you* remember the Reich side is the wrong side to be on."

"I don't understand, monsieur," said the short gendarme.

"I said, bon voyage," Valentin said, his voice trailing off as the Metro stopped and he walked off.

"Bon voyage," the short gendarme said as he looked at Valentin quizzically.

Less than two minutes later, three men in black uniforms approached, one holding a leashed shepherd.

"This is a paper check," said the first man. "Show your identification. Hurry with it."

Valentin now regretted *not* getting off at the Opera metro station to avoid all these checks, but perhaps the *same* fatheads *wouldn't* check next time.

"Let's have everything in your pockets," the same man said.

Valentin handed over his opera ticket, his cash, and avoided his pencil flashlight.

"You're going to write about tonight's concert?" asked the man.

"Yes - if I can ever make it through all of these identity checks."

"Come," he said, his expression serious.

For a moment, Valentin thought his six-month agent tenure suddenly ended in six hours.

"We'll escort you," the man said. "We'll personally introduce you to sentries and gendarmes on the way, tell them who you are."

"Thank you."

The men walked hurriedly up the Rue Royale, all the way to the Boulevard Haussman.

"Follow Rue Auber down to Palais Garnier from here," said the man holding the shepherd. "You may be stopped again since there are many patrols around the Kommandantur's office just around the corner, but when they find out *who* you work for, you'll be fine."

"Thank you."

"We look forward to your review, Monsieur Delcourt."

Yeah, me too, Valentin thought, a review akin to nothing reviewed recently for the only music he'd heard recently was his own - where the only audience were the birds and the neighbors of Shelby's Creek.

"To know the cause why music was ordain'd! Was it not to refresh the mind of man. After his studies or his usual pain?"

— Shakespeare

Paris, France
Palais Garnier
May, 1943

Chapter 41

Valentin sat on the stone stairs and stared into a large dark puddle from the recent rain.

Yes, he remembered the moments playing here, the moments sitting here as he was now, and of the family who shared this with him who were now gone.

But he could help bring back two of them and, at the risk of principles, *he would*.

A couple of officers, a few soldiers, and a couple of citizens dressed in their finest, now filed toward him.

He pulled out pen and paper, made notes for his review and then walked up the stairs into the building, into the foyer, to the concessionaire.

"No," she said, "I can't upgrade your ticket. All *premiere* seats are reserved always for the officers."

He placed fifty francs in front of her.

"Well, I guess we *do* have a seat closer to the stage."

He walked down the hallway occupied by several uniformed officers who stood beneath a grand chandelier . . . yes, if I can figure a way to drop that chandelier, I may get a *premiere* seat after all . . . .

Just then, the concert doors opened.

He stepped inside the dimly lit hall, glanced at the gilt bathed in golden light, at the multi-tiered balconies on either side of the grand staircase . . . Gosh, it brought back many memories of many concerts and thought curiously how he agreed with Hitler: Sacré-Coeur was as hideous as the opera was heavenly. And also thought how - like Hitler - Sacré-Couer will one day collapse beneath itself.

"Time will tell," he imagined Mom saying. "Time changes everything - waits for no one."

Below, in the amphitheater stage, several concert members were sitting, fine-tuning instruments - mostly older men - mostly balding, domed heads that gleamed as if polished in oil.

He found his seat, watched the premiere stalls and boxed balconies fill with high-ranking officers in full-dress uniforms.

Then he noticed a pretty, young blonde with Lana Turner looks sitting in a box seat alone and looked at her for some time - wondered if she came alone or if she'd soon be with some pudgy, middle-aged general.

Well, since officers' wives were not allowed in Paris, women with officers were considered either collaborators or prostitutes and hoped his Lana Turner fit neither mold.

He glanced to other box seats to where egg-faced, monocled officers barely moved - their torsos and heads in rigid pose.

He shook his head - never would've guessed l'Opera would fill with such military guile - proving place and power, but ersatz power like ersatz coffee - medals and ornaments, mentality and ideology, temporary and superficial - more ersatzism, less Fascism.

Now the house filled with eagle medallions flashing notably in the dim lighting - the few exceptions - classily-dressed couples and singles - probably enemy and French, the latter possibly nouveau riche payola collaborators, payola black marketers, or, of course, old wealth - which he guessed fit the elderly man now sitting beside him.

"Hello," Valentin said, extending his hand to the man wearing wire-rim spectacles with a shock of white hair and a groomed white goatee like a Saanen.

The old man put out a limp hand to shake without looking away from the stage, but Valentin could see his eyes: intelligent, impatient.

"Can you tell me why there are so many children at this concert?" asked Valentin.

"Les Jeunesses Musicales de France," the man said, more grumble than mumble.

"I beg your pardon?"

"A program for the brats of Paris to attend concerts, etcetera, etcetera. Of the tens of thousand of brats I've been forced to deal with at concerts for the past year, at least *one* better turn out to be *half* as good as Cortot."

Valentin thought to mention that he was to interview Cortot, but sensed even *this* missive would *not* impress *this* curmudgeon. "Have you seen this chamber orchestra before?" he asked instead.

The old man shrugged and then spoke as if by great effort, his timbre low, gruff, "They're an eclectic group - some of the Berlin Symphony sent here to perform especially this week for General von Zimmerman."

"Say, I didn't get a program..." said Valentin.

"Ravel and Debussy are the only works I know for tonight, the only *French* works anyway," said the old man, his tone now rushed and impatient. "If this place plays more Wagner or Mozart, I swear I'll shoot bloody Hitler myself. If that mucking Das Rheingold plays here one more time, I'll join the commies on the mucking Eastern front! I can deal with the oft-repeated performances of Verdi's *Rigoletto* or even Gounod's *Faust*, but no more *Walkure* - I'll be seeing sauerkraut in my dreams!"

Valentin hoped, for this old man's sake, that there *weren't* any collaborators or occupiers nearby. "And for tonight, what about conduct..."

"And for maestros, it's either Clemens Krauss or Hans Knappertsbusch or some other such foreign name that takes a glass of water to spit out!"

"Who ever loved that loved not at first sight?"

— Shakespeare

Paris, France
Palais Garnier
May 1943

Chapter 43

*V*alentin suddenly felt happy, the happiest he'd felt since leaving Shelby's Creek - here I am at one of my favorite places in the world - about to listen to some of the finest music in the world - even if there is complete chaos in the world.

No, the latter doesn't matter - not now.

The latter will be addressed in its own time, in its own place, but *that* place is *neither* here nor *now*.

Again, like Mom said, "Time waits for no one." But when the time in front of you is quite possibly - some of your *best* time - love it - yes, *love it* - *before* it leaves you.

He turned again to the old man beside him. "Say, did you say you saw Honegger's *Antigone*?"

"No - Pfitzner's *Palestrina* last year - if *that* makes you happy."

Valentin grinned and looked up to his Lana Turner. "Say, do you know who that pretty blonde might be up in the box seat?"

The old man shrugged. "There are *always* pretty blondes sitting beside *uniformed* officers at l'Opera, at Comedie-Française, at...wherever. Her name's Annabella Waldner - secretary of the military governor of Paris . . . ."

"What?"

"Pay attention . . . that curled blonde in the box seat is here every concert - the finest of the Reich's, belle époqué," he said, now looking through his opera glasses at her, smiling an elfin smile and then turning his opera glasses to the stage. "Some of tonight's performers are Paris regulars - like this girl walking on stage who does a fine job with the oboe."

Valentin forgot immediately about his Lana Turner, his attention locking on a lady with waist-long, bronze-tinted hair - dressed to the nines - wearing a bright blue silk gown with shining silver spangles - standing statuesque, Choupinette-slender - now moving with the natural grace of a young cat.

Then, halfway across stage, she turned to the audience and smiled - her eyes *very* merry.

Valentin watched every move she made - could tell - whether walking, sitting, or standing, she knew poise - whether taught - as with the rich - or natural as with those who appear rich. And yes, the high, but fine cheekbones - light skin - long legs - suggested possible Norman lineage - northern French for sure.

"Isn't she a sight to behold?" asked the old man.

Valentin nodded, but said nothing.

Other performers walked onstage with the primitive, uncultivated keenness of feral animals compared to her, he thought - some short, some tall, fat, thin, bald, unkempt... None as perfect as the mold that made *her*, none with the grace *she* beheld.

"I said, isn't she a sight to behold?" the old man asked, louder.

Valentin still said nothing as he wished she'd walk again across the stage's width or length or whatever - wished to paint her in front of the stage's Foyer de la Danse - wished she forgot something - had to return to the stage - see her walk, see her smile, see her . . . .

"Your goggles," said Valentin to the old man, not taking his eyes from her.

"What?"

"May I borrow your goggles?"

"Before the concert...yes, during the concert...no. I intend *not* to miss a moment. This is my first outing since *The Damnation of Faust*."

"Were you lead?" asked Valentin under his breath as held his hand for the goggles, not looking away from her.

"What?"

"Mephistopheles...is...lead for *Damnation of Faust*, is he not?"

"It sure as hell isn't Joan of Arc," said the old man.

Valentin put the goggles to his eyes, gazed at her, felt suddenly as though Palais Garnier was short of air.

She wore no jewelry upon her smooth, cream-colored skin except for a pearl necklace that cast a radiant, ivory pallor that only enhanced her elegance.

242

Gosh, he wished the maestro to break his baton, his leg, his nose, anything to delay the concert so the old man wouldn't demand the goggles back, for their magnified glass now showed her high cheekbones and almond-shaped eyes, now looking down to smooth out her dress. And he wondered what her legs were like beneath the flowing bulk of the long gown - wondered how her hands looked up close, hands of a lady meant to make music, paint art, hold and feed a child . . . .

No, no woman ever struck me so immediately as being so beautiful, he thought.

"I wanted to marry your mom the second I saw her, and I wanted my best man to be the French peasant who introduced me," Dad used to say.

"Your grandma struck me like a lightning bolt when I first saw her," Grandpa used to say.

Well if a thunderbolt was stronger, that's what *this* felt like, he thought but wasn't sure about asking the old man beside him to be a best man for pointing her out.

Yes, he was smitten, definitely smitten.

She was incredibly, superbly beautiful.

If she looked his way, should he smile?

Should he not stare?

Should he applaud after the applause stopped to get her attention?

No - I'm not used to feeling self-conscious, but now I *am.*

He watched her place sheet music on her music stand; place the oboe reed to her full, rosebud lips.

Yes, every movement she made seemed subtle, but strong.

And her earnest, smooth, freckled face was cherubic - as an angel kissed her cheek - and she *became.*

Then she smiled the merry-eyed smile again and he found himself smiling.

Yes, for all her physical beauty, she possessed also an inner...

"Give me the damn goggles," the old man said.

"The concert hasn't started yet," Valentin said, still not taking his eyes from her.

"The moment maestro steps on stage, you better hand them over, or I'll punch your nose, young man."

243

"Yes, sir," Valentin said, now fully committed *against* the "best man" idea with the old man.

He moved the goggles back down to view her hands and then up to her face again and startled to see her looking *right* at him.

He jerked back and his elbow poked the old man in the forehead, knocked his glasses from his face.

"What the hell are you doing?" the old man said, bending down to pick up his glasses, getting elbowed in the forehead again as Valentin also bent over to retrieve them.

"I'm so sorry," Valentin said, still bending down, but peeking over a seat to see if she still looked his way, and since she did, he immediately pointed to the fat tuba player and muttered gibberish.

"What the hell you are talking about?" the old man said, rubbing his forehead. "Give me my damn goggles."

"Sorry, monsieur," Valentin said as he pulled a paper tablet from his shirt pocket and glanced up to see she still looked his way with a trace of a smile playing at the corners of her mouth.

He looked quickly down at his tablet and wrote gibberish.

"I should report you to Director Jean-Louis Vaudoyer," said the old man.

"Once again, please accept my apologies, monsieur," Valentin said, forgetting that he already had an interview set up with Vaudoyer, but remembering instead, *her* smile.

"Director Vaudoyer is a friend of mine," the old man said, still fuming.

Sure, Valentin thought, drop a name, feel important. Too bad we can't all go by first names to increase familiarity and decrease name dropping. Though there was *nothing more* he wanted *now* than *her* full name - *first, second, last, and all aliases.*

Then the bright ceiling stage lights came on and the performers and their instruments were bathed in an ashen gold glow.

Among the musicians with chromed domes, the young lady with the silk-smooth ginger-blond hair sat still, staring at the sheet of music before her.

Then she looked up and he looked away and then back to see her scan the crowd, but not really seeing the crowd, as if seeing only the concert that lay before her.

She pushed her hair back away from her high cheekbones, tucked the strands behind her ear.

Gosh, she could hire *me* for *free* to do that, he thought.

Then she looked again in his direction and he didn't look away from her now.

In that light, *nothing* seemed as cherubic as she, he thought - in that light, her merry eyes twinkled now as she looked directly at him and he felt his face blush, his mouth go dry.

"There's the maestro now," the old man said. "Hand over my goggles or I'll hand over a fat lip."

"Thank you, sir," Valentin said, giving up the goggles.

Gosh, if there was a wish I could wish, it'd be to approach *her* after the concert to ask if she'd go out for a real espresso, a private, after-curfew conversation and a *real* date *uninterrupted* by gendarmes, soldiers, shepherds, old men. . . .

The hall lights faded completely now as l'Opera House's historic statuettes and stone carvings became silhouettes, the ornate tapestry displayed dimly.

Then the maestro swept across the stage, sprung up to his podium, bowed quickly, waited for the applause to end, and turned to the orchestra with his baton raised.

Palais Garnier fell silent.

"Truly fertile Music, the only kind that will move us, that we shall truly appreciate, will be a Music conducive to Dream, which banishes all reason and analysis. One must not wish first to understand and then to feel. Art does not tolerate Reason."

— *Camus*

Paris, France
Palais Garnier
May, 1943

Chapter 44

Valentin watched her eyes, now focused intently upon her sheet music - yes - her head and arms poised perfectly - as if a cast could be made of her to replicate for the Louvre . . . then her delicate fingers positioned precisely. "If music be the food of love, play on..." he said, almost unconsciously now.

"What?" said the old man. "*Why* are you quoting Shakespeare?"

"Nevermind," said Valentin, thinking now how he *wasn't* in the mood to *say sorry* for *anything.*

The maestro dipped his baton.

Valentin watched her begin to play Dubussy's "Prelude to the Afternoon of a Faun,"- her sound like a whisper - the tone sotto voce - notes like a thrush at break of day.

Then the wind section joined in and she played with great élan, the orchestra with equal verve.

He watched her fingers move with the energy of an efficient machine, as if they had a life of their own - wished to be sitting beside her playing Bach in A major . . . no . . . preferably not Bach . . . or Mozart - but he'd succumb - to play *beside* her.

The maestro raised his baton high.

In a flash, he swung it down fully and the strings opened up, which then thundered from the amphitheater stage.

The whole orchestra chimed in.

Yes - right now he loved life - right now - in occupied Paris - there were *no* rules - *no* curfew - *no* intimidation . . . . No...there's only Debussy - and - for him - an intriguing lady nearby - looking demure, sincere, intelligent - unaware an American in the audience *cannot* take his eyes *off* of her.

And as he watched her, he stopped listening to decipher errors, flat notes, wrong notes - listened *only* to what he saw *in her* - and thought how, as a symphony performer, you never hear the music the way the audience does - just as you may not see a person or place as well - *until* you are *away* from them.

Well, he wasn't sure what she heard - or what she saw - but from where *he* sat, he *knew* what he heard - and - for possibly the first time in his life - *knew* what he saw.

Perhaps I can meet her after the concert - perhaps backstage, in the wings, in the rehearsal room, in the foyer, upon the marble staircase, or the Palais Garnier, or - anywhere - perhaps across the street at the café . . . yes . . . he'd even be her personal velotaxi or her horse ride home if he could meet her . . . .

Now the symphony played Mozart's "Eine Kleine Nachtmusik - Andante."

Yes, wisely chosen, Valentin thought, to balance the Frenchness of Debussy.

Next was Tchaikovsky's "String Quartet No. 1 – Andante." No, unwisely chosen - no balance to the makeup of this ethnic audience.

But then if music hath charms to soothe a savage breast - perhaps even the savage breasts in uniforms in this audience . . . if music is food of us that trade in love - and perhaps *now* is *my* time - *now I* am the trader bidding on such 'food' . . . .

Now she took center stage and played only with the piano - Liszt's "Liebstraume" . . . .

Good Lord, she plays so beautifully - so incredibly, beautifully, he thought and thought of La Bruyere: "A fine face is the finest of all sights, and the sweetest music is the sound of..." the sound of...he couldn't remember.

But her face was definitely the finest - and her music the sweetest of sounds - and he wondered what her voice sounded like. It must sound like . . . a thrush - in spring, a . . . whippoorwill - in winter, a...fowl - in fall? He laughed to himself. Stop it, you sap. You're giddy as a schoolgirl with a schoolboy crush . . . .

And he grinned. Yes, I'm in a 'willing suspension of disbelief . . . . Hell, here I am in the middle of Paris, in the middle of France, in the middle of a war, and all I can think about is this heavenly, angelic lady playing heavenly, angelic music.

The maestro turned to the audience and pointed to her now.

The audience applauded and she stood and bowed.

The maestro turned back to the symphony, raised his baton, and the orchestra opened up with Beethoven's "The Storm; Symphony No. 6 in F 'Pastorale.'"

This was followed by "Also Sprach Zarathustra," one of his all-time favorites, one of Hit's all-time favorites - and why not, he asked himself? Why let some "Zarathustra" connection with Hit put a black mark on art? Why let some dictator dictate *how* a composition will be remembered instead of *how* it was meant to be remembered by its composer: pure, artful, inspired, natural. The same with "Ride of the Valkyries," known for its own agenda for the enemy - but to him it was simply a *rousing* piece of classical music, like Tchaikovsky's "1812," like Khachaturian's "Sabre Dance," like Mussorgsky's "Night on Bald Mountain," like Sousa's "The Thunderer March," like Mouret's "Rondeau," like Chopin's "Revolutionary Study," or Rossini's "William Tell Overture."

Yes, these are all commanding compositions from composers from countries as varied as colors in a rainbow - a good mixture of music by a good mixture of composers - Italian Rossini, Russian Tchaikovsky, French Debussy, American Sousa, Polish Chopin, German Wagner, Russian Khachaturian, French Mouret, Russian Mussorgsky . . . . No . . . perhaps a Russian Orthodoxy wouldn't appreciate corn on the cob in Iowa as much as an Iowan Presbyterian wouldn't appreciate Borsch soup in Russia - any more than a Catholic Frenchman wouldn't appreciate Kielbasa sausage in Poland, as much as a Jewish Pole wouldn't appreciate escargot in France - any more than an atheist Italian wouldn't appreciate hot dogs in America, as much as a Baptist American wouldn't appreciate gelato or risotto in Italy - any more than a Lutheran German wouldn't appreciate lentils or momos in Nepal, as much as a Hindu Nepalese wouldn't appreciate bratwurst or labskaus in Germany - such minor differences in lands - such minor differences in foods - such minor differences in faith - such *major* wars make.

He glanced to *her* again and realized quite suddenly and quite conscientiously *how* far - just how *very far* he was - from Shelby's Creek.

"Surely the day will come when color means nothing more than the skin tone, when religion is seen uniquely as a way to speak one's soul; when birth places have the weight of a throw of the dice and all men are born free, when understanding breeds love and brotherhood."

— *Josephine Baker*

Paris, France
Palais Garnier
May, 1943

Chapter 45

Valentin continued to grin as he watched *her* and his mind continued to race for ways to resolve his current dilemma of this current war.

Now "Moonlight Sonata" played - a perfect song to be loved by *all* cultures, *all* religions, *all* over the world - no matter the composer's, the listener's or the performer's country, faith, favorite food, or language - no bias, no prejudice, no ethnic division.

Yes…music is its own language - without condition - without prejudice - without rules or treaties. And when music melds from one culture to the next, why couldn't cultures meld from one culture to the next? Its too bad, too bad people aren't as harmonious, as simple, as genius as music.

Enough…he told himself. I can't stop the war now, but I can start an accord now…perhaps…with *her*.

Then the maestro bowed and there was a short intermission.

Valentin caught himself grinning again. And again, he spoke aloud. "In sweet music is such art, killing care and grief of heart fall asleep . . ."

"Again with the Shakespeare?" said the old man said. "If I wanted theatre, I'd have gone to Grand Guignol instead of l'Opera."

"You have a problem with Shakespeare?" asked Valentin, tongue in cheek.

"Trust me, Monsieur - I'll make sure Director Vaudoyer gets a seat for me much closer to the stage – much, much farther from you next time."

"Again with Vaudoyer?" Valentin mumbled.

Then the maestro returned, bowed, waved to the symphony, and the crowd clapped.

He raised his baton and all fell silent.

The symphony burst into Verdi's, "Anvil Chorus."

Yes, a piece strongly encouraged by uniforms in the audience, Valentin thought.

Bach's concerto in F minor, "Largo," followed - then Mozart's "Andante from Piano Concerto No. 21 – then Schubert's Andante . . . .

But now he listened less and watched her more, for, as beautiful as the music was, *she* was much more so, and there was never music he enjoyed so much - for now *was* the music - yes, *she's* the music.

Then, to him, ninety minutes passed as one.

And, after the applause, bravos, encore, and more bravos, the stage emptied, the lights dimmed, and most of Palais Garnier vacated.

Then a man walked in the middle of the stage with a microphone. "It's half past the hour. Catch your last train in time."

Valentin waited, hoping against hope she might show once more onstage.

Yes, if she showed, he'd approach her with some cockamamie line of questioning - where she'd played - where she'd perform next - where she'd like to go for a coffee - where she'd like to find a café - where she'd like to walk along the quay for a tête-à-tête about Monet or even Manet - if worse came to worse . . . .

No, she was not coming back, he told himself.

But *I'll* be back and she'll be back - hopefully.

Darnit, why didn't I arrange an interview with members of the symphony? Yes, I own the credentials to make it look good. Yes, I have the knowledge to make it look *really* good.

"We're closing the doors," hollered a commissionaire - "Last metro in fifteen minutes."

Valentin looked at his pocket watch. Yes, I must hurry.

He stood, turned, and looked once more to where she'd sat and to where her music stand still stood.

And now he kept looking back as he walked fast down the aisle, down the long set of red carpeted marble stairs to the lobby, where he rushed to the doors.

As he exited the doors, he thought how his demeanor had changed from when he entered them.

Yes, in the last couple of hours he'd entered a portal he sensed might change his life - as though a new life began the moment she smiled that merry-eyed smile.

No, she hadn't said a thing, didn't need to.

She only smiled and that was everything he needed to know or would ever need to know, just like Keats, or was it Yeats - he didn't care.

Funny, he thought - how only a month ago I felt finished with women, hell, two hours ago.

And now, I feel that I've begun and ended - not with women - but with *this* woman.

Gosh, in that moment she walked onstage, in that moment she looked at me, I felt I knew her all my life.

And in his mind now she looked at him again, her eyes matching his, her merry-eyed smile meant for him.

"Yet in your warm golden hair, downward flowing, I find Nirvana and leave you unknowing."

— *Stephane Mallarme*

Paris, France
Palais Garnier
May 1943

Chapter 46

*V*alentin glanced over to Rue Scribe where cafés usually bustled with a steady hum of people conversing and partying after a concert.

But now it was quiet as a wake.

And all side streets were quiet.

And all corrugated shutters of all homes closed as though trying to keep *out* the occupation.

He checked behind and around to see if *she'd* leave in a car, a gazozene, a velotaxi, or a bike.

But she seemed already gone. He'd waited too long inside for her to return to the stage.

"Need a ride, monsieur?" shouted a young male voice from a lone velotaxi at the curb. "The last metro just filled with the last of the concert audience and musicians, and you've got a little under thirty minutes before curfew."

Valentin nodded, jumped into the small-shelled contraption and bumped his head on its roof. "Ouch," he said, now crouching in the cab. "Rue de la Huchette, please."

The cabbie stood on his pedals and pushed hard to get the bike going. Then he pedaled like a madman and the velotaxi wheeled down the street.

Valentin looked out the window and back for *her* once more, but she was long gone.

He quickly noticed how Paris had become suddenly, strangely silent and remembered Rosy saying soldiers no longer walked the streets at night unless required, for fear of assassination. Plus, midnight curfew scared the populace home early. Plus, enemy regulations forbade soldiers to approach French women during daylight, so at night, under guise of blackout, any soldiers brave enough to be out became aggressive and women, in turn, were inside homes by sundown, as if vampires roamed the streets. Plus, the limited Parisian money was spent on food, not entertainment.

Yes, that was probably the main reason: other than soldiers, collaborators, or black marketers, who could afford to go to a revue at the Casino de Paris when money went to buy beans, swede, rutabagas, coffee, and cabbage?

But, whatever the reason, at night, the City of Light was not only a city of almost no light, but also a city of hushed ghosts.

Now a couple of the ghosts showed in the forms of silhouetted sentries and moved at a snail's pace, guns jutting from their sides, their robotic route like carousel ducks at a county fair.

"Rue de la Huchette," said the cabbie.

Valentin kept his head low, exited the velocab, paid the cabbie. "You'll be fit for the next Tour de France," he said.

"That's my hope," the driver said, grinning, his voice frantic, his face wet with sweat. "I still have time for one more pickup. Good night, monsieur."

Valentin walked to Hôtel Normandie, sat on its front steps, and listened.

No noise, no sound, not even a whisper on a wind.

Yes, a city shrouded, perhaps by soldiers, but also shrouded from sound.

Yes, all seemed silent, as if he were sitting on the porch step of his cabin at Shelby's Creek in midsummer at midnight.

Across the street, at Le Panier Fleuri, all four levels of all eight windows were closed now in accord with curfew.

But he sensed eyes behind those shutters watching, waiting for the day when, once again, they'd open those shutters to *unoccupied*, summer Paris breezes.

Then he sensed something above him and looked up to the moonlit roof, at the zigzag flight of several bats dropping, rising, like wind-driven kites. No wonder the women were safely inside their homes by sundown, he thought.

And then he hoped, especially, that the oboe player had arrived in *her* home safely, safe and with good people.

And now he murmured a prayer for the first time in what seemed a long time.

About the Author

Mark Matthiessen was born and raised on a 160-acre farm in Shelby County, Iowa.

He graduated from Clarke College, a private liberal arts school, with degrees in Print Communications and Psychology.

After college, he worked for a computer firm, writing tech manuals, while also writing travel and feature pieces for local magazines. He moved from Alaska to Florida to Europe in the last 10 years and has authored more than 200 travel articles for national and international magazines.

In the year ahead, he plans to revisit France and Germany to continue work on the next book in this series. In between, he resides in Shelby County, Iowa on the family farm, now being worked by the fifth generation of his family.

This is a composition of fiction. The characters and situations are resultant for the author's inspiration and imagination. Any similarity to actual situations or people should be considered as fiction or coincidence.

Apropos, there is a contingent that this novel reflects historic truths, facts and realities.

NOW AVAILABLE

Shelby's Creek: Green Eyed Europe

Made in the USA
Las Vegas, NV
25 February 2024